blackbird
singing

blackbird singing

jay amberg

**A Tom Doherty
Associates Book
New York**

BLACKBIRD SINGING

Copyright © 1998 by Jay Amberg

A Forge Book
Published by Tom Doherty Associates, Inc.
175 Fifth Avenue
New York, NY 10010

Forge® is a registered trademark of Tom Doherty Associates, Inc.

Design by Lynn Newmark

Library of Congress Cataloging-in Publication Data

Amberg, Jay.
    Blackbird singing / Jay Amberg. — 1st ed.
        p.   cm.
    "A Tom Doherty Associates book."
    ISBN 0-312-86554-6 (alk. paper)
    I. Title.
PS3551.M19B58   1998
813'.54—dc21   98-21182
                                                          CIP

First Edition: October 1998

Printed in the United States of America

0 9 8 7 6 5 4 3 2 1

For Katie, Megan, and Lily

acknowledgments

Thanks to John Manos—neighbor, friend, and editor. And thanks, once again, to Andrew H. Zack for his continued support and guidance.

chapter 1

The thin, pretty nine-year-old gymnast performed an aerial on the balance beam. Her form perfect, she stuck the move without flinching. Her skin was the color of teak, and her wavy black hair was pulled back in a single thick braid. Her almond-shaped eyes were bright with concentration. The gym, clean and well-lit, had a floor exercise mat near the door, a runway and vault along the far wall, two sets of uneven bars, and three balance beams at different heights.

Ken Culhane's blue nylon warm-up suit swished as he entered the gym and sauntered by a diminutive gymnast finishing her tumbling run with a flip-flop, flip-flop layout with a full twist. He stopped by the gymnastics coach, a short, sturdy, dark-haired woman in a warm-up suit that matched his, put his hand on her shoulder, leaned down, and whispered, "The ice queen called. She wants the little princess outside in five minutes so they can meet the team plane." He ran his hand through his blond hair, leaned back, and rolled his eyes. "All hail the conquering hero."

The coach nodded to Culhane. "It's okay," she said in a thick Eastern European accent. "She's been virking hard." As the gymnast set for her dismount, the coach, stepping over to spot her, shouted, "Strong, Tonya! Now!"

Tonya Walker hit her dismount, took a half-step forward, caught herself, threw her arms in the air, and grinned.

As she hugged Tonya, the coach said, "Nice virk, my little champion. Your mother, she is on her vay to take you to the airport to meet your father."

Tonya tugged at the strap of her leotard, turned toward Culhane, flashed a winning smile, and asked, "Really?"

"You bet, champ," he answered. "Let's go. She'll be here soon, and you know she doesn't like to be kept waiting."

Tonya skipped ahead of Culhane across the gym floor. When he reached the corridor, she was already halfway down the carpeted hall pushing open the locker room door. Inside, she spun around and dunked an imaginary basketball into the janitor's gray rolling Dumpster left near the first row of lockers. She opened her locker and, before taking out her red-and-black Chicago Bulls sweatsuit, lifted her small gold and diamond ring from the shelf and slipped it onto the ring finger of her right hand. As she leaned over to pick up her shoes, a burly, bearded man in a navy blue janitor's uniform stepped quickly from the shower stall, grabbed her from behind, and cupped his black-gloved hand with a chloroform-soaked rag over her mouth and nose. She was able only to snap up her hand and claw for a second at his cheek before she passed out.

"Bitch," he muttered as he picked her up. He nudged the locker shut with his elbow, carried her to the Dumpster, shoved her in, and covered her with a black plastic bag. Before pushing the Dumpster from the locker room, he wiped the blood trickling down his cheek, took a cellular phone from his pocket, and punched the North Ridge Gymnastics Center number. When Culhane answered, the man said, "Hello, I'd like some information about classes for my daughter." He then clicked the phone against the rim of the Dumpster and added, "Ah, excuse me, can you hold while I check that call? Thank you."

The man cracked the locker room door, glanced both ways along the empty corridor, and wheeled the Dumpster past the open office door, where Culhane, still cradling the receiver and tapping the fingers of his free hand on the desk, had his back to the hallway. When the man reached the service entrance at the rear of the building, his mouth twisted into a mirthless smile.

chapter 2

Ignoring the reporter's shouted questions, Tom Hopkins brushed past the television crew shooting through the North Ridge Gymnastics Center's glass doors. As he entered the center, he nodded to the uniformed officer guarding the door, pointed over his shoulder with his thumb, and asked, "What the hell's Pit Bull doing here, Billy-boy?"

The officer, a thin, young man with sallow skin, grimaced. "They got here right when we did, sir," he answered.

Hopkins glanced at his black military watch and shook his head. He was six-three and, though past forty, still lean. His dark brown hair was starting to gray at the temples, and his hazel eyes were clear. His khaki pants, button-down blue shirt, and blue blazer were neat despite the fourteen hours he had already worked. He had been North Ridge Police Department's Investigations Unit Commander for less than three months. "Jesus," he said. "How'd those jackals find out?" He scratched the side of his nose. "Where's Banks?"

The young officer pointed down the hall. "In the office

with the coaches. Beltram and Maniatis are searching the building and grounds."

When Hopkins entered the office, Sergeant David Banks, a large black man built like a defensive lineman with a bull neck and shaved head, stood over Ken Culhane, who sat in the chair at his desk. The gymnastics coach, clutching her hands tightly in front of her, stood to their left. Her lips were pursed, and her dark eyes were watery. A stout, swarthy man in a brown suit and starched white shirt leaned against the wall glowering at Culhane. His arms were folded across his chest; his coat bulged under his arm where a gun hung in a shoulder holster.

"Commander Hopkins," Banks said, moving back a step, "we got us a situation here that looks real bad." He glanced at his open notebook. "This is Nadine Byrzinski. She runs the place. And Kenneth Culhane, her assistant." He turned toward the other man, who had stood away from the wall and dropped his hands. "This is Anthony Ignacio, the Walkers' chauffeur."

Cocking his head, Ignacio growled, "Security. I handle security for the Walkers."

Hopkins nodded to each of them, glanced at the red-and-black sweatsuit next to the pair of black children's Reeboks on the desk, and said to Banks, "What do we have?"

"Tonya Walker's missing. When Mr. Ignacio arrived to pick her up, she wasn't here." Banks pointed the notebook at Culhane. "Mr. Culhane, here, insists Mrs. Walker called and picked the girl up earlier, but . . ." He slapped the notebook against the palm of his hand.

Hopkins turned to Ignacio. "Any chance Mrs. Walker . . . ?"

Ignacio shook his head vehemently. "No. No way," he said. "No way. When Tonya didn't come out with the other kids, I checked the locker room. Her stuff was still there so I paged Mrs. Walker." He looked over at the wall clock between the framed posters of Nadia Comenici and Mary Lou Retton. "She was outta her fu . . ." He shook his head again. ". . . She was, uh, very upset. She's on her way over here from a meetin' downtown. Should be here any minute."

Culhane clutched the arms of the chair. "Mrs. Walker called here," he snorted at Ignacio.

"All right, okay," Hopkins said, turning back to Culhane. "When was the last time you saw the child?"

Culhane ground his heels into the carpet. "When she, ah, went into the locker room. I got stuck on the phone. With, ah, some parent."

"So you didn't see her leave the building?" Hopkins asked.

"No, I, ah, figured she just scooted past the office."

The coach smiled sadly. "Tonya, she is a very . . ." She hesitated, searching for the correct English word, ". . . a very energetic girl."

Hopkins took a deep breath and exhaled slowly. "Did any of you call the television station?"

"Unh, unh," Culhane answered.

The coach shook her head and then rubbed her eye with the heel of her hand.

"Me?" Ignacio scoffed. His smile was antagonistic. "No way in hell."

"Sergeant Banks," Hopkins said as he motioned toward the doorway.

When they were in the hall, Banks whispered, "This is some serious shit, Hoop. Sky Walker's kid missing. Shit's gonna hit the fan big time."

"We've got to assume the worst," Hopkins said, scratching his nose again. "You've gotten a description of the girl, what she was wearing?"

Banks nodded.

"Put it out on all channels," Hopkins said. "Have the E.T.s go over the locker room, every goddamned inch of it, before anybody else can get in there and further muck up the evidence. Get the fugitive procedures going. I want everybody in on this. The canine unit. Everybody. Let me know immediately what Beltram and Maniatis turn up." He glanced again at his watch. "When Mrs. Walker arrives, keep Pit Bull away from her."

"You got it, Hoop," Banks said as he turned toward the front door.

"And contact the Chief," Hopkins called after him. "He'll need to know what's going on."

No one was speaking when Hopkins reentered the office. He walked over to the desk and frowned down at the sweatsuit and shoes but didn't touch them. "All right," he said. "Let's start at the beginning. Who was here?"

The coach looked at the poster of Nadia Comenici doing the splits on the balance beam. "Just me and Ken," she said. "And the girls on the traveling team."

"You have practice regularly on Sunday nights?" Hopkins asked.

"Yes, vee do," she answered. "From 6:30 to 8:30 for the advanced girls." She looked into Hopkins' face for a moment. "It is the only time I can give to them vithout . . ." She waved her hand. ". . . Being interrupted."

"How many girls?" Hopkins asked.

"Six, tonight," she answered. "And no parents. They get in the vay so I do not let them stay." Anticipating his next question, she took a clipboard from the desk, slid out a sheet of paper, and, her hand trembling, handed it to Hopkins. As he scanned the printed roster, she said, "Just the bottom five and Tonya. Laurie Anderson, she vasn't here tonight."

"It's the slowest time all week," Culhane said. "Nobody's around." He drummed the arms of the chair. "Nothin' ever happens."

"Somethin' happened," Ignacio grunted.

"Okay, okay," Hopkins said, looking at Ignacio. He pointed to the sweatsuit and shoes and asked, "How'd this stuff get in here?"

"I brought 'em in from Tonya's locker," Ignacio answered.

"You removed items from her locker *after* you knew she was missing?" Hopkins asked, his voice flat and calm.

"Yeah . . ." Ignacio realized the implication of his answer. "I was just tryin' ta . . ." He shut his mouth and slouched back against the wall.

"The other girls," Hopkins asked the coach, "would they've been in the locker room after practice?"

"Yes," she said, "and me and Ken, too, after Mister Ignacio told us . . ." Her voice trailed off as she shrugged.

"Was there anything missing from the locker?" Hopkins asked. "Anything that should've been there that wasn't?"

"No." Ignacio scowled. "Wait. She was wearin' the gold ring Sky . . . her father . . . gave her when she won the State meet last year." He straightened and took a step away from the wall. "She told me on the way over it was lucky. It was why the Bulls won today."

When Hopkins glanced at the coach, she shook her head. "Tonya did not have the ring on," she said. "She knows better than to vear it during practice."

Hopkins took a deep breath. "I'm going to need a statement from each of you," he said. "And I'd like you to take polygraph tests down at the station."

Ignacio, who'd begun to pick at the skin by his thumbnail, muttered, "A lie-detector test?"

Hopkins stared at him. "Yes," he answered. "It's routine in . . ."

Sergeant Banks leaned in the doorway. "Commander Hopkins," he said, "the girl's nowhere on the premises, but Beltram's turned up something you should see out by the service entrance."

Hopkins nodded and then turned back to the others. "The polygraph's routine in missing-children cases," he said. "Anyone connected to the crime scene. Even family members." He glanced at each of them and added, "Officer Banks will take you to the station. I'll be there as soon as we've got the building and grounds secured."

Hopkins headed for the service entrance as the others went to the front door. When he was rounding the corner at the end of the hall, light and dark shadows swam around him. Looking back, he saw that the television crew's lights flooded the building's front entrance. Monique Jones-Walker stood in the doorway accosting those leaving the building. Backlit by the TV light, she shimmered in a pale green linen suit that, even at that distance, accentuated her figure.

While Hopkins hurried back along the corridor, Jones-Walker assailed the coach. "What's going on here?" echoed in the hallway. "Where is my daughter?"

"Mrs. Walker," Hopkins said as he approached the group. He gestured toward the door. "Sergeant Banks, please take . . ."

"Who are you?" Jones-Walker demanded, her tone imperious. Her large, almond-shaped eyes glistened darkly with anger.

Hopkins reached out, not quite touching her arm. "Mrs. Walker, please . . ." He nodded to Banks, who whisked the others out the door and past the TV crew. "I'm Thomas Hopkins, North Ridge Investigations Commander," he said as pointed his hand toward the office.

"Where the hell is my daughter?" Jones-Walker's voice was icy. Her eyes fixed on Hopkins.

chapter 3

James Robert Saville spun in his wheeled, swivel armchair across the carpet of his sound-proofed basement office. Paul McCartney sang to him, "Blackbird singing in the dead of night / Take these broken wings and learn to fly / All your life / You were only waiting for this moment to arise" through the electrostatic headphones connected by the fifteen-foot cord to the Bang & Olufsen amplifier and sound system. The office, which he always referred to in his rambling rants on the Net as the Command Center, had spotless white walls and clean white counters and cabinetry. He'd homebrewed the fully integrated electronic array—everything from the 796 STX computer with its multiple hard drives (sporting fifteen gigabytes of memory), sound and video boards, and twenty-one-inch monitor to the Spandex and fiber-optic dataglove for the 3D immersion system he'd almost perfected before this current operation had engrossed him—and he was quite sure that nobody, nobody anywhere, was farther into cyberspace, deeper into the WELL, hotter with a flame. White-hot, he was, a supernova.

Saville was thirty-nine years old, not quite six feet tall, pudgy, and balding. His skin was pallid, and the pink, puffy welt where Tonya Walker had scratched him ran across the acne scars on his cheek. With his left hand, he grabbed a fist-ful of Cheetos from the bag caddy he'd rigged between his lap-top and the two modems on the counter. He stuffed the Cheetos in his mouth and, as he fastidiously wiped his hand with a Wash n' Dry, glanced up at the twenty-seven-inch color television monitor suspended from the ceiling just like those in sports bars and airline waiting rooms—only his featured the latest twin-tuner Picture-in-Picture amenities so he could stay abreast of his sources, scroll and swap at will. And here it was now, the Reebok ad with Sky Walker leaping, double-pumping, seeming to stroll almost leisurely through the air, and then jamming the ball.

Saville took the two-liter bottle of RC Cola from the elec-tric, air-cooled bottle dolly on the floor and washed down the Cheetos with a long swig. He then lifted the headphones for a moment to confirm that Tonya Walker was still screaming that constant, repetitive yawp of hers, took his glasses from the top of the scanner, and leaned forward in the chair. With his cramped right hand, half-covered by a canvas and plastic carpal-tunnel wrist brace, he lifted the super-remote he'd built, toggled from CD to Video, and jacked the sound. Columns of figures appeared on the laptop and the STX's monitor. It was all about to begin. He was at the peak of the mountain, ready to take wing, to soar, to fly above the feeding frenzy. His eyes gleamed.

The TV screen, the Videot Box, cut to a somber an-nouncer, who, with the image of Robert Walker over his shoulder, said, "As fans swarm the airport to welcome the Bulls home after their stunning victory over the New York Knicks, WLN *News at Nine* news has learned that overwhelming personal tragedy is facing Sky Walker when he and his teammates land at O'Hare in the next few minutes."

"You got that right!" Saville, still wearing the headphones, yelled at the Videot Box. He snatched more Cheetos and scarfed them, chewing vociferously.

"Here now," the announcer continued, "reporting live from the Gymnastics Center in suburban North Ridge, is Jack Bollinger with WLN's exclusive coverage of the story."

Jack "Pit Bull" Bollinger, standing by the gymnastics center sign on the wall near the front door, held the microphone close to his mouth. His short, graying hair looked silver in the light. The collar of his trademark trenchcoat was turned up despite the early June temperature hovering above sixty. "Thanks, Bill," he said, his voice gravelly. He checked his watch for effect and turned slightly to stare directly into the camera. "At exactly eight-twenty-four P.M. this evening, an anonymous caller informed this reporter that nine-year-old Tonya Walker, Sky Walker's only child, had been abducted from this gymnastics center."

"Sic 'em, Pit Bull!" Saville shouted, his eyes darting from the Videot Box to the three videotape recorders stacked on the counter to his right. All systems were full ahead go.

Bollinger gazed for a moment at his dog-eared notebook. "North Ridge police," he said, "have not yet released an official statement, but a few minutes ago, as a police officer escorted three people from this building, WLN news anchor Monique Jones-Walker arrived at the site and confronted the police investigators."

The screen cut to video footage of Jones-Walker approaching the gymnastics center door, turning toward the camera, and hissing, "Get out of here, Jack! You've got no business here." She passed the young policeman holding the door open for her and stopped abruptly in front of Officer Banks and the three other people about to exit. Her shout of "What's going on here? Where is my daughter?" was clearly audible before the door shut again.

Saville guffawed, leaned back in his chair, rotated 360 degrees, and played a long riff on his air guitar, the fingers of his gnarled hand plucking the imaginary notes of John Lennon's "Helter Skelter."

On the screen, Jack Bollinger shook his head. "The three people taken away in the squad car," he said, "have not been officially identified, but one was definitely Anthony Ignacio, the Walkers' bodyguard. The other two were both wearing North Ridge Gymnastics Center warm-up suits. At this time, Monique Jones-Walker remains in the building with a North Ridge police official." Bollinger glanced again at his notebook. "We can also confirm that police investigators are at the site, and all North Ridge police and rescue personnel have been ordered to report to police headquarters. That's it for now, Bill."

The TV screen split to include the somber announcer, who folded his hands on his long, uncluttered desk. "Thanks, Jack," he said. "Please stand by to update us on any further developments."

Bollinger nodded, and the screen cut to a close-up of the announcer, who cocked his head and, with his voice low, almost reverential, added, "We can only hope for the Walkers' sake, there's been some mistake, some terrible error here." He took a long, slow breath. "In any case, our thoughts and prayers, and those of all Bulls' fans, all Chicagoans, and all Americans are with the Walker family." As he turned, the screen cut to a wide-angle shot of him. "Stay tuned to WLN *News at Nine*'s exclusive extended team coverage of this tragedy. Our own Wendy White will report from North Ridge police headquarters, and Carl Marinelli, who's already at O'Hare, will fill us in on the situation there. We'll have it all for you after these brief messages."

Saville snatched the super-remote, stabbed the mute button with his thumb, and, as the TV screen cut to a McDonald's ad, slumped in his chair. He yanked off his headphones, heard the child's incessant yelping, and pulled off his glasses. The light faded from his eyes, and his chin fell against his chest. He brooded for a moment before turning slowly toward the Command Center's opposite wall where his costumes hung in a neat row and his disguises lay carefully arranged on the white metal shelves. Gloves were a necessity, of course, and the mask was a must.

chapter 4

The door opened, and a shaft of light lanced the darkness. When the overhead flicked on, Tonya Walker, hunched naked in the corner on the tile floor, stopped her safety yell. Though she was no longer vomiting, she was still dizzy. Her stomach was queasy, and her head throbbed. She squeezed her eyes shut against the blinding light and squinted at the doorway. For a second, her spirit took wing beyond the leather straps shackling her ankles to the wall. Her father stood there, bathed in light.

Then, she recoiled. It wasn't her father at all, but some hideousness, some shorter, rounder being in dark overalls and gloves and a mask of her father's face, the mask that so many of the fans wore at the United Center in that special cheering section behind the scorer's table. The Beast loomed above her, just out of reach of her cuffed hands. He spoke in a voice too high to be her father's. "Look at this mess you've made, young lady. Your mother's angry. Angry that you're gone, young lady. Angry that you left the gymnastics center without her permission." It was a man's voice, but higher, a woman's, too. "She's upset. And you know what happens when she's angry and upset." The voice cracked. "You know what'll happen to you now!"

As her eyes adjusted to the light, Tonya glanced around the small room. The walls, floor to ceiling, were covered with white ceramic tiles. A toilet and washbasin stood against the far wall, and shower heads, pointing down toward her corner, jutted from the remaining three walls. A single round floor drain lay like a full moon in the center of the floor. Dual exhaust fans purred high up near the silver ceiling. Although she was cold and afraid, she sat up straighter; goose bumps spread across her skin, spotted with dried vomit. She sucked in her breath and began her safety yell again. Deep from within her stomach, the "Huh! Huh! Huh!" rose, burst, and echoed around the room.

"Stop it!" the voice shrieked. "Stop it, or you'll regret it, young lady! I'm warning you!"

Tonya's braid came loose, and twisted clumps of thick hair hung down to her shoulders. Her ribs stuck out each time she took a breath. As she continued to yell, she glared defiantly at the man. He was bigger than her mother, and wider, but he was nowhere near the size of her father. A line of pale skin appeared below the mask as he shook his head vehemently and screamed, "Shut up! Stop it! Stop it! Stop it!" He stepped forward and raised his hand. She stared at the shaking hand which seemed swollen, as though there were a mitten or a second glove beneath the work glove.

The hand swept down, crossing the overhead light like a shadow, and swatted her head. Her forehead and nose bounced against the floor tiles; silver bees swarmed around her, buzzing in her ears, and the room swirled. Warmth spilled over her upper lip and down her chin. She raised her head, spat the warmth from her mouth, and tried to shake free of the bees.

"No! No! No!" the voice shrieked. "No, Sarah! Sarah! Sarah!"

And then the room turned gray, the door slammed, and the world closed into blackness.

chapter 5

The telephone cradled between his shoulder and ear, Tom Hopkins stood in his cramped corner office of North Ridge Police Department's Investigations Unit. For as long as he could remember, the office had been called the "fishbowl" because it was separated from the hallway by a brick and glass wall and from the rest of the unit's office by wood and glass partitions. At any time, anyone who wanted to could see his cluttered oak desk, computer stand, gray steel file cabinets, and low wooden bookcase stuffed with manuals. His detectives' desks ran along the two longer walls of the large rectangular outer office. Cork boards crammed with memos and bulletins hung above each of the desks. The entry to the office faced the building's main corridor; the two doors at the far end led to the unit's interview rooms.

When Hopkins saw Peter Mancini hurrying along the corridor, he hung up the phone, scuttled out of the fishbowl, and met the police chief at the door. Mancini, paunchy, fifty-four years old, and just over six feet, was wearing the starched white

shirt, dark tie, and blue dress uniform he always wore in public. His black hairpiece was perfectly groomed, but perspira-
tion lined his forehead below it. "I got here as fast as I could,"
he said, his voice almost breathless. "We were just leaving the
symphony when I got the page." He glanced through the windows at the detectives working the phones. "This is unbeliev-
able, Hoop."

Two uniformed officers rushed by them into the Investigations Unit office. Hopkins shook his head. "Yeah," he said.
"It's already starting to spin out of control."

Mancini ran his tongue across his capped teeth. "It's the
only thing on the radio. All the way back from downtown,
every station was airing reports that Sky Walker's little girl had
been kidnapped in North Ridge." With 185,000 people,
North Ridge was not only Chicago's closest northern neighbor but its largest suburb—a city with a diverse population
and complex urban problems of its own. In the three years
that Mancini had been police chief, the department's motto
had changed from PROTECTION FOR A SAFE CITY to SERVING
THE PEOPLE AND COMMUNITY. The first chief to come from
the Technical Division rather than Field Operations, he had
rankled a number of senior officers not only by bringing the
entire department on-line but also by instituting problem-
solving approaches that bypassed traditional rules and regulations. His promotion of Hopkins had been popular with the
younger officers but caused two disgruntled veteran watch
commanders who had vied for the position to take early retirement.

"It's even worse than the media jocks know," Hopkins said.
"Nothing adds up. There's been no attempt to contact the
parents. No ransom demand. But WLN News was tipped fifteen minutes before we were notified. Bollinger was already at
the site when I arrived."

"Pit Bull? He knew before we did?"

"It looks that way."

"Haul that son of a bitch in here."

"I sent Beltram out to get him when we were at the gym, but the bastard bolted. The line from WLN's lawyers is that the station got an anonymous tip, and Bollinger checked it out. Nothing more."

"Yeah, right." Mancini took a clean white handkerchief from his pocket. "Any witnesses?"

Hopkins shook his head. "Sunday night's apparently the slowest time all week. A closed practice for the competition team—just the kids and the two coaches. No parents allowed."

"What did you find at the site?"

"The E.T.s are still working. We got nothing from the locker room. The other kids were in there after the Walker girl. And her belongings were removed before we got there."

"Hell," Mancini said, wiping his forehead with the handkerchief. "It's going to look like we botched things already."

"It's not a total wash, though," Hopkins said. "The alarm on the service entrance had been bypassed. Rewired so that it could be opened by remote. And there was an empty janitor's cart out back. We may get prints or fibers from it."

"Sounds like an inside job."

"Looks that way." Hopkins led Mancini along the hallway. "But the Walkers' bodyguard and the only two other people at the site, the coach and the guy in the office, all passed polygraph tests. And get this, the guy says Monique Jones-Walker called just before the abduction—and his polygraph results back him up."

They entered the records office and headed between the rows of desks, computer terminals, and filing cabinets toward a painting of a New England ice skating rink hanging on the far wall.

"And our initial canvass," Hopkins said, "turned up a kid

in the neighborhood who insists he saw a Jeep out by the service entrance at about the time of the kidnapping."

"Let me guess," Mancini said. "The Sky Walker Special Edition Grand Cherokee. Bulls' red with black trim and oversized tires."

"You got it." Hopkins took down the painting, set it against the wall, and peered through the one-way viewing port into the small, stark interview room where Monique Jones-Walker was taking a polygraph test. Facing him, she sat on the other side of a small wooden table, her suit jacket off, the top button of her white blouse unfastened, and her sleeves rolled up. The polygraph's black straps covered her forefinger and her upper arm like a blood pressure band. The wide black strap across her chest pressed her breasts upward. "And Mrs. Walker arrived at the center in a red Grand Cherokee less than an hour later." He stepped back a couple of feet.

Mancini looked through the port, whistled softly, and said under his breath, "Whatever's happening here, one thing's certain. The TV doesn't do the lady justice."

Hopkins shook his head, smiled wryly, and waited for the Chief to draw his gaze from the port.

"How did you get her to submit to the polygraph?" Mancini asked.

"She wasn't happy. Refused at first. But I explained that it was routine for everyone connected to a missing child case." He smiled. "And I pointed out to her that though it was voluntary, refusing to take the polygraph might be misinterpreted . . ." He shrugged. " . . . In fact, had been misconstrued in the past, even on her own news program, as a tacit admission of guilt. Or at least as an attempt to hide damning evidence."

Mancini took another look through the port, turned, and asked, "What about Sky Walker?"

"We called the Bulls, and they were able to get him off the

plane on the runway at O'Hare before it reached the gate. The media's infesting the terminal." Hopkins glanced at his watch. "I sent Dave Banks to pick him up. We'll bring him in through the security garage."

"Good," Mancini said. "The front lot's already full of reporters. I had to run the gauntlet just to get in the door." He paused. "You know, you actually have to *push* through those assholes."

Hopkins smiled. As the department's public information officer, he'd had a lot of experience with the press, "Pit Bull" Bollinger in particular. A series of rapes at a rapid-transit stop near the university had set off Bollinger's unique style of "investigative" sensationalism a year earlier, and neither he nor Mancini was naive about aggressive journalists. But he could feel the difference with this case—the frenetic camera crews and reporters outside like a pack of hounds, all baying for answers at the sight of any official face. "I think it's going to get worse," he muttered. He looked through the port at Jones-Walker, who was standing and removing the polygraph's arm band. Her face was expressionless, her eyes cold. "I told them we'd have an official announcement in another twenty minutes. You want to handle it?"

"Yes." Mancini raised his hand. "With your input, of course." He cleared his throat. "Are the missing-child procedures all operational? Have we got all our bases covered?"

"Yeah," Hopkins answered as he rehung the painting. "Everything's up and running. We've got a team at the Walkers' house. Put a tracer on the phones. Got the girl's bedsheets for the canine unit." They walked back through the records office. "We've given the description of the Cherokee to PIMS and the State Police Emergency Network. And we've sent a poster of the girl out over the NCIC Network. I was on hold at the FBI when you came in."

"The Feds?" Mancini asked. "That may be a little premature, Hoop. I don't think we need to involve them until we've got a better idea of what's going on." He scratched his chin. "Let's take care of the media first, and then . . ." Shouts in the hallway interrupted him, and he and Hopkins rushed through the records office doorway.

Robert "Sky" Walker, facing Monique Jones-Walker in the corridor, shouted, "I asked *why* you weren't there to pick her up?" His voice boomed in the hallway. Standing with his hands on his hips, he looked even larger than six-ten and two hundred and forty-five pounds. His gray-green, hand-tailored Italian suit fit impeccably. His black hair was closely cropped, and the beard he had been growing throughout the NBA playoffs was neatly trimmed. His eyes were wide with anger and fear.

Jones-Walker took a deep breath and said defiantly, "My meeting ran late."

"Your meeting?" Shaking his head, Walker looked away. The noise in the Investigations Unit office subsided for a moment as the officers gaped through the glass partition at the Walkers.

"Yes," she said. "My meeting." She stared at her husband as he buttoned and then unbuttoned his double-breasted jacket.

Sergeant Banks, standing to the side and behind Walker, caught Hopkins' eye.

Hopkins, who could not remember ever before thinking Banks looked small, stepped forward and said, "Mr. Walker, Mrs. Jones-Walker, there's an interview room at the other end of the office." He pointed to the Investigations Unit door. "Perhaps, we . . ."

"I've been in that interview room, Mr. Hopkins," Jones-Walker snarled through her teeth.

"There's a different room, ma'am," Mancini said as he approached the couple. "You'll be more comfortable." He extended his hand. "I'm Chief Peter Mancini. We're doing everything possible to see that there's a successful resolution to this matter." As he shook Walker's hand, he added, "Mr. Hopkins here, our Investigations Unit Commander, will apprise you of what's already being done."

As Walker's massive shoulders sagged, Sergeant Banks stepped around him and held the door open. Walker ducked his head as he entered the office. Ignoring everyone staring at him, he crossed the room with long, deliberate strides.

A table and lamp stood at each end of the plaid couch along one wall in Interview Room A. A framed Andrew Wyeth print of a meadow at dusk hung on the beige wall above the couch. Matching green armchairs faced each other across a low coffee table. Walker slumped into the chair to the right of the couch, leaned forward, his knees almost touching his chest, and rubbed his face with his hands. Jones-Walker, sitting in the chair against the opposite wall, crossed her legs and straightened her suit skirt.

After Hopkins shut the door and took a seat on the couch, he said, "In situations like this, it's best to begin with . . ."

"I can't believe this," Walker said. His huge hands shaking, he looked at the ceiling. "You do everything possible . . ." Beads of sweat ran down his temples. His eyes welled as he gazed at his wife. "Jesus Christ, Monique, what's happened to my Tonya?" His deep, plaintive voice reverberated in the small room like a tolling bell.

chapter 6

At 12:15 A.M., Jack Bollinger slung his trenchcoat over the partition of his cubicle in the WLN newsroom. He set a steaming mug of coffee between the piles of folders on his desk, sat down, and switched on his computer terminal. By the time he had left the North Ridge Gymnastics Center, the place had been overrun with police and the press and all manner of gawkers. Tape of his initial report, particularly the clip of Monique's mini-rant, had circumnavigated the globe in the first hour, and, after the cops had begun to harass him, he'd slipped back to the station and done live updates every twenty minutes until midnight.

Reporters from around the world were already converging on North Ridge, descending on Chicago like hyenas in heat, but he'd scooped them all. He'd been first, the top dog, so far ahead of the pack that the others were hopelessly yapping at his ass. He relished his nickname, Pit Bull, took it always as a compliment, even when it was used in a derogatory tone. He wasn't pretty enough—or, frankly, enough of a backslapper and bootlicker—to be offered an anchor spot or his own specials, but everyone knew that once Pit Bull sank his teeth into a story, the truth, no matter how rancid, would be bared to the bone. And this story was, as he'd already been informed, the crime of the century, the scoop of a lifetime.

After logging onto the computer, he stood and scanned the newsroom, normally a tomb at this time of night, watching the peons scurry about. The brouhaha had temporarily abated, but there were still two dozen station-serfs pulling all-nighters, scouring the morgue, looting the archives, slap-dashing, throwing together anything to keep WLN out in front of the competition—where *he'd* put the station. The flow of energy in any crisis was phenomenal, and this was going to zone nuclear before it was over. He caught a glimpse of the titsy young, exquisitely nubile Columbia College intern as she bustled by with a stack of tapes. She exuded carnality and gravity-defying wonders. He sat again and sipped the strong, bitter coffee, hot and black as always—no yuppie latte or mincing mocha or cutesy cappuccino for him, and definitely no faggoty decaf.

Checking his e-mail, he found, just as he'd expected, another communiqué from the kidnapper. One of the NBC dweebs had already nicknamed him the Skyjacker—just the sort of inane and misleading drivel you got from those pretty boys. This lunatic was a snatcher, *the Snatcher.* And his message now was characteristically curt and condescending—

Kudos, Pit B!
Good show!
Atta, boy.
The best bones ever will be tossed your way soon.
Sit.
Stay!

But it was to him, and him *only*. Patience wasn't his long suit, but this story was monumental, and he'd stand by, as long as necessary, for the Snatcher's next dispatch. He scratched his scalp, and a little more dandruff settled onto his shoulders. In the meantime, he could scope the station scuttlebutt, see how the honchos had reacted to his scoop. He was even more tempted to browse through his collection or maybe join one of his more esoteric chat groups, but that wasn't exactly politic with all the current hotfooting in the newsroom. This story, *his story*, was going to eat air so fast that every interview, no matter how mundane, every sound bite, every snippet of info would run and rerun to keep feeding the voracious tube. He'd known well before the brass confirmed it that WLN and the networks and superstations and any other station that could muster the manpower would begin round-the-clock coverage by daybreak.

Shortly after dawn, Tom Hopkins climbed the breakfront along the Lake Michigan shore. To the west clouds billowed above the trees, but the sky was clear over the lake. The water glistened—far out sparkling sunlit gems and inshore tumbling silver. He sat on a boulder just above the roistering surf. Waves broke in a turbulent roar, the water exploded in front of him, and the rip-rap below him gleamed. In the distance, Chicago's skyline wavered in haze the sun was just starting to burn off.

He had slept for two hours, awakened suddenly to a surge of images from the night before, splashed cold water on his face, called into the department to learn that there had been no new developments, pulled on shorts and a faded Notre Dame sweatshirt, and jogged from his garage apartment along the quiet streets and back through the park to the shore. He'd grown up with the lake, fishing along the finger piers with his father, riding bikes with buddies to the beach, and watching submarine races with girlfriends in high school. And, the last few years, since his divorce, whenever he'd needed to think, whatever the season, he'd come to the lakeshore early, before other people were around, and let the waves speak to him. The more raucous the lake, the more settled he became.

He had heard other cops say that there was invariably one case that they never quite got over, that affected them more than all the others, that haunted them still—and he'd awakened knowing that Tonya Walker's abduction would be that case for him. He gazed at vapor rising above a damp chunk of driftwood jammed between the boulders. He had no idea how things would turn out. The newspapers and the morning TV news shows had splashed the story around the world, flooding the media and drowning all other stories. Rumors were already swirling, and already there were troubling inconsistencies—Jones-Walker's apparent phone call and her failure when answering some of the polygraph questions about the meeting she'd attended, the sighting of the red Jeep, the rewired alarm at the gymnastics center's maintenance entrance, Sky Walker's obvious anger at his wife, and, most ominous of all, the TV station's having been contacted before anyone even knew that the girl was gone. But there was still no ransom demand. The kidnapper had simply vanished with the child.

As the waves beat the rocks, he thought of the pictures and descriptions of Tonya Walker sent out over the Internet. And then he thought of his own seventeen-year-old daughter, Cari. If anything happened to her, he'd be devastated. He couldn't imagine how he would've reacted had she been abducted when she was nine. It involved thinking about the unthinkable. He breathed the cool, damp air and squinted at the sun and dazzling lake. Each wave, for one brief moment before it broke, was a smooth, curling wall of light brighter than fire. Flaming wall upon flaming wall.

chapter 7

James Robert Saville dimmed the
Command Center lights and cracked the washroom door. He
still wore the overalls, but the Sky Walker mask and the gloves
were neatly stowed in their spots on the shelves. When his
eyes adjusted to the darkness, he could make out the girl in the
scant light filtering over his shoulders. She was huddled, asleep
on her side, her cuffed hands under her head. Her tangled
hair covered her eyes; dried blood caked her chin. Her nakedness, like everything else, was part of the master plan, another
of the hooks for the media. It meant nothing to him, but it'd
beguile that pervert and the other media morons. And anyway,
it was necessary for sanitary reasons. She would have to be
cleaned up, of course, and the blood and puke and urine on the
floor tiles would need to be washed away.

He bit his lip. He hadn't intended to hit her, but that incessant yelling had gotten to him. And that defiance in her
glare—it had been so much, too much, like that look of

Sarah's. He hadn't counted on her reminding him of Sarah. Personal involvement with the girl was the last thing he needed on this operation. That French bitch was right. Attachment *was* the great fabricator of illusion. *Reality* was only attained by someone detached.

He shut the door, sat in the swivel chair, and rotated twice. Too wired to sleep after what he was sure was the most brilliantly conceived and perfectly executed kidnapping ever, he'd spent the night first watching more of the "returns" from the media and then checking out the NCIC electronic poster—the likeness was excellent, but nothing compared with what the Netheads and the media morons would see in another hour. Toward dawn, to placate himself, he'd logged through an anonymous posting into a hot tub for a scalding hot-chat with MEGAMAX and his VALKYERIE in San Francisco.

He ate a couple of handfuls of Cheetos, swigged some RC, and wiped his hand on a Wash n' Dry until every bit of the orange residue was gone from his fingers. With the kid in the washroom, he'd have to go upstairs to shower. It was to avoid just such inconveniences that he'd had the washroom installed when he'd designed the Command Center. Over the past three years, he'd grown used to working for his corporate clients for days on end in the Command Center with no breaks except to shower and eat. The sun never rose or set in the Command Center, and staying on task had been what, he knew, had made him the best. His clients had been more than happy to pay his exorbitant fees even though they'd never known who he really was or even in what state he was located. And his fees had risen astronomically as he'd cracked larger and more sophisticated systems, stolen more deeply sensitive and confidential information, and ultimately planted smarter and more powerful electronic bombs that had taken out whole systems, whole companies. But none of those corporate gambits, brilliant

though they'd been, had been nearly so intricate, so meticulously planned, so stunningly executed, or so personally satis-
fying as this operation. All the world would watch, indeed,
hang on his every move, as he finally balanced the ledger, set
the record straight, made his indelible mark, flew high above
the masses.

He turned and stared at the open shelving. Perhaps the
blood and puke on her face would be good, a bonus that would
make the shots even more enticing to the media morons. Yes,
he'd clean her up after the shots, not before. And the whole
world would see what had become of Monique-the-Media-
Babe's treasured daughter. He got the Skywalker mask, the
work gloves, and his still-video Xap Shot camera, already
loaded and ready to go. Grinning behind the mask, he slipped
into the washroom, flicked on the light, and slammed the door
behind him.

Tonya raised her head, eyes blinking, disoriented, wondering
where she was. "Mom," she mumbled. "Dad?" She shut her
eyes against the flash of light and covered them with her cuffed
hands.

"Hands down!" screamed the high-pitched voice. "Smile
for the camera."

Memory of what had happened returned with the sound of
the voice, and she squirmed away until the straps chafed her
ankles. The Beast was back, the Beast with her father's face,
the dark shadow looming in all that light. She licked her dry,
encrusted lips, dropped her hands, and opened her eyes just as
another flash blinded her. She shook her head, but the Beast
would not go away, so she drew herself up on her hands and
knees and then raised herself further and began her safety yell
amid more flashes.

*   *   *

He kept his angle high, to diminish her, and aimed always toward the corner so the pigs'd have no clue about where she was incarcerated. The yelling did not bother him as much this time because her open mouth and closed eyes made it look as though she were screaming in pain. When he had taken the tenth shot, he stepped back and said, "Time to clean up, young lady!" At the door, he turned the shower handles to full blast, flipped the fan switches, watched for a moment as the water from all three spigots pelted her, and then slipped back out to the Command Center. The entire shoot had taken him less than two minutes.

The water was hot and, seeming to come at her from everywhere, quickly drenched her. Her ankles and wrists stung where she'd yanked against her bonds. She stopped yelling, threw her hair back out of her face, and wiped the caked blood from her mouth and chin. She gingerly touched her swollen nose, blew the dried blood out, breathed in, and coughed pink phlegm from her throat. Her forehead had a bump, and her head where he had struck her was sore, but she felt better, not quite as queasy as before. But where was she? Why was she trapped in this bright steaming cave with the Beast? Was her mother really angry at her? She hadn't *wanted* to leave the gym. And what about her father? He'd for sure come to get her. Or send Anthony. When Anthony'd dropped her off, he'd promised to pick her up. And her mother'd always told her Anthony'd be there if anything went wrong. It was Anthony's job. "Mom," she repeated, her eyes stinging in the heat. "Dad? Please . . ."

*   *   *

James Robert Saville took the videodisc from the Xap Shot camera, inserted it into the computer's auxiliary drive, and scanned the photographs. He soon rejected four of them, three that weren't clear enough and one that was too graphic. He wanted the photos to be sensational, her nakedness and bondage and bloodiness obvious, but not so lurid that the legitimate press and the networks would refuse to glut the world with them. Titillation was the goal, of course, not overt pornography, which might detract from his mission. The other six would do just fine. Cleaning his glasses, he mused about his plan to release one photo every two hours, each routed through different hubs so that they'd be untraceable, and all billed to, and seeming to have originated from, the same Los Angeles address. It was all too easy, really.

He put on his glasses and examined the six photos again. They were good, very good, diminishing the child just so. She was less defiant, more vulnerable. Less like Sarah. Not really at all like Sarah. He sucked in his breath. He had to keep his distance, safe within the glacial ring. Involvement meant pain, pure searing agony. And that wasn't going to happen again. Ever. Letting out his breath, he decided to go first with the shot of her hunched on all fours, sideways to the camera, her mouth open in a silent scream. The photo of her covering her face with her cuffed hands caught his eye. That little gold ring might prove quite useful if anyone dared to doubt his tenacity or his will.

chapter 8

At **8:15 A.M.,** seated at his desk, Hopkins finished leafing through the lead sheets on red Skywalker Grand Cherokees and gazed for a moment at his daughter Cari's framed senior portrait half-hidden by a pile of file folders. Her ash-blond hair fell to her shoulders, her green eyes were bright, and her smile was wide.

Barely controlled chaos reigned in the Investigations Unit office. The emergency telephone lines, installed overnight, rang incessantly, and Hopkins had already assigned one uniformed officer to screen the scores of volunteers, detectives from other departments, and people from the community who wanted to help with the investigation. Outside, the reporters and newscasters hummed like locusts. Reluctant to relinquish any control over the case, Chief Mancini had not contacted the FBI at all during the night. But the Bureau's director had called early that morning and insisted that, at the very least, an agent from the Behavioral Science Unit be assigned to the case as an adviser.

Before eight o'clock, Hopkins had debriefed the evidence technicians who had found both fibers and drops of blood on the janitor's cart outside the gymnastics center's service entrance. He'd also sent a new team over to the Walkers' house to relieve the officers and the department's consulting psychologist, who had spent the night there. The stacks of lead sheets were already too large to analyze, much less follow up, and the investigative teams were sifting through the more than seventy possible Tonya Walker sightings in northern Illinois and southeastern Wisconsin alone. There were scores of possible sightings in other states, a smattering from Canada and Mexico, and even one from Germany and another from Jordan. Red Skywalker Jeeps had been checked out all over the Midwest, but two leads on the sheets in front of him had especially grabbed Hopkins—one of a Jeep rented from Hertz at O'Hare Airport the previous Friday and the other of a Jeep stolen Saturday night in Milwaukee.

A bald, tan, incredibly fit-looking man in his middle fifties glided through the office door with Meghan Ross, the bright, attractive young officer Hopkins had assigned to fend off the media and public at the department's front entrance. When she pointed to Hopkins, the man patted her on the shoulder, let his hand slide down her arm, and whispered in her ear before turning his attention to Hopkins. "Thomas 'Hoop' Hopkins," the man said as he entered the fishbowl, "this is a pleasure." His dark worsted wool suit draped neatly over the tops of his black leather slip-ons. His gold and diamond tie pin glistened, and his smile shone. He slipped a gold case from his suitcoat, deftly snapped out a gold-embossed business card, and handed it to Hopkins. "Bert Adelman, Tom," he said. "Robert Walker's attorney and agent."

Hopkins scanned the card, which read,

Albert I. Adelman, MBA, JD
Walker Management, Ltd.
The Skywalker Foundation
Chicago • New York • Los Angeles

The lower corners of the card held phone and fax numbers for the offices.

Hopkins traced the edge of the card with his thumbnail, cocked his head, and asked, "What can I do for you, Mr. Adelman?"

"Well, Tom," Adelman answered, glancing around the room. "We need to talk. Somewhere less congested, if possible."

Suspecting that the purpose of the lawyer's visit was to offer a reward, Hopkins did not see the need for privacy or a lengthy conversation. He scratched the side of his nose. "I'm pretty busy right now, Mr. Adelman."

"Call me Bert, Tom," Adelman said. His eyes narrowed. "And you're not too busy to hear what I have to say. It pertains directly to the case."

Hopkins nodded. "Five minutes?"

"Less than that," Adelman answered, smiling amicably.

Hopkins led him to Interview Room A, where he had met with the Walkers the night before. Adelman sat on the couch, tugged at his gold and diamond cuff links, and leaned forward. As Hopkins took the armchair to the right, Adelman said, "I need to apprise you of two issues, Tom." When he held up the index and middle fingers of his right hand, his University of Chicago class ring gleamed in the light. "Firstly," he continued, glancing at his Philippe Patek watch on its dark alligator band, "in less than forty-five minutes, I will hold a press conference at the Walker house during which I will announce that Walker Management is offering a two-

million-dollar reward for information leading to the safe return of Tonya Walker."

Hopkins nodded.

"And," Adelman went on, "each of the major corporations
whose products Sky endorses—Reebok, All-Sport, Chrysler/
Jeep, Hertz, and Burger King—has offered to match that
sum." He sat back, hooked his arm along the top of the couch,
and crossed his legs.

Startled, Hopkins said, "Twelve million dollars? The
ransom demand, if and when we receive one, may not be
that high."

"Exactly." Adelman smiled. "Anyone with information will
be compelled to come forward."

Hopkins thought about it for a moment, patted the knees
of his khakis, and said, "Fine. It can't hurt."

Adelman leaned forward again. "Furthermore," he said,
"we're poised to provide considerable aid with the investigation." He paused, but Hopkins, who did not like the sound of
it, made no response. "Late last night," Adelman continued, "I
contracted with the firm of Baker and Bransfield to pursue a
private inquiry into Tonya's disappearance."

Hopkins exhaled slowly. "The 'investigators to the stars'?"
he asked. "That may prove counterproductive, Mr. Adelman."

"And that attitude, Tom," Adelman said as he fingered the
knot of his dark burgundy silk tie, "is exactly why we're having this little chat. The Walkers have authorized me to do
everything possible to ensure that Tonya returns home safely."
He stared at Hopkins. "And Baker and Bransfield, whatever
your misinformation about the firm, is top-drawer, an excep-
tional resource." He smiled cordially. "It's a done deal, Tom.
Don't take it personally. Cameron Bransfield, a good friend of
mine, flew the red-eye from L.A., and at the press . . ."

Meghan Ross, the officer who had accompanied Adelman

to the Investigations Unit office, poked her head in the doorway and said, "Pardon me, Commander Hopkins. Mr. Bollinger is here." Ross was twenty-seven years old, slim and sinewy, and almost a foot shorter than Hopkins. Her uniform fit snugly over her lithe runner's body.

Hopkins smiled at her, glanced over to see Adelman eyeing her, and said, "Keep him on ice until after the ten A.M. briefing."

Ross had been training with Hopkins to be the department's assistant public information officer, and they had developed a subtle, almost telepathic ability to communicate with each other. She returned his smile, shifted her eyes fleetingly to the doorway, and said, "He apparently has information relevant to the investigation. His exact words were, 'crucial, absolutely critical.' "

Hopkins nodded. Standing up, he said, "If you'll excuse me, Mr. Adelman, I'll be back in a minute."

Anger flashed momentarily in Adelman's eyes, but he said, "Of course, Tom." Before Hopkins even turned to the door, he was slipping his cellular flip-phone from his pocket.

chapter 9

As soon as Ross and Hopkins left the Investigations Unit office, Ross took his elbow to stop him. Her eyes, blue-green in the light, betrayed her anxiety. "Hoop," she said, "something's wrong." Energy flowed through her grip. "I don't know what Pit Bull's got, but he's acting weird. Creepy, conspiratorial. He left the camera crew out by the van, and he's cut out all that tough-guy crap of his. He kept talking to me in a sort of whisper."

Hopkins wasn't sure what Bollinger was up to, but he knew that dealing with him and Adelman at the same time would be tricky. "Stick with me on this one, Meghan," he said as they began walking again. "I may need you to handle Adelman."

"Okay, Hoop. That old goat in there thinks he's slick, huh?"

Hopkins smiled. "Be careful, Meghan," he said. "He's got to be a pretty savvy player to be Walker's agent." Touching her forearm, he added, "When you get a chance, tell Maniatis to run a background check on Mr. Adelman."

Halfway down the main corridor they met Chief Mancini

and a short, handsome, sturdily built black man in a khaki summer suit. Hopkins slowed but did not stop.

"Hoop," Mancini said, "we were on our way to your office." He clicked his teeth. "This is Carl Henderson, the FBI agent assigned to the case."

Hopkins paused and said, "Tom Hopkins, Agent Henderson." A records office clerk carrying a stack of printouts scurried by them.

"Good to meet you, Mr. Hopkins," Henderson said in the slow drawl of his native Texas. His handshake was firm. His thick neck and sloping shoulders were vestiges of the NCAA wrestling championship that had indirectly led to the Rhodes Scholarship, Yale Law degree, and meteoric career in the FBI's Behavioral Science Unit.

"This is Officer Ross," Hopkins said as he stepped back.

While Ross shook Henderson's hand, Mancini suggested, "I thought you could get Agent Henderson up to speed, Hoop."

"Yeah, sure," Hopkins answered. He glanced back toward the Investigations Unit office. "Can you give me ten minutes? I've got Walker's lawyer in the interview room and Bollinger in the lobby."

"No problem," Henderson said. "I'll wait in your office."

Frowning, Mancini said, "Pit Bull's in the lobby?"

"Yes," Ross answered. "He asked to speak to Hoop personally."

Still glowering, Mancini said, "Hold onto him, Hoop." He ran his tongue over his front teeth. "He's got some serious explaining to do about how he got to that gym before we did."

Hopkins and Ross found Jack Bollinger sitting in one of the brown plastic molded chairs that lined the wall opposite the glass entranceway, guarded by the young uniformed officer who had been at the gymnastics center. He stood stiffly, looking out at the reporters, cameramen, and technicians who were milling about in the crowded lot and talking in small knots as though they were waiting outside the gate of some theme park or ball game. Beyond them, a line of television vans, with mini-satellite dishes and raised signal processors, lined the driveway and street. Three network helicopters hovered above the trees.

Bollinger stood up and, shaking Hopkins' hand, said, "Jack Bollinger, WLN News." His voice was low but not nearly as gravelly as the voice he used on the air. Without makeup, his skin looked waxen; the circles beneath his eyes were dark, and his temples and cheeks were marred by pockmarks.

"I remember you, Mr. Bollinger," Hopkins said.

Bollinger held up a manila envelope. "This was faxed to the station forty minutes ago. To my attention." He looked over at Ross.

"Officer Ross is privy to anything you show me, Mr. Bollinger," Hopkins said.

Bollinger glanced again at Ross, smirked, and said, "All right, if that's the way you want it." He handed the envelope to Hopkins, stuffed his hands in his pants pockets, and shifted his dark eyes from Hopkins to Ross and back.

Hopkins slid the fax from the envelope, and the instant he saw that it showed Tonya Walker naked, bloody, on all fours, handcuffed, and shackled to the wall, he sucked in his breath, and muttered, "Goddamn it . . . goddamn it."

Ross, looking over his elbow, shuddered and whispered, "Oh, Jesus." She sagged for a moment against his arm and then stepped back and straightened up.

Bollinger rocked back and forth on his heels, his eyes gleaming.

"What came with this?" Hopkins asked. Despite the churning in his stomach, he kept his voice even. "Where's the cover sheet? What'd it say?"

Bollinger took his hands from his pocket and rubbed his forefingers and thumbs together. " 'A gift for WLN News,' " he answered. " 'Sic 'em, Pit Bull.' "

Hopkins stared at the photograph. The child's wordless cry rang in his ears. "Where'd it come from?" he asked.

Shrugging, Bollinger squinted at Ross for a moment.

"What're you going to do with it?" Hopkins asked.

"That copy's yours," Bollinger answered. The corner of his mouth turned up.

"I meant, what is the station going to do with the photo?"

Bollinger shrugged again. "We've *got* to run it," he said.

"When?" Hopkins asked.

Bollinger glanced at Ross, licked his lips, and said, "My producer gave me fifteen minutes to inform you before we cut to a newsbreak."

Hopkins smiled sardonically. "Thanks," he said, holding Bollinger's gaze. "You know, this, coupled with the contact last night, makes it look like the perp's got something going with you and WLN."

Bollinger continued to rock on his heels. "Yeah. So what?"

"Does it occur to you that the guy's using you?"

"I've thought of that," Bollinger said.

"But you're going to broadcast the photo anyway?" Hopkins asked.

"Are you kidding?" Bollinger retorted, pointing to the photograph. "Millions of viewers'll tune in to get a glimpse of that." His gravelly on-air voice slipped out for the first time. "And anyway, if we don't run it, the guy'll sure as shit find somebody else who will."

Hopkins slid the photograph back into the envelope and turned to Ross. "Will you escort Mr. Bollinger to Interview

Room B?" he said. "I want him to make a statement for the record." He tapped the edge of the envelope against the palm of his hand. "Both about this and last night—how he found out about the kidnapping. We'll need a copy of the cover sheet and any other information the station's got on the source. Tell Beltram I want him to handle it personally." He looked at Bollinger and asked, "Did you ever work with Mrs. Walker?"

"Monique?" Bollinger said. "Yeah. What of it?"

Hopkins nodded thoughtfully, caught Ross's eye, said, "Excuse me," to Bollinger, and started back along the corridor.

"Look, Hopkins," Bollinger called after him, "I didn't *ask* to get involved in this."

Hopkins stopped, turned, cocked his head, waved the envelope once, and said, "Neither did Tonya Walker."

chapter 10

Enthralled, James Robert Saville surfed the channels. As the thumb of his impaired hand struck the super-remote's buttons, he saw his work everywhere. Lunatic scurrying and glib blathering far and wide, high and low, coast to coast, pole to pole. Everywhere! In the ceaseless pontifications of politicos—from podunk mayors to foreign premiers, from the president mouthing prayers to the speaker of the House haranguing the hoi polloi over their pathetic paucity of values. Downtown at the United Center and at loads of arenas and amphitheaters across the country, legions of fanatics, garbed in red-and-black Bulls gear, gathered to wail and gnash. In the Lose-iana hamlet where Skywalker hatched, the folks scratched, benumbed. Inside the gymnastics center, the news geeks poked and peeked now that the pigs had vacated. At the North Ridge Pig Depot, the vanguard of the invasion pressed on, a phalanx of interlopers and their electronic arrays in full siege! And, ultimately, at the Walker manse itself, the quivering helicopter shots showed the vast fleet of media vehicles out front beyond the fence—and even the lake out back flashed and clapped its approbation! It was such a bravura blitz! And they were all, everywhere, his convoys, his army, his stormtroopers goose-stepping to his anthem, so masterfully commanded that they marched inexorably on, only vaguely aware, not yet fully cognizant, of his dominion!

WLN had run the first photo, of course, showing it five distinct times during the ninety-second newsbreak. Pit Bull, that muddleheaded mutt, had kept his paw raised the entire night. But then the station had procrastinated almost an hour before airing the image, which was absolutely unacceptable. The copies later faxed to the networks, the wannabe networks, and the superstations had all made the airwaves in under ten minutes. And now the photo, too, was everywhere, even the Spanish and Polish channels. Omnipresent, it was. Omnipotent, he was, the commander-in-chief of the whole assault, the entire theater!

He removed his headphones, heard that irksome, unremitting yelp, shook his head, and pushed his glasses up on his nose. He reached over to the box of individually wrapped Hostess chocolate cupcakes on the counter, lifted one out, carefully unwrapped it so that no chocolate morsels fell onto his equipment, and jammed the cupcake whole into his mouth. Rubbing his fingers and thumb together on a Wash n' Dry, he gazed at the wall clock. In five minutes, the press conference at Walkerville on the Lake would begin. And that, he knew, would be carried live by all the stations. Everybody. Everywhere.

He chewed and swallowed the cupcake, took a triple-belt of RC, and sat back. The scratch on his cheek itched and, as he ran the tip of his finger along it, he remembered he should feed the kid. She'd be dry by now, she and the washroom spotlessly clean again. No more blood or puke or urine. He scooped four cupcakes from the box and lined them on the counter in front of one of the scanners.

Tonya Walker was ready for the Beast this time. Crouched in the corner, leaning forward to hide much of her body, she shouted louder as soon as she heard the click of the door. Her hair, still damp, dangled in thick clumps around her face. When the lights went on, she raised her head and squinted defiantly at the shadow circumscribed by all that brightness. Her antagonism seemed to stop the Beast for a moment, but then he was squatting in front of her, those small eyes deep within that large mask of her father's face. When she stopped her safety yell, he leaned forward as if to get a closer look at her bruised forehead and swollen nose. She snapped out her arms, but the cuffs slowed her, and she missed the mask by an inch.

The Beast lurched backward, almost toppling over, and then the voice was screaming, "Stop that, young lady! That's not nice! Don't you ever try a stunt like that again!" The Beast stood over her, just out of her reach. "Do you hear me, young lady? Never, ever do that again!"

There was a long, silent stalemate, and then the Beast stooped and the voice became softer, almost gentle. "Here's your breakfast, young lady. Be a good girl, and finish all of it. Don't spill!"

She stared at the four cupcakes and the twenty-ounce plastic bottle of Orange Crush standing on the tiles. She was suddenly famished, but she did not touch the food. She had to be strong. Her father would come, she was sure, and she'd hold out until then. She would not eat in front of the Beast, would not give him the satisfaction.

*   *   *

Back in the Command Center, James Robert Saville leaned
against the door he'd just slammed. Breathing deeply, he tore
off the mask and muttered, "Little bitch! Stop defying me!"
Then his shoulders slumped, and he shut his eyes. He shook
his head sadly and murmured, "You never would play the
game. All you had to do was play the game like me. Just give
in to her once in awhile. Not fight her at every turn. And it all
would've been different. Everything would've been okay."

He opened his eyes and glanced up at the television monitor, where Albert Irwin Adelman, sartorially splendid as always,
was standing on the Walkers' front porch speaking into a bank
of microphones. "Wait, Bertie!" he yelled at the screen. "You
can't start without *me*!" Yanking off his gloves, he lunged into
his chair. He fumbled for his glasses, slipped them on, pulled on
his headphones, boosted the sound, and heard, ". . . Management and the five corporations I've just mentioned have pooled
resources to offer rewards totaling twelve million dollars."

As Adelman paused to let that sum sink in, Saville grinned
euphorically. He'd estimated five million—tops. "Way to go,
Bertie!" he screamed. Not that the amount really mattered to
the master plan, but twelve million was truly ludicrous, too
much to be believed. He drummed on the arms of his chair
and began to titter. Twelve million, and the fun had just begun.

As Adelman explained the various ways that information
might be forwarded to the police or directly to Walker Management, Saville leaned forward, elbows on the counter by
the 796 STX keyboard, and spoke aloud to the man, his words
coming in a rush. "So, Bertie, your *audible* voice is just as flat
and boring as your letters and memos. And that snobby, nasal,
overeducated, U. of C. and Harvard tone of yours, Bertie!
You'll lose that, you bagel bastard, when I'm done with you."

Neither of the Walkers was present on the porch. "This is your show, huh, Bertie!" he yelled at the Videot Box. "Your fucking fifteen minutes of fame! Not Monique-the-Media-Babe's! Or her all-star husband's! The Pres, Bertie, can't get this kind of coverage! This is it, Bertie! *The* moment! Yours, Bertie. All yours!" Saville continued chattering rapidly at the television, the morning's crystal scintillating in his central nervous system. He wasn't hooked, he knew. In fact, he had only disdain for anybody who *needed* meth. He had control over it, used it sparingly, only in special moments. And this was one of them. When he'd stepped out of the hot shower, he'd been losing altitude fast, not yet in a tailspin, but definitely at the moment to kick in the afterburners. And now he was soaring again, which was fine. It really was.

He'd procured the meth himself, of course. You couldn't be too careful. The stuff on the street just wasn't pure. Who knew where the hell it came from or what it'd been adulterated with? So he'd simply broken into a pharmaceutical company's computer system, ordered the uppers using an HMO's account, and erased his tracks. A piece of cake, really. No problem at all. "You're grabbing the spotlight," he hooted at Adelman, "but that's okay, Bertie! In cyberspace, info is money, huh, Bertie? And you got lots of both." He guffawed. "I know exactly what you're cooking up for Monique-the-Media-Babe! Hey, I know every deal you've cut, every move you've made, in the last two years. And every buck you've wagered, Bertie! Every fucking bet you've laid! I know when you're gonna take a dump even before you do! How about them bagels, Bertie!"

He stood suddenly and gaped at the Videot Box. Off to the right behind Adelman was a tall, chiseled, broad-shouldered man. His hands were clasped behind his back, and his feet were spread in a military pose. The blond hair falling across his forehead made him look much younger than his forty-six years. Saville slid the super-remote onto the counter, tapped the laptop's keys with his left hand, and stared at the STX's monitor until he'd isolated and enlarged the image. The man's teal shirt was open at the collar, and a gold and diamond crucifix hung from the gold rope chain around his neck. "So Cameron, my man," Saville yelled, "you made your plane. Good going, dude! Glad you've joined up because the surfin' we're gonna do'll wipe you out! Wipe you out, motherfucker!"

He took off his glasses and rubbed his sweating neck with his shirt sleeve. It was hot, too hot, in the overalls, but he had a lot of work to do. And he needed to get cracking if he was going to finish checking his information sources before the next police press briefing. It was happening fast, so fast that lesser intellects couldn't keep up, couldn't make the exquisite sense of it all, couldn't detect the order embedded in the chaos, the logic he'd imposed. "Hey, Bertie," he hollered, "time to shut up!" He had things to do, not just surfing his sources but selecting the next photo and deciding if Pit Bull and WLN deserved another chance to do the job right. Busy, he was, busy, busy.

chapter 11

Shortly before ten o'clock, Meghan Ross brought Hopkins' daughter, Cari, in to see him. Hopkins, arranging his notes for the press briefing, stood up and hugged his daughter. Cari stepped away and gave her father a hard high-five, her North Ridge High School class ring glinting in the overhead light. She was tall and willowy, almost six feet; her hair was pulled back in a ponytail, and she wore no makeup. When she was younger, people had told him she should be a model, but she loved sports, especially basketball, and, until she was a sophomore in high school, had avoided dresses and seen boys primarily as worthy competition on the court. She had started to date regularly but still went to her senior prom with her neighbor, the boys' team's point guard against whom she'd played one-on-one since fourth grade.

"I got out early because I only had one final," she told her father. She glanced out at the office where detectives and uniformed officers were talking on phones, filling out lead sheets, and charting the investigation on a large display board set up near the interview rooms. "I saw you on TV last night, and I, uh, just wanted to see if you're okay."

"Thanks, Car," he said, "I'm doing fine." He shrugged. Despite the fact that they still lived in the same town, he had seen his daughter only intermittently in the last year. His garage apartment was too small for her to spend the night, and, though they scheduled weekly visitations, his work and her school life often upset their plans. He'd gone to most of her home volleyball and basketball games and every play-off game in both sports, but he hadn't played anything but horse with her in three years. His competitive streak still shone whenever he set foot on a court, and he knew that giving one's daughter a facial was bad form. "I've got this press thing in a couple of minutes," he added, rubbing the back of his neck. "Tests go okay?"

"Yep!" She smiled. "Aced 'em all so far. Physics tomorrow, and I'm done with high school *forever.*"

"Good," he said as he picked up his notes and the accordion file he'd need for the briefing. "Well . . ."

Ross touched Cari on the arm. "Maybe it'll help the old guy if you're at the briefing," she said to the girl. "You know, if any of the reporters get too pushy, you can throw an elbow their way."

Cari grinned at her father, and he flashed Ross a grateful smile.

The site for the briefing had been moved outside of the department's front entrance to accommodate the mob of reporters. Under a cobalt sky, more than a hundred journalists and newscasters and their crews formed a tight semicircle around the makeshift dais and podium. Flanked on his right by Chief Mancini and on his left by Agent Henderson of the FBI, Hopkins outlined the progress of the investigation. At first the questions were routine, and he fielded them adeptly, deferring to Mancini on interdepartmental issues and to Henderson when, given the huge sums bet on the NBA play-offs, questions of Mafia involvement came up. Then, a young female reporter from the *Chicago Tribune* asked him to verify rumors circulating that the kidnapper on more than one occasion had contacted Jack Bollinger rather than the police. Nodding, Hopkins answered, "As Chief Mancini mentioned during last night's briefing, the perpetrator notified WLN news *before* the abduction was reported to the police." It was warm in the sunshine, and sweat trickled down his neck and back. "And this morning, a personal note to Mr. Bollinger was faxed to WLN with the lurid photograph of Tonya Walker."

"What did the note say?" the reporter asked.

Hopkins glanced at Henderson. "We cannot at this time," he said, "discuss the content of the note." He looked over at Bollinger, who had positioned himself in the front line of reporters just to the left of center.

Bollinger had put on a striped tie, and the pockmarks on his face were covered with makeup. With all of his colleagues focused on him, expecting him to respond to the question about the note, he cleared his throat and smiled sourly. His voice a notch deeper and even more gravelly than usual, he asked, "Is it true, Commander Hopkins, that Monique Jones-Walker was forced to take a lie detector test last night?"

"No, it is not true," Hopkins answered. "Mrs. Jones-Walker, as well as others who had been at the crime scene, *voluntarily* submitted to polygraph exams. As you well know, Mr. Bollinger, the polygraphs are standard procedure in missing-children cases."

"And the results?" Bollinger snapped as other reporters called out questions.

Hopkins glanced furtively at Mancini, who was wiping the palms of his hands on his uniform, and said, "We're not at liberty to discuss the results except to say that they were generally satisfactory."

"What, Commander Hopkins, does 'generally satisfactory' mean?" Bollinger yelled, his tone contentious.

"It means they were generally satisfactory," Hopkins said flatly. Turning toward other reporters, he saw Cari at the periphery of the group. Although her thumb was raised in a silent salute, she was grimacing.

Hunched in his seat in the Command Center, James Robert Saville peered up at the television screen, spellbound by the press conference. Amid the storm of shouted questions, Bollinger was barking, "What about the call Monique Jones-Walker made to the gymnastics center just before the kidnapping? Can you explain that? And the red Skywalker Grand Cherokee the eyewitness reported—what about that? Was it hers? Didn't she arrive later in a red Jeep?"

Saville leapt from his chair and boogied around the room wildly flailing his air guitar, the headphones' cord trailing him like a guitar cable. "Tharaway, Pit Bull!" he shouted up at the Videot Box, where the other reporters were buzzing and braying. He loved Pit Bull's schtick. The guy certainly deserved first shot at the next photo. He was earning it, all right.

On the Videot Box, the police commander—Thomas Hopkins, Hop the Hoopmeister of old—was saying, "Mr. Bollinger, the investigation will follow all leads, but we have not drawn any conclusions. And I don't believe it would be a good idea for you to draw conclusions, either."

Saville snorted. "Yeah, right!" he yelled. "You got a prayer! They'll be hanging Monique-the-Media-Babe by noon." He stifled another laugh. "And then they'll be after Bertie's ass. You ain't seen nothing yet!" Hop was a newbie, hadn't even been a player when the master plan was first developing. Leapt on stage only three months before the opening. But here he was, sweating bullets—and the real barrage had barely begun.

On the Videot Box, the Hoopmeister, turning his attention from Bollinger, said, "Any other questions?"

A reporter near the back of the crowd shouted, "Commander Hopkins, you characterized the photograph of Tonya Walker as 'lurid'—have you been able to establish a psychological profile of the kidnapper?"

Saville squatted on the arm of his chair and squinted up at the screen. Just before the camera cut away, he glimpsed behind the reporter a young blond woman who reminded him of Sarah. Not really all that close a resemblance, maybe, but close enough. "Well, well," he murmured, "you must be the young Hopster. The little Hoppette. Your yearbook picture really doesn't hack it. We'll have to freeze you when we review the tape of this sitcom! Maybe even print you out!"

On the screen, the FBI agent stepped toward the microphone and said, "We're dealing with a dysfunctional human being . . ."

"Dysfunctional!" Saville shouted at the screen. "The whole goddamned country's dysfunctional! The whole fucking world, you moron!"

". . . But it would be premature," the FBI agent continued, "to hazard a guess as to the exact nature of the disorder we're dealing . . ."

Chief Mancini leaned over in front of Hopkins and, his mouth too close to the microphone, said, "Whoever we're dealing with here, I assure you of one thing. We're going to bring him swiftly to justice." He ran his tongue along his lower lip. Sweat dripped onto his starched shirt and uniform jacket. "Anyone who would do that to an innocent little girl is a coward. A coward and a pervert."

"Coward! Pervert!" Saville screamed at the Videot Box. "You fucking rug-roofed pig!"

"Mark my words. He'll make a mistake. In fact, he's already made several," the police chief continued as Hopkins tried subtly to wedge himself between Mancini and the microphone.

"Mistakes?" Saville screeched. "I don't make mistakes! Your fucking parents made the mistake!"

Henderson attempted to step in front of the Chief, too, but Mancini continued, "He's apparently taking his own deficiencies out on a helpless child."

Saville was out of his chair again, hyperventilating, his hands shaking with rage, his face raised close to the screen. "Deficiencies! What the hell do you know about it, Pig?" he shrieked, saliva spewing from his mouth. "We'll see who's deficient, you pompous shit! You'll pay for this!" He hammered the counter. The fat-assed bastards with all their regulations and relegations, exclusions and expulsions, disavowels and dismissals—none of them had ever understood him. Not in school. Not on the job. They'd never gotten it. Never. They were too deficient to ever get it. And this fucking chrome-domed neo-Nazi was going to pay big time for his ignorance. Big time!

He slammed his headphones to the floor and slumped back into his chair. Except for the small voice still squeaking in the headphones, it was quiet. Too quiet. The kid had stopped her yawping. But he had no idea when. What'd she heard, he wondered, and why was she so silent? He tried to catch his breath as he took the Skywalker mask from its shelf. His hands still quivered while he struggled with the gloves. It was too hot in the mask, and sweat stung his eyes. He lowered the climate control setting to sixty-five, dimmed the Command Center lights, flung open the washroom door, and flicked on the lights.

A scream caught in his throat. She crouched in the corner sneering at him, her teeth bared, her eyes gleaming, and her hair pulled back in a tangle. Black shit covered the walls all around her. She had soiled the walls with her . . . No, it was just the cupcakes. She'd smeared the cupcakes all over the walls as high and far as she could reach. "You little bitch!" he howled. "You think this is funny! You'll . . ."

As he stepped forward, the soles of his boots stuck to the tiles. Wheeling, he saw orange-brown blotches on the walls. She'd shaken the bottle of Crush and sprayed it everywhere. "Goddamn you!" he roared. "Damn you to hell!"

She smirked at him as he came toward her, sniggered at the squeaking boots. "Wipe that smile off your face, young lady! Don't you ever laugh at me." He raised his arm to hit her, to beat her so badly that she'd never laugh at him again, but he stopped himself. She glared up at him, her eyes blazing, her expression so much like Sarah's it was uncanny—just too weird. She *was*, for a moment, Sarah.

His whole arm shook as he backed away. He gasped for breath, tasted the sweat and fury in his mouth. "You'll pay for this mess, young lady," he hissed. "Do you hear me?" His voice was shrill. "You listen to me, young lady. Don't ever pull a stunt like that again! You'll regret it! Regret it, do you hear me?"

chapter 12

Hopkins had selected Interview Room B because it was stark, private, and relatively quiet. He and Agent Henderson sat on one side of the table, and Bert Adelman sat on the other. A clear plastic pitcher of water and three glasses stood next to the tape recorder by Hopkins' left hand; two file folders lay on the table in front of him. After Chief Mancini's televised comments about the case, the day had gone from bad to worse. At two-hour intervals, three additional photographs of Tonya Walker, each as shocking as the first and each accompanied by a personal note, had been faxed to Jack Bollinger, and WLN had wasted no time in airing them. Bert Adelman's offer of the twelve-million-dollar reward had quadrupled the number of calls coming into the lead room, but the only possible breaks came from the fax accounts and the car rental agency. The ultimate source of the faxes was untraceable because they had been routed through hubs in California and New York, but an FBI computer crimes team in Washington, working under Henderson's orders, had already located the account billed for the faxes—AIA Development, Ltd., of Beverly Hills. North Ridge detectives investigating leads on the red Skywalker Grand Cherokee had discovered that the Jeep rented at O'Hare Airport had also been billed to an AIA Development MasterCard account. The follow-up call Hopkins had made to Monique Jones-Walker's producer had been even more unsettling. None of this information had leaked to the media yet, but Hopkins, who had seen one of the teasers for the afternoon news touting "Monique Jones-Walker's possible involvement in her own daughter's abduction," feared the worst. He finished rolling up the sleeves of his blue oxfordcloth shirt, pressed the record button, and said, "I asked for this interview, Mr. Adelman, because of evidence gathered this afternoon. At your request, Mr. Henderson is sitting in."

Resting his muscular forearms on the edge of the table, Henderson nodded to Adelman.

"There are two, actually three, issues," Hopkins continued, "that I believe you can shed light on, Mr. Adelman."

Adelman sat back in his chair, crossed his legs, and turned a little away from the table. He wore the same suit and tie he had worn that morning, but he had put on a fresh shirt. His black leather briefcase stood on the floor next to him. The interview had been scheduled for 4:00 P.M., but he had arrived twenty minutes late.

Hopkins opened the top file folder, took out a sheet of paper, and asked, "Mr. Adelman, what can you tell us about AIA Development?"

Adelman leaned forward, folded his hands on the table, and said, "Why exactly do you need to know, Tom? And what conceivable connection could AIA have with the Tonya Walker investigation?" His tone was far less amiable than it had been that morning.

Henderson leaned forward as well, took the sheet of paper

from Hopkins, and said, "Mr. Adelman, please understand that we are not assuming an adversarial position here." His drawl was slow, but Hopkins had been impressed by his calm astuteness both during their initial conversation after Bollinger had delivered the first photograph and throughout their later meetings. "Mr. Hopkins simply needs to establish the veracity of certain information that has come to our attention during the course of the investigation."

Adelman looked for a moment at Henderson, turned his gaze to Hopkins, and said, "As the name suggests, AIA Development is a real estate venture. I formed it last fall."

"And," Hopkins asked, "what connection does it have to Walk . . ."

"It's completely independent," Adelman interrupted, "of either Walker Management or the Skywalker Foundation."

Hopkins nodded. "And it's wholly owned by you? You're sole owner?"

Adelman glowered at him. "As you no doubt are already aware, Tom," he said, "AIA's a limited partnership with four other principals."

"And one of the principals is Cameron Bransfield?" Hopkins asked.

"You seem to have it all figured out already, Tom," Adelman said sarcastically.

"Thank you, Mr. Adelman," Hopkins said. He listened to the relentless ringing of the telephones in the outer office. Like all those intriguing but ultimately false leads, this meeting, he realized, though absolutely necessary, would produce nothing but antipathy.

Sliding the sheet of paper across the table, Henderson said, "If you'll peruse this invoice, Mr. Adelman."

Adelman gazed at the sheet and then pushed it back at Hopkins. "What is this?" he demanded. "A joke?"

"Mr. Adelman," Hopkins said, "that copy of the Hertz

rental agreement is real. And it's no joke—or at least not my joke." He shuffled the folders, drew four sheets from the second one, and passed them across the table. As Adelman scanned the pages, Hopkins poured water for himself and Henderson. "Would you like some water, Mr. Adelman?" he asked.

Looking up from the papers, Adelman shook his head and then said, "Yes. Yes, I would."

Hopkins poured the water, set the glass in front of Adelman, and glanced at Henderson.

"Mr. Adelman," the FBI agent said, "all four photographs faxed to Mr. Bollinger thus far have been billed to your development company. I expect that WLN is receiving another one, even as we speak. And it, too, I'm quite certain, will be billed to you."

Adelman shook his head slowly, tapped the papers with his forefinger, sat back, and looked away at the walls, all of which were bare except for the one-way viewing port that reflected the light like a mirror. Raising his hand as if to wave the information away, he said, "This is absurd." His voice was nasal, devoid of emotion. "You can't possibly think that I'm involved in Tonya Walker's . . . in all of this." He glanced from Henderson to Hopkins.

Hopkins took a sip of water, put down the glass, and said, "No, Mr. Adelman, I don't think you're involved. You're certainly not stupid enough to bill the vehicle or the faxes to your own company."

"Mr. Adelman," Henderson said, "I have concluded, sir, that the perpetrator has thoroughly infiltrated your business systems, obtained access to your accounts, and perhaps even altered your records. My assumption is that he—or they—have done this while seeking information on the Walkers."

Adelman drank half the water. "I'll get Baker and Bransfield on this immediately," he said.

"With all due respect, Mr. Adelman," Henderson said, "this hacker appears to be more than a bit sophisticated."

"Mr. Henderson," Adelman answered, fingering his University of Chicago ring, "I spend my life routinely handling problems far more complex than some computer nerd's diddling with corporate records."

"That may be true, sir." Henderson's tone was courteous. "But I have authorized an FBI team to look into this matter and, thus far, they haven't found any trace of this 'computer nerd' in AIA's or Walker Management's files."

"The FBI's going through my computer records?" Adelman asked, his tone incredulous.

"A search warrant's been obtained, sir," Henderson answered. "And the team's only examining them for signs of tampering that might present a pattern or, if we get lucky, a trail."

Adelman pursed his lips and stared at Henderson. Sweat beaded on the top of his head among the few wisps of greying hair. "What exactly do you plan to do with all this information?" he asked.

As Hopkins reached over, took back the four sheets of paper, and refiled them, he said, "At this time, there are no plans to release any of it publicly."

"Thank God for small favors," Adelman scoffed.

"But," Hopkins went on, "my guess is that if the information doesn't leak to the press soon, the perp'll make sure Bollinger gets it anyway."

"Speaking of media problems . . . ," Adelman said.

"Mr. Adelman," Hopkins interrupted, "I mentioned that there were three issues. The car rental invoice and the fax bills are the first two." He paused, scratching the side of his nose. "While speaking with Mrs. Walker's producer earlier today, I learned that she abruptly left yesterday evening's meeting to make a phone call in private after you paged her."

Adelman rooted through his briefcase and pulled out a red

and black folder with Walker Management emblazoned in gold letters across it, laid the folder on the table, and folded his hands on it. "What are you implying now, Tom?" he asked, his voice cold. "That Monique and I were organizing Tonya's abduction? Or merely that she and I were involved in a tryst?"

"Did you page her?" Hopkins asked.

"I did not." Adelman brushed the red and black folder with the side of his hand.

"But," Hopkins said, "Mrs. Walker's producer . . ."

"Her producer's misinformed about who paged her," Adelman said.

"Mrs. Walker, during my initial interview with her and during her polygraph exam, failed to mention the page or her leaving to make a call. Any idea why?"

Adelman lowered his eyebrows, leaned across the table, and said icily, "I have no idea. You'll have to ask Monique about that, won't you, Tom?" He sat back and opened the folder. "Now, are you through?"

"Not quite, Mr. Adelman," Hopkins answered. "If I may be blunt, does it occur to you that the perp has a fixation with Mrs. Walker—and maybe you, too?"

"Or, Tom," Adelman snapped, "maybe he—or, more likely, they—figured out a way to get to Sky Walker, play games with the media, and yank your chain all at the same time." He slipped a sheet of Walker Management letterhead from the folder and slid it across the table. Speaking to Henderson but looking at Hopkins, he said, "This is a request from the Walker family—and we realize, of course, that it's in no way binding . . ." His voice became softer, once more that of the slick negotiator. ". . . that you, Mr. Henderson, or, if necessary, one of your superiors in the FBI, assume full responsibility for the investigation into Tonya's disappearance. We simply cannot allow Tonya's welfare to be dependent on the actions of some suburban police department. And furthermore, the Walkers request that you, Mr. Henderson, and you alone, act as the investigation spokesman during media briefings."

Anger rose in Hopkins' belly, but he said nothing.

Henderson took longer to read the document than he needed to. Then he gazed directly at Adelman and said, "I understand full well the need for a more global perspective on this case, sir. But the investigation is, by definition, a joint operation, requiring both local and national resources. And, sir . . ."

"I appreciate that," Adelman said, his tone oily. "But Tonya's abduction is, as I've been trying to elucidate, an event of national, even international, significance. And it's the Walkers' feeling that the FBI could better direct the investigation than a suburban . . ." He waved his hand. "As to the role of spokesman, not only are you far more qualified than Mr. Hopkins or his Chief, but, let's face it, the fact that you are black provides an excellent image vis-à-vis the media."

"May I remind you, sir," Henderson said, "that I'm here by invitation of the North Ridge Police Department." He shook his head. "And, sir, race is not an issue."

Adelman stared at Henderson again. "Neither you nor I believe that," he said, his voice low and blunt for a moment. "And anyway, the crux of the issue remains the case management. If the abduction was as well executed as it seems to have been and if, as you say, both the Walkers' and my computer records are at risk, it stands to reason that a group with considerable manpower and resources is at the center of it." He twisted his ring. "The possibility of Mafia involvement, for instance, is not being properly investigated by the local authorities." He looked again at Hopkins. "The Las Vegas odds on the NBA Finals have, as you are probably not aware, already shifted dramatically. A hundred million dollars, maybe more, is at risk depending on whether Sky Walker plays."

Hopkins took a deep breath and asked, "Did you hear *any-thing* I was telling you about the perp?"

"Yes, Tom, every word." Adelman's tone was condescending. "But the tampering with Tonya's clothing at the gym and your Chief's debacle at this morning's briefing . . ." He shrugged. "The Walkers just aren't sure that anyone in this department understands what's happening here."

The ire rose in Hopkins' chest and filled his lungs. He ran his hand through his hair and, barely able to keep his voice even, asked, "The Walkers, Mr. Adelman? Or you?"

Adelman shook his head disdainfully. "Understand at least this, Tom," he said as though having to repeat himself to a child, "As far as you and your department are concerned, I am the Walkers' sole representative in this matter."

Hopkins leaned forward and smacked the tape recorder's off button.

Henderson took a long sip of water, carefully folded the sheet of Walker Management stationery, and then ran his finger along the edge to crease the fold. "Fine, Mr. Adelman," he said, "I agree with you that there are national and international ramifications to this case, that the investigation must broaden in scope. And, I'll present your request to the North Ridge officials and to my superiors at the Bureau." His voice became lower, his drawl more pronounced. "But for what it's worth, sir, I happen to agree with Commander Hopkins that the perpetrator's got some twisted thing going with the Walkers—and even you—that's got nothing to do with the latest Vegas line or any other business."

chapter 13

At dusk, Hopkins drove his silver-gray
Taurus through the gauntlet of media vehicles parked on either side of Lincoln Avenue. Reporters and technicians sat on
hoods, smoking and talking, seemingly ready to mobilize in a
minute if the Walkers moved from their house. The patrol-
man guarding the driveway waved him by, and he stopped in
front of the wrought-iron gates. He looked up at the closed-
circuit television camera on the white steel pedestal, pressed
the intercom button, and said, "Thomas Hopkins, North
Ridge Police, to see Mr. and Mrs. Walker." Late in the afternoon, after a couple of tense conferences, Carl Henderson
had been made co-head of the kidnapping investigation, with
Hopkins retaining only his command of the local detectives.
He had also been relieved of his role as media spokesman. Additional FBI personnel had already moved into the Investigations Unit office. Allegations about the Grand Cherokee and
the faxed photographs being billed to AIA Development had
aired on the network evening news programs—along with

promises from the news anchors that there would be much more about Albert Irwin Adelman and his financial dealings on the nightly news. While at his garage apartment to shower and change clothes, Hopkins had turned on WLN to see the most recent photograph of Tonya Walker, a shot of her with her hands raised, covering her eyes. The gold ring her father had given her showed prominently in the photograph.

As the gates swung slowly open, Hopkins gazed across the wide expanse of lawn and sculpted evergreens at the three-story mansion looming on the bluff above Lake Michigan. The terra-cotta clay tiles of the multilevel roof held the day's last light. The wide eaves, casement windows, and the horizontal reaching lines of the white stucco façade were reminiscent of the earlier, smaller Prairie School houses in the Chicago area. The mansion, flanked by oaks and pines, intimated stability and roots.

He parked next to the coach house, a building slightly larger than the house he had lost to his wife in the divorce settlement. Four of the five garage doors were shut, but the red Skywalker Grand Cherokee stood in the open bay. The American flag on the nearby pole riffled in the breeze; a single star glinted in the darkening sky above the tops of the trees. Power cords used during Adelman's press conference still ran across the mansion's tiled front steps and porch. A helicopter roared in from the south and hovered above the lawn, its lights and cameras following him as he approached the house.

When Anthony Ignacio, wearing a black leather shoulder holster over his white shirt, opened the front door, he frowned. As Hopkins stepped into the huge foyer, his Nikes squeaked on the marble floor. The silver-white walls rose three stories to a domed ceiling. A magnificent crystal chandelier hung above him, and a grand staircase wound to the second floor. The dark frame of Ignacio's Smith & Wesson

.357 Magnum gleamed in the chandelier's light, reminding Hopkins of David Banks' adage that no one who really wanted to should ever be allowed to carry a gun. Hopkins' own standard-issue .38 service revolver was in a holster discreetly clipped to his belt.

"I'm here to see Mr. and Mrs. Walker," Hopkins said.

"I'll check if they're available," Ignacio answered. As he retreated toward the closed door at the back of the foyer, Monique Jones-Walker stepped from the living room and waved him away. She wore a yellow sundress with a scooped neckline. Her hair was pulled back from her face, and she seemed to glow, brown-gold, in the light.

"Your technical team's in the kitchen," she said to Hopkins. "There's more room for them to operate in there."

"Actually, I stopped by to talk with you and Mr. Walker for a moment, if I may," he answered.

"Together or alone?" she asked.

"It doesn't matter, whatever is better for you."

She nodded, turned, and, without a word, led him through the opulent mauve and teal living room past the white grand piano into the library. She sat in the dark leather armchair, crossed her legs, and gestured toward the leather couch.

The burgundy carpeting was plush. Spread above the couch and lining the opposite wall on either side of the single high leaded-glass window were scores of framed photographs of Sky Walker playing basketball, shaking hands with presidents, posing with actors and other sports figures, and greeting corporate executives and foreign dignitaries. A massive glass-front mahogany trophy case dominated the third wall. Filled with testaments to Sky Walker's talent, it held among the lesser trophies and plaques the NCAA tournament Most Valuable Player trophy he won his junior year at Georgetown, the NBA Rookie of the Year trophy he earned the following

year, three NBA Defensive Player of the Year trophies, two
NBA MVP trophies, two NBA Finals MVP trophies, an NBA
all-star game MVP award, an NCAA championship ring, two
Olympic gold medals, and three NBA championship rings.
Hopkins stopped, frozen for a moment, then turned slowly, his
mouth agape, trying to take it all in.

"They do have that effect on men," she said.

As he sat on the couch, he smiled in embarrassment.

She pointed to the bookcases filled with vellum-bound
volumes that rose from floor to ceiling on both sides of the
doorway. "The books are mine," she said. "Collecting anti-
quarian volumes is a hobby of sorts." Her tone was caustic.
"Not a bad hobby, really, for a prime suspect in the kidnapping
of the century."

Folding his hands in his lap, he said, "No one in the department or the FBI believes you had anything to do with
your daughter's abduction, Mrs. Walker." Her reaction the
previous night and her attitude now perplexed him, but he
knew that parents of abducted children often exhibited inap-
propriate responses, even indifference or hostility.

Her almond eyes fired for a moment and then returned to
their cold, hard brightness. "Tell that to my brethren in the
media," she said. "And to the world."

He nodded.

She glared at him. "Don't you for a second, Mr. Hopkins,
think you understand anything about me. What I'm going
through, and what I'm feeling." Her voice was icy. "Nobody
can possibly understand."

He sat with her in silence for a minute before he said, "As
far as I've been able to determine, Mrs. Walker, Bollinger did
not get his information from anyone in the police department.
Do you have any idea who might've leaked the information?"

She gazed out the window at the gathering darkness. "I

tried . . ." When she looked back at him, her eyes were moist. "I tried to work for a while this morning. I got in touch with people at the station through e-mail and the phone, people that I thought were my friends. I let my guard down with a couple of them. Told them what happened last night." She pulled at the hem of her sundress. "I'm not sure which one . . ." As she stared across the room, her eyes hardened again. "That peckerwood, Jack Bollinger, is out to get me," she went on. "I saw the press conference. I know what the bastard said."

He watched her long, thin fingers, the nails polished almost to the color of the carpeting, pick at the hem of her dress. "Why?" he asked. "Why does Bollinger . . . ?"

She shook her head. "Maybe because I got the assignments he wanted. And he thinks it was because I was black and a woman, not because I was a better journalist—which I am." She flicked the end of a loose thread. "Or maybe because I find him laughable. Jack'll chase any skirt, hit on anything that twitches. Even the college interns. The younger the better."

Hopkins sat back and brushed the back of his hand across his face. "Mrs. Walker," he said, "what evidence we have suggests that it's not just Bollinger. It seems as if the perpetrator has some personal . . ."

"Vendetta, Mr. Hopkins?" she said, pain flashing fleetingly in her eyes. "He's got my daughter. And he's smearing obscene photos of her across the world. It couldn't be more personal."

He nodded slowly. "Mrs. Jones-Walker," he said, "there's something I'm confused about . . ."

"Only one thing?" Her tone was derisive.

Letting her comment pass, he said, "Your producer told me that you left yesterday's meeting for a while after Bert Adelman paged you."

"That's right."

"To call Mr. Adelman?"

"Yes. But I couldn't reach him." Her expression was impassive again.

He leaned forward, resting his forearm on his knees. "But Mr. Adelman told me he never paged you."

She sat back in the chair and folded her arms across her chest. "I received that page, Mr. Hopkins. If you'd like, I'll submit to another poly . . ."

"That's not necessary," he said. "But it is, you'll admit, quite a coincidence that you left the meeting to make a call at exactly the same moment Ken Culhane insists he got a call from you."

"Jack Bollinger's already noted that particular irony on the evening news, Mr. Hopkins." She stared past him at the photographs on the wall.

He wanted to find out why, if she was telling the truth, getting immediately in touch with Adelman had been so important that she'd interrupt the meeting, but he realized that neither she nor Adelman would likely tell him. "Have you talked to Mr. Adelman since our meeting this afternoon?" he asked instead.

"Yes, Mr. Hopkins." Her tone betrayed nothing.

"So you know the extent to which the perp's trying to get inside your head?"

The corner of her mouth turned up. "As ill-advised as your Chief's comments this morning were, they were absolutely correct. I understand perfectly that the pervert who's got my daughter wants to destroy me and my family."

"Any idea who it might be?"

"I told you last night, Mr. Hopkins, I don't know anybody who'd do anything like this. And that was before I had a sense of how sick the bastard really is." Gazing down at her hands, she spoke slowly. "Not everybody in the industry likes me. I've made enemies. But it's inconceivable that anybody'd do something like this." She took a deep breath, exhaled, and looked out the window again. A floodlamp had come on, lighting the American flag against the dark trees and sky.

chapter 14

After stopping in the kitchen to talk for a moment with his trap-and-trace team who, twenty-four hours after the abduction, still had no word from the kidnapper but only dozens of crank calls from people who had the Walkers' unpublished number, Hopkins went down the basement stairs. "You've seen the shrine," Monique Jones-Walker had told him at the end of their interview. "If you want to talk to Robert, you'll have to visit the sanctuary." At the bottom of the basement steps, he opened a steel door and, as he descended another flight of stairs, heard the sound of a basketball bouncing on a hardwood floor.

Sky Walker turned when the door opened. Sweat was pouring from his head, dripping from his beard, and streaming down his chest onto his soaked red tank top. His legs below his baggy black shorts were thin, but his shoulders were broad and bulky. A tattoo of a sharply angled S on an octagonal shield gleamed on his dark skin above his bulging right bicep. The gym, carved out of the basement and sub-basement, was semicircular, six feet wider than the old NBA three-point arc. Doors were set into the walls at the corners of the baseline, and overhead lamps with steel mesh covers hung from the twenty-foot ceiling. Forced air hummed from the vents. Walker palmed the basketball, cocked his head, and said, "Mr. Hopkins, I was wonderin' when you'd show up here."

Walking across the court to where the basketball star stood by the free throw line, Hopkins said, "Can I ask you a few questions, Mr. Walker?"

"Do I have a choice?"

"Yeah."

Walker gazed down at the the basketball and then bounced it sharply to him. "Bert tells me you played the game," he said.

"Yeah."

"You have a handle?"

"Hoop. First Hop, then Hoop."

"But you gave up the game?"

Hopkins spun the ball and bounced it twice. "I blew out my knee my sophomore year at Notre Dame."

"The Fightin' Irish, huh?"

"Yeah." Hopkins spun the ball again and then swished an eighteen-footer. "What the *hell's* a Hoya?" he asked.

Shaking his head, Walker said, "Right." He retrieved the ball, looked at it for a moment, and asked, "You got any kids?"

"One. A daughter graduating from high school next . . . this week."

Walker squinted up at the lights and then, while passing the ball back, asked, "What'd you need to talk to me about?"

Hopkins dribbled the ball, moving a couple of steps farther back from the basket. "I wanted to see if there's anything you've thought of that might help us find Tonya." He nailed the jump shot.

Walker grabbed the ball again. "Hoop . . . Can I call you Hoop?"

Hopkins nodded.

"I've thought about nothin' else since last night." Walker bounce-passed the ball back hard. "I didn't sleep or eat or nothin'. I keep goin' into her room, reachin' for her, but she's not . . ." His voice cracked, and he stared again at the lights. "This may not've been my best season, comin' back from surgery and all. But it's been my sweetest. Even playin' hurt every night." He stretched, kneading his lower back. "Nobody believed I could get us into the Finals. Not with me still bein' less than a hundred percent. But I said I would. And we're here." He gestured for Hopkins to shoot.

The ball hit the front of the rim, bounced off the backboard, and fell through the net. Walker snared the ball and winged it back even harder.

His hands stinging, Hopkins moved a few steps to his right.

"It's not public yet," Walker said, "but I'm not gonna play in tomorrow night's game." He lifted the red tank top and mopped his face. His stomach was hard and flat. "One last ride, one more ring was all I wanted. But it means nothin' now. It ain't worth shit to me now." The pain in his voice deepened. "Without Tonya, nothin' is."

"Any idea who might've done it?" Hopkins asked. He held the ball until Walker gestured again, and then he buried the twenty-four-footer.

Walker let the ball bounce and roll dead against the wall. "No," he said. "None." He trotted over and scooped the ball from the floor. "All I wanted was for Tonya to have somethin' normal in her life. You know, I was goin' to hire her a private coach." Guilt and bitterness crept into his voice. "I'd already set up a gym for her." With his free hand, he waved toward the other end of the house. "But I wanted her to be with other kids, to be part of a team. To have somethin' that was all hers,

somethin' besides bein' Sky Walker's little girl." He stared
down at his black Reebok Skywalkers for a minute, looked up,
and spun the ball behind his back to Hopkins. "I'd give anythin' to have Tonya back, Hoop. Anythin'.'"

Hopkins nodded again. "Hiring Cameron Bransfield, was
that your idea?"

"No," Walker answered. "It was Bert's. Me and Monique
told him to do whatever he had to." He leaned over and wiped
his hands on his socks. "I play ball. Bert takes care of business.
And I've done real good by Bert. I've got more money than I
dreamed was possible growin' up." He shook his head. "And
Bert's the guy that did all the deals. Got all the endorsements."

"And having the FBI take over the investigation, that was
Bert's idea, too?"

"Yeah. Bert's . . . and Monique's."

Hopkins drained his fifth consecutive shot. "Had Bert told
you about the AIA stuff that came out in the news today?"

Walker wheeled, snared the ball, and dribbled fast a dozen
times. "I knew he had some big real estate deal cookin' out in
L.A." He held the ball, staring for a moment at the NBA logo.
He then looked at Hopkins and said, "I've been in the spotlight a long time, Hoop. If I told you I liked it, I'd be lyin'. I've
been sick of those media guys, their constant shit, for years.
But it's parta my life. And I should've known what was comin'
today. What those media pricks would do to Monique and
Bert when they got the chance. But that's the media. All they
ever wanna do is tear people down. Bert's into the media, just
like Monique. They handle as much of my public stuff as I can
get away with missin'. But I should've figured the media'd
turn on 'em, attack 'em faster than anybody." As he whipped
the ball back to Hopkins, he asked, "What sort of animals eat
their own kind, Hoop?"

Hopkins didn't have an answer. He bounced the ball,

squared his shoulders, and shot. Walker sprang forward and swatted the ball back at him. Hopkins ducked away, stumbled, and turned.

Walker's eyes were narrow. "Find my Tonya, Hoop," he said, his voice choked. "You gotta find her, man."

chapter 15

James Robert Saville removed his glasses and wiped his forehead. "Paint It Black" howled in his headphones. He'd showered again and boosted the air in the Command Center, but he'd still worked himself into a sweat. Too much to do. Too many loose ends. Too many proverbial irons in the fire at one time. It was good he was flying. Maybe not good, but necessary. Otherwise he'd never keep up, never stay on top of everything. He had to check his sources and review his tapes, especially the one of the young Hoppette and that rug-roofed pig wigging out. And he had to keep up with his research. He'd bombed plenty of systems in cyberspace. But this was different, real-world stuff. He needed just the right materials. And clear directions. Those militia bozos on the Net were mostly full of shit. And fucking contradictory. But he was working his way through it. And he pretty well had it now. Procuring additional materials, though, meant another sortie. More stores and people. More potential problems. Bombing systems was one thing, but this was another.

He glanced over at the cigar box resting next to the surgical gloves, scalpel, gauze, and tape on the scanner cover. The embossed white Dunhill logo stood out on a deep blue oval centered on the white lid. It'd been risky to procure the box. It was so much messier out there in the world. Things tended to spin out of control. But it'd been worth it. Getting the big pig's own brand was a nice touch. Very nice, indeed. Amazing what MasterCard bills and store records and all the other electronic minutiae in cyberspace told you about some dildo's personal habits!

Nailing the big pig and punishing the kid all at once—it was perfect, really. She'd been bad, very bad. She had to be punished. It was absolutely imperative. If he didn't discipline her, he'd lose control, slip from the ring. That wouldn't do at all. And that fat-assed pig! Nobody called him names anymore and got away with it. First there'd be the little predawn surprise. And then later, when the pigs persisted, there'd be the Big Surprise! His reconnaissance had shown him that the big pig didn't sleep much. Got up early. Making the delivery would be tricky. More than tricky, dangerous. But the gift, the little surprise, had to be waiting on his doorstep in the morning. Pit Bull and the other media morons were going to go ape-shit over this gambit.

He put on his glasses and got back to work, first checking the AIA action, sneaking in through B & B. Cam Bransfield's surfers were hacking the AIA files all right, just like the FBI jockeys, looking for footprints, a trail, any sign he'd been there—even a wormhole. How predictable! And, how futile! Couldn't any of these fools figure out that he'd already cracked Baker and Bransfield's security, too? The idiots!

He jerked his fingers from the keyboard, leapt back, and, rolling the chair away from the console, scowled at the computer screen. It *was* a trap. The morons had figured he'd cracked B & B. They were laying for him. He ripped off the headphones and flung them against the washroom door, the cord wiggling like a snake. Leaning forward, barely touching the console, he quickly erased his tracks before escaping. Then, clutching the arms of the chair, he mentally scrolled through his defenses. They were elegant: his trip wires were intricate and artful, his armor impregnable—barriers set, shields and detectors up and running. He couldn't be attacked. Or could he? His heart raced. His breathing was quick and shallow. Sweat stung the scratch on his cheek. No. He was just being paranoid. It happened sometimes when you were flying.

And then he started to laugh, a malicious high-pitched tit-ter that reverberated around the Command Center. He slumped against the back of his chair, unable to stop cackling. Bransfield's boys were surfing while the Wizard himself hid behind them setting the trap. The FBI, with all their covert-op geeks and dweebs jetting the Net like stealth fighters, should've thought of that. His shoulders were shaking with laughter; his eyes began to twitch. Bransfield was laying a trap for him, all right. And tomorrow morning, after he'd made the delivery and sent the ransom demand and finished all his other work, he'd stroll into Bransfield's trap, right on cue—and then he'd blow Bransfield, that too-smart-for-his-own-good meis-ter motherfucker, right out of the water. Laughing hysteri-cally, he leaned forward, unable to catch his breath. Work on the pigs' Big Surprise had to wait while Cam Bransfield blasted into orbit! It was all going to be too wild—even wilder than he'd planned.

chapter 16

Just after one o'clock in the morning, Tom Hopkins climbed the ramp from the department's underground garage to the back parking lot. It had been an exhausting day, but he felt too unsettled by everything that had happened to be tired. When he reached the lot, he breathed the cool night air deeply and gazed up beyond the lot's lights at the stars blinking among intermittent clouds. There were, for once, no reporters, no television cameras, no hovering helicopters. He rolled his neck, exhaled slowly, and took his car keys from his pocket.

As he crossed the lot toward his Taurus, he heard, "Hey, Hoop!"

Meghan Ross sat on the hood of her black Nissan. Rubbing the back of his neck, he turned toward her. A line of freckles ran across her nose, her light brown hair was pulled back in a claw clip, and she looked young and clean and unspoiled by her work.

"I thought you'd headed home," he said.

She slipped from the hood of her car, brushed off her uniform pants, and said, "I've been, uh, thinking . . . it's this case . . . It's all I've been able to think about."

"I know what you mean," he answered. His uneasy feeling that morning that the case would consume him had not abated at all. And nothing that had happened that day had relieved the knot forming in his stomach. He had not been able to shake the deep sense that he had to do something fast, but, having been stripped of much of his authority over the investigation, there was nothing he could do except have his detectives check out the local leads, sift and sort the information, evaluate it carefully, and hope there'd be a break. And yet he knew full well that the longer any missing-child case remained, the less the chance it would be solved. The critical first twenty-four hours had come and gone.

"That was shitty, what they did to you this afternoon," she said. "The Chief should've stuck by you."

"After what he'd said at the briefing, I don't think he was in any position." He shrugged. "And anyway, money talks—even in this kind of thing."

Staring down at her hands, Ross said, "I can't get those pictures out of my mind. I see them all the time." She wiped her hands and looked up at Hopkins. "The perp's such a sick son of a bitch."

He nodded. "He's also very smart in some warped way I don't quite get. I'm stuck with the idea that he knows everything. That he's spent a hell of a lot of time digging into the Walkers' lives and the lives of the people connected to them."

"And maybe our lives, too," she said. She clasped her hands and asked, "Do you think he's local?"

"If you mean North Ridge, probably not. But the area, Chicago. Definitely." He spun his keys around his forefinger. "Adelman and the media and everybody else keep seeing some goddamned conspiracy that I just don't think exists. I mean, the perp could hack the computer systems from anywhere in the country. Hell, from anywhere in the world. But he's been around here. He'd staked out the gymnastics center. Had to've been in it more than once before. Probably wired the alarm earlier in the week." He reversed the spin on the keys. "He's obviously got some twisted relationship with Monique Jones-Walker. And he sure as hell didn't choose Pit Bull by chance."

"You know," she said as she took her car keys from her uniform pocket, "I got the feeling today that Pit Bull *liked* that picture. He was sort of getting off on it."

Hopkins, who had noticed the same thing, answered, "Yeah. And when he went after Monique, he was having *too* much fun." He shook his head and looked out toward the road where a half dozen television vans were still parked. "By the way," he added, "thanks for your help with Cari."

"She's a good kid." She turned and unlocked her car door.

Hopkins nodded. Despite her parents' marital problems, Cari had not fallen apart—perhaps, he thought, because, unlike most adolescents, she had understood that she was not the cause of her parents' estrangement. As he opened the door for her, he asked, "How's Dan? Things going better?"

"He's still bugging me to tie the knot." The man she lived with, a commodities broker at the Board of Trade, had asked her to marry him a month before, but she had refused. She smiled ironically. "I thought a woman approaching thirty was supposed to get the nesting instinct. But something inside me keeps holding me back. And he's pretty used to the fast track, to things running his way." She shrugged. "When I tell him he needs to be patient, he doesn't like it much. But I can't . . ." Her voice trailed off.

They stood in silence for a minute, Hopkins thinking about how his marriage had slowly dissolved. He had never considered himself a loser. Schoolwork had always been easy for him, and his junior and senior years in high school, the basketball teams he'd captained had made the Sweet Sixteen and Elite Eight in the state tournament. His freshman year at Notre Dame, he had played more than twenty minutes a game on a team that earned an NCAA bid—not a small accomplishment for a program overshadowed by the Golden Dome and a legendary football program. Even his career-ending knee injury had been a blessing; he'd begun to take his courses seriously and graduated magna cum laude in pre-law. He'd avoided law school, instead finishing at the top of his police academy class. And the job at the police department in North Ridge, just south of his hometown, had been an excellent match. Promotions had come quickly, and his marriage, at twenty-four, to the willowy young lawyer already on track to be a partner at Armstrong & Willis, one of Chicago's oldest and most prestigious firms, had seemed a dream. With Cari's birth the next year, his life had been for a while complete. But over the years neither he nor his wife had been able to put their relationship above their respective careers. Their divorce had really been the first time he had thought of himself as anything other than a winner. The ensuing deaths of each of his parents, fifteen months apart, had drained him, and it was only with the promotion to Investigations Unit commander that he'd felt the self-doubts dissipating.

"You dating much, Hoop?" Ross was asking him.

He started, lost in his thoughts, almost missing her question. "Yeah." There was no shortage of attractive divorcées in his life, but he'd found himself breaking off whenever one of them started to use the word *couple* to describe the relationship. "But nobody special."

She reached over and touched his forearm lightly. "Maybe . . . Maybe there'll be a break in this thing tomorrow."

"Yeah," he answered, not really believing it.

She got into the car, and he shut the door. After she started the engine, turned on the headlights, and fastened her seatbelt, she waved to him through the window. He watched her drive off, her brake lights blinking before she turned onto the road by the television vans.

chapter 17

When his phone rang at 4:38 A.M., Hopkins was already awake, one hand behind his head, staring into the darkness. Ross' statement that the kidnapper seemed to have dug into all of their lives had rung him awake half an hour earlier and had been cycling through his mind ever since. If she was right, the perp would have hacked not just the Walkers' and Bert Adelman's systems but also the department's computers and PIMS, the network that connected Chicago's suburban police departments, and perhaps even the State Police and FBI networks—and who knew what else? He wondered if it would be possible to trace the perp or trap him, not through the phone system, but through the computer networks. He didn't know, but he was sure Paul Kim, the department's systems manager, would have an idea.

After the phone's third ring, he cleared his throat, fumbled for the receiver, and said, "Hopkins."

"Hoop," Sergeant Banks said, "we got us a problem at the Chief's house. A package. Looks like a bomb."

"A bomb? At Mancini's?" Hopkins asked. He turned on the lamp by the bed.

"Yeah," Banks answered. "Bomb squad's already here. But I thought you'd want to know. I'm betting the Chief's gonna need to talk to you soon as he calms down."

"Yeah," Hopkins said. "Thanks, Dave. Good you called." He sat up on the edge of his bed, blood pounding in his temples, and murmured, "What the hell?"

Light was beginning to spread in the eastern sky and birds were singing as Hopkins drove through North Ridge. His eyes itched, and he felt grimy and sluggish from the lack of sleep. Bedlam greeted him as he approached Mancini's house. Flashing lights wove through the branches of the trees lining the parkway. Squad cars, fire department rescue vehicles, and television vans clogged the street. A crowd milled across from Mancini's redbrick colonial. The North Suburban bomb disposal van stood behind Mancini's blue Oldsmobile Eighty Eight in the driveway. Helicopters drowned the birdsong.

Hopkins left his car, pulled on his dark nylon NRPD windbreaker, and, elbowing away the microphones jammed in front of his face by shouting reporters, pushed through the crowd toward the house. Jack Bollinger, already broadcasting, stood just outside the police cordon. Turned so that the camera angle caught the house's front door over his shoulder, he was growling, ". . . responded as though this was a bomb threat, reliable sources have informed this reporter that the delivery made to this residence sometime around four A.M. is not an explosive device, but rather a gift for Peter Mancini, the North Ridge police chief." His voice sounded like a truck rolling over stones. He was clean-shaven, in full camera-ready makeup; his trenchcoat collar was turned up as though a wardrobe mistress had arranged it for him.

When Hopkins stopped near Bollinger, a reporter careened into his back, her microphone stabbing his kidney.

Without glancing at him, Bollinger cleared his throat and continued, "The North Ridge police department, according to a recently retired senior officer, is simply ill-equipped to handle a case of this magnitude. At this time, we can only venture a guess as to the nature of the gift the kidnapper has left Chief Mancini, but, even with the FBI now running the investigation, doubts persist about North . . ."

Hopkins strode through the cordon and halted again by the bomb van. Brian Murphy, the North Suburban bomb-disposal officer, was stowing a portable X-ray machine in the back of the van. Stocky and balding, he wore a black uniform and armored vest.

"Morning, Murph," Hopkins said. "What've you got?"

"Hey, Hoop," Murphy said. He shook his head. "It's not no bomb." His tone somber, he added, "The Chief said for you to go in soon as you got here." He gestured toward the half-open front door.

When Hopkins stepped inside the house, he saw Banks and Mancini standing next to the long oval table in the dining room to his left. Mancini was saying, ". . . want everything analyzed, even the cotton." Hopkins had never seen the man looking so shaken. He seemed pasty, worn out, deflated like an old balloon. His toupee was off, and his scalp was sweating. The flaccid skin of his neck drooped down to the graying hairs matted in the V of his T-shirt. His hands wrung the back of the chair. Banks needed a shave, and his uniform shirt, with the sleeves rolled up above his thick forearms, was rumpled. A white Dunhill cigar box lay closed on a clear plastic evidence bag on the table near them.

"Morning," Hopkins said. "Marilou, everybody, all right?"

Banks nodded, but anxiety shone in his eyes.

Mancini rasped, "Close that door, Hoop."

Hopkins shut the door and entered the dining room, the relative quiet almost eerie.

"We got to get this guy fast," Mancini said. His knuckles were white from gripping the chair so hard.

Hopkins looked from Mancini to Banks, who gestured toward the cigar box.

"We got to nail the pervert to the wall," Mancini muttered.

Hopkins took out and opened his Swiss Army knife, a birthday gift from Cari. When he glanced at Mancini, the Chief said, "Go ahead."

Using the knife blade, Hopkins raised the lid. A putrid odor made him shudder. A note, printed in 24-point black boldface, read,

> **Hey there, you rug-roofed PIG**
> **Here's a gift, your favorite CIG**
> **Don't ever call me names, you DIG!**
> **Or your next gift'll be real BIG—**
> **The mangled corpse of the little JIG!!!**

Hopkins looked quizzically at Banks and Mancini. The Chief gaped at the cigar box as though it were going to explode. Banks set his jaw, but pain still showed in his eyes. Hopkins tilted the lid until it fell back, slipped the knife's blade under the note, and lifted the sheet of paper. His hand trembled as he stared into the box. "Oh, Jesus," he murmured. "Jesus Christ."

The thin, bloodless gray-brown finger nestled in a thick bed of clean white cotton. Near the severed end, the little gold championship ring gleamed.

Hopkins let the note drop back over the finger and flipped the box top shut. As he closed the knife, his hand would not stop quivering. When he was sure his breathing was under control, he asked, "Where was the box?"

"Out there," Mancini said, still staring at the box. "On the front stoop." He sucked in his breath. "He called. The perp called. Woke me up. Said there was a gift for me at the front door. I thought it was a goddamned bomb. Called Murph in." He looked up, seeming to really notice Hopkins for the first time. "What in God's name am I going to say to Sky Walker? That I shot off my big mouth, and now I got his daughter's finger in a goddamned Dunhill box?" He wiped his scalp. "God, I wish it *was* a bomb."

chapter 18

The nightmare was always the same: He is nine years old, short for his age, chubby. He cowers under the kitchen table. His mother is screeching at his older sister, ". . . and don't you ever talk to me that way again, young lady! I work twelve hours a day at the station to support you ungrateful brats!" His mother is wearing a beige tweed suit. She is pretty, her blond hair permed, her lipstick red, too red.

"Get off it, Mom," his sister screams. "You love that shitty job. Your phony smile plastered all over the tube!" She is fifteen but looks older. Her blond hair is straight, falling over her shoulders to the top of her halter. She's pretty, too, like his mother. Not like him. Nothing at all like him.

"Don't you ever use that word, young lady, or you'll . . ."

"Shitty! Shitty! Shitty!"

His mother slaps her hard across the face.

Tears fill his sister's eyes, but she doesn't give an inch. "Where've you been this time, *Mom*?" she yells. "Off to Vegas with your producer again?" She's practically spitting the questions at his mother. "You leave us here alone for days. No money. Practically no food. What are we supposed to do, *Mom*? I'm the one bringing up the little bastard. If it wasn't for me, he wouldn't even . . ."

"Shut that mouth of yours, young lady! Or I'll shut it for you!"

He can't stand it anymore. They've been battling like this for hours, days, months, his whole life. It's all his fault. It's always his fault—and he can do nothing at all about it. He curls up by the table leg. Covers his ears with his hands. But he can't look away. He can never look away.

"You don't even know who his father is, you . . . you slut!"

His mother is sputtering, "Never say . . . never . . . !" She's beating his sister, pounding her head with closed fists. "You'll regret to your dying day that you ever . . ."

His sister is crying now, hysterical, tears streaming down her cheeks as she pushes away her mother, who stumbles against the table. He can't see it, but he knows his mother's grabbing for the heavy metal ruler he'd been using to draw his rockets and spaceships at the kitchen table.

His sister plants her feet. She's crying so hard she can barely get the words out. "You slut . . . slut . . . slut . . . You . . . whore!"

His mother steps away from the table, her legs just out of his reach. She's swinging the ruler. It almost misses, nicking his sister's bare shoulder. A thin line of blood appears. Hyperventilating, tears falling to the floor, his sister gapes at her shoulder. "Go ahead!" she wails, her head thrust forward in defiance. "Just . . ."

He lunges at his mother as she raises the ruler again. His shoulder bumps her leg, knocks her off balance for a moment. Shrieking, he hooks his right arm around his mother's ankle.

She smacks his head with the ruler.

His sister screams, "No! Leave him alone!"

Turning, his mother swings the ruler wildly, slashing his sister's jaw. Blood erupts.

They are all howling now, not words but sheer sound, a cacophony.

Blood cascading down her neck and spattering the floor, his sister careens around the table. She flings open the door, plunges out, and vanishes into the night. Disappears forever.

His mother is dragging him, still clinging to her leg, toward the open door. Her rage turning on him, she stops suddenly, leans down, and pummels his back with the flat edge of the ruler. When he finally lets go, she stamps his right hand with her spiked heel. He feels no pain, no pain at all. But as she stamps again and again, he hears his knuckles crunching, the bones shattering under her heel. "Help!" he howls. "Sarah! Don't leave me! Help me, Sarah!"

James Robert Saville woke with a start. The Command Center whirled around him. He'd heard something. A scream. His sister Sarah's! No. The kid's. He felt like he was going to puke. His skin was clammy, his whole body sweating. That goddamned dream again, more real even than that horrendous night. It made him sick—always. The only thing in the world he still feared. Despised it. Hated ever going to sleep. Couldn't do a thing to stop it. Nothing.

His cheek damp with drool, he raised his head from the console, reached for his glasses, and scowled at the clock. Almost oh-five-fifty. He'd been out of commission for over an hour. Must have been the cool night air. He swallowed the rising bile, wiped his face with his shirtsleeve, and stared up at the Videot Box. The sound was off, but there was Pit Bull, on cue as always, the rug-roofed pig's pen behind him, silently spouting. The sortie'd been a success. A huge success. Magnificent. He'd been stealth itself. And now the big pig was paying.

What next? The ransom demand and the call. Another fine touch, almost as nice as the cigar box. And then he'd deal with Cameron Bransfield, the systems-meister, whose trap was going to spring, all right! Everything coming in its correct order. That's the way to get things done.

But the girl was screaming, just like Sarah. Just like Sarah. She wouldn't stop screaming. Not that infernal yell this time, but screams of pain. He shook his head, reached for his headphones. But it would do no good. Unable to ignore her, he sank back in his chair. Even if he jacked the headphones into the stratosphere, he couldn't escape what he'd done.

Tonya Walker hunched hard and low against the wall farthest from the door. Her screams echoed in the darkness. The horrible pain throbbed where her finger should be, crossed the palm of her hand, and shot up her arm. She was dizzy, nauseated, the smell of vomit all around her. Her throat burned; her head thundered. She'd awakened to the pain, thought her finger had dislocated, just as it had once before during a tumbling run in her floor routine. When she had reached for the ring, there had been nothing there but a thick bandage. And then she'd remembered the Beast coming at her with a damp cloth, pulling her head back by her hair as she struggled to gouge him with her nails and teeth, and jamming the cloth over her nose and mouth. The Beast had stolen her ring, cut off her finger to get it.

When the door swung open and light flooded the room, she hugged her knees and buried her head. She tried to make herself smaller, a part of the wall, as small as a speck of paint. The pain was immense, but she willed herself into silence.

Wanting no sound at all to give her away, she tried to stop breathing. Her eyes were so tightly shut that gold and silver circles spun before her.

The voice was softer, seemed almost to be sobbing, but she would not look up, would never again look at that hideous Beast. "You had to be punished," the voice was blubbering. "Had to be. For the mess you made. But it's over now. Do as you're told, and there'll be no more pain. I promise you, young lady. I promise, no more pain." The Beast was shuffling around, sniffling, sliding things onto the floor. When her stomach rumbled, she pressed herself still harder against the wall, trembling, trying to stop the sickening spinning, biting her lip, focusing only on the gold and silver circles. "It'll be over soon," the voice said. "They won't dare ignore me now. They know they have to take me seriously."

The door closed, but the light remained on. She waited until she was sure the Beast was really gone before letting a long moan escape. She lifted her head, turned, and squinted through her tousled hair into the brightness. Just beyond the dried vomit on the floor tiles, a tall plastic bottle of Evian stood next to a small translucent brown vial and a neat line of individually wrapped Hostess Twinkies. Whimpering, she raised her cuffed hands together to inspect the bandage. The stump was carefully wrapped with gauze and tightly taped, but dried blood spotted the bandage and her other fingers. She became aware that with her hand raised the pain was not quite so awful. Keeping her hands up, she leaned back against the wall and glanced at the vial and the bottle of water.

When she reached for the vial, pain almost overwhelmed her. Cradling the vial in her uninjured hand, she caught her breath and then examined the prescription label. The name— Acetaminophen Codeine 30 mg—meant nothing to her, but the white tablets, visible when she held the vial to the light, looked like oversized aspirin. She braced the vial between her knees, stripped off the plastic seal, and tried to unscrew the cap. The movement sent hot bolts up her arm, and, gagging, she dropped the vial. Blinded by pain, she felt hot tears running down her face.

chapter 19

When Hopkins arrived at the house just after 6:00 A.M., Anthony Ignacio, bleary-eyed and surly, kept him waiting in the foyer while he went upstairs to get the Walkers. Unshaven and uneasy, Hopkins stood under the massive chandelier, wondering how he would react if he were in Sky Walker's position. He had convinced Mancini that they could not wait until later in the day to inform the parents about the finger. Jack Bollinger had already announced to the world that the package was a gift from the kidnapper, and it was only a matter of time before the perp leaked information about the Dunhill box's contents to the media. And no parent, Hopkins knew, especially not Monique Jones-Walker, should receive this sort of news from the likes of Jack Bollinger.

In less than two minutes, the Walkers appeared together at the top of the winding staircase. They hesitated, seeming to know that he was the bearer of some horrific news. Then, Sky Walker took his wife's elbow and led her down the stairs. At the foot of the stairs, she pulled the lapels of her red silk bathrobe closer around her neck, straightened her shoulders, and asked, "What is it, Mr. Hopkins? Is it the ransom demand?" Her hair was uncombed, but her eyes were clear, as though she had been awake for some time.

Hopkins shook his head, glanced at Sky Walker, and then looked her in the eye. "No, Mrs. Walker," he answered. "Would you like to sit down?" He gestured toward the living room and library.

"No," she said. "We've been watching TV. What does the package have to do with us?"

Their eyes never parted. He took a deep breath and exhaled slowly.

"Please, Mr. Hopkins," she said.

"The package contained your daughter's . . . Tonya's . . . ring finger."

Sky Walker gasped. His shoulders sagged, and he turned away, staring through the living room into the library as though searching there for some rational explanation.

Monique Jones-Walker's face turned to stone. "What?" she asked.

Hopkins did not repeat himself.

"No," she said, her eyes still locked to his. "There's some mistake. There's got to be."

"It's possible, Mrs. Walker," Hopkins answered. "Nothing's been analyzed yet. But I don't think so. Her . . ."

"You're wrong," she hissed. "It can't be."

Hopkins inhaled, shook his head, held her gaze, and said, "Mrs. Walker, her ring, the gold championship ring, was there."

Sky Walker, his head bowed and his shoulders quivering, leaned against the wall. Gasping, unable for a moment to catch his breath, he looked as though he would retch.

"No, this is not happening," Jones-Walker insisted. "It's all some cruel hoax. You've got it all wrong."

Walker raised his shoulders, turned, and cinched the belt of his black robe. His eyes welling, he began to put his arm around his wife's shoulder, but she brushed past him and stalked up the stairs, the hem of her bathrobe billowing behind her.

Hopkins put his hands in the pockets of his windbreaker and stood silently with Walker for a minute after she was gone.

"You sure?" Walker asked, his voice distant.

Hopkins nodded.

They were silent again for a while before Walker took a deep breath and said, "Jesus, Hoop, I just don't know if I . . ." His eyes were cloudy, despondent. He clutched his beard, exhaled, and, shaking his head, added, "I can't take much . . . This is too much to . . ." He wiped his eyes, gazed up at the chandelier, and took several more deep breaths. Then, focusing on Hopkins, he asked, "Would you like some coffee? Can I get you some coffee?"

"Thanks, no," Hopkins answered, taking his hands from his pockets.

Walker glanced up the stairs, stepped toward the doorway at the rear of the foyer, and turned back to Hopkins. "How 'bout orange juice?" he asked. "It's fresh squeezed every mornin'."

Hopkins nodded. He had a meeting with Henderson at 7:30, but clearly Walker wanted him to stay, probably had something more he needed to say. He followed Walker into the kitchen, a vast room with French windows that faced east and the lake. The white walls and custom-built cabinetry, all natural spruce with white Carrara marble panels, made the room sparkle in the early-morning sunlight. The uniformed officer manning the trap-and-trace equipment at the south end of the kitchen took off his earphones and waved to Hopkins but seemed to understand that it was not the time to strike up a conversation. As Walker and Hopkins passed the large cooking island in the center of the room, a dark-haired maid in a black uniform said, *"Buenos dias."* Walker and Hopkins sat at the circular glass table in the wide alcove protruding east, surrounded outside by a patio and then the lawn, the bluff, and the shimmering lake.

The maid brought a mug of coffee for Walker, who said, *"Gracias,* Consuela." He pointed to Hopkins and added, "O.J., *por favor!"*

They sat silently for a few minutes, gazing out at the glimmering morning. The maid brought Hopkins a tall glass of orange juice that tasted sweet and cold. The phone rang, and Hopkins glanced over his shoulder at the officer who, after ten seconds of listening through his earphones, shook his head. A red-winged blackbird, the triangle on its wing more orange than red, lighted on a chaise longue out on the patio. Feathers twitching, it seemed to look in on them.

Walker stared out at the blackbird singing the same series of notes over and over. "Hoop," he said, "I told you last night that all I wanted was my Tonya back." His voice was low, almost a whisper. "But now that I know the dude's hurtin' her . . ." He pushed the mug away. "Now I know the terrible things he's doin' to her . . ." He looked into Hopkins' eyes. "I want to see the dude fry. And, Hoop, I shouldn't be saying this to you, but I *will* see him dead. I promise." His eyes blazed with wrath.

"We'll do everything we . . ." Hopkins began.

"I'll see him dead, Hoop," Walker repeated, his voice still quiet, as though he were speaking to himself rather than to Hopkins. He brushed his hand through his hair, picked up the mug, and gazed out the French windows at the blackbird.

Hopkins ran his finger along the condensation on his glass.

As the silence loomed between them, the blackbird took wing, its orange-red marking flashing for a moment in the sun. "Hoop," Walker finally said, "I'm still gettin' a whole lot of pressure to play tonight. That tub-o-lard general manager, the sponsors' reps, even Bert, are all on my case. They're all tellin' me I owe it to Tonya." He shook his head slowly. The mug looked like a demitasse cup in his hand. "But I don't see it that way. Not at all. They don't know what's inside me."

Hopkins nodded. "You do what you need to do," he said.

Walker looked him in the eye. "Exactly. I love the game more than all of them put together." He tapped his stomach. "But my gut's tellin' me I can't play. Not with Tonya gone. Not after what's happenin' to her. And I ain't gonna play." He folded his hands around the mug, making it disappear from sight except for the steam swirling in the light. "I ain't ever gonna play again 'til I get my Tonya back."

Hopkins thought he understood. Walker's great loves, the game and his daughter, were somehow intertwined in the man's mind, in his soul even, and without one there'd be no other. Hopkins respected that, but he could also imagine the pressure Walker would feel as the days passed and Tonya was not returned. Walker was far too important an icon in the United States and around the world; no one would ever leave him alone with his grief and fear and anger.

"Can I see it, the ring?" Walker asked suddenly. "I'd like to see it."

Hopkins hadn't expected the request. "That should, uh, be possible," he answered, "once the FBI's evidence technicians are done with it."

Walker put down the coffee mug and leaned forward. "I really would like to see the ring," he said, his voice a sad whisper.

Seeing the ring, some tangible evidence of his missing child, seemed crucially important to Walker. "I'll make sure you get the chance," Hopkins answered as the telephone rang again.

"Commander Hopkins," the trap-and-trace officer called, "I think we got something here."

Hopkins looked at Walker, sprang from his chair, and hustled across the room. The maid, who had been putting more oranges into the squeezer, froze with half an orange in her raised hand. As Hopkins leaned over his shoulder, the officer, a wiry man with a long nose and rimless glasses, rewound the tape and said, "It's short, less than twenty seconds, but it's the first thing that's sounded like it could be from the perp."

Walker came up behind Hopkins and peered down at the officer. All incoming calls had been routed directly to the Walkers' voice mail so that the police could screen them—and every call was automatically taped. The officer took off and unplugged his earphones. "Ready?" he asked before pushing the play button.

The flat, unemotional voice on the tape said, "Time to check your e-mail, Monique. You have exactly forty-eight hours if you want to see Tonya safely returned."

"Your wife has an office at home, right?" Hopkins asked.

"Yeah," Walker answered. "Upstairs, off our bedroom."

"And a modem?"

"She's got so much electronic stuff up there," Walker said, "she's connected to everybody in the world."

"Can she . . ." Hopkins began.

"Play that tape again," Walker said, his voice deep and compelling.

Hopkins turned and looked at Walker, who glared down at the tape recorder as though all his pain and anger might blow the machine apart.

The second time through, Hopkins recognized the voice as well.

"That's Bert," Walker muttered. "It's Bert." He turned and swung his open hand at the nearest cabinet. The marble panel shattered, splintering onto the counter and floor.

chapter 20

At 7:10 A.M., Hopkins sat at the glass table in the kitchen's alcove with Carl Henderson and the Walkers. The French doors were open, and the azure sky, sunshine, and cool breeze belied the mood of those present. A tray of bagels, cream cheese, and fresh fruit lay untouched in the center of the table. Jack Bollinger had broken news of the finger ten minutes before, and every other station had already picked up the story. *Good Morning* had already run a piece on the disfigurement of kidnap victims, which had apparently been produced just in case something like the severing of the finger occurred. Hopkins had turned off the little Sony on the counter when the Walkers returned from getting dressed. He now scanned for the fifth time one of the copies of the ransom demand Monique Jones-Walker had printed from her e-mail. The note read:

> **MONIQUE, BABY:**
> • **$48 million—that's the demand!**
>   **Has quite a RING to it!**

- **48 hours—that's the time frame.**
  Make sure you put your FINGER on the cash!

- **$48 MILLION in 48 HOURS—**
  or YOU and SKYWALKER never see the Little
  Princess alive again.

- **$$$$$ to be delivered per instructions to follow!**
- **No DELAYS!**
- **No EXCUSES!**
- **No TRICKS!**
  Or hcr HAND will be next!!!

"How do we know it's real?" Jones-Walker asked Henderson as she tapped a copy of the ransom demand. Since she had comc back downstairs, she had not mentioned what had happened to her daughter, but the muscles in her face were taut and her voice was strained—as though she were holding back the emotion through pure force of will.

"We don't," Henderson answered. He straightened the knot of his tie. "But it makes reference to the ring and the finger, and it was posted at 6:20, almost half an hour before news of the finger aired." He spoke slowly, his drawl elongating what he said. "And the forty-eight million in forty eight hours is typical of the games this guy's playing."

"Where the hell is Bert?" Walker asked. "He said he'd be here ten minutes ago." He lifted but did not drink his third cup of coffee. A pair of Band-Aids covered the cuts on the heel of his hand.

Ignoring her husband's question, Jones-Walker asked Henderson, "So you think it's just onc guy now, too?"

Henderson glanced at Hopkins. "Yes," he answered. "It seems more than likely."

"And what about these games you mentioned?" she asked. "What do you mean?"

"It looks like everything's a game to this guy," Henderson answered. "And everything's a symbol." He pointed at a copy of the ransom demand. "His routing this, for example, through Walker Management's Chicago computer."

"He goes to a lot of trouble," Hopkins added, "to add an overlay of meaning to everything he does."

Jones-Walker glanced at Hopkins, turned back to Henderson, and said, "Like involving Pit Bull, contacting him even before the . . . before it happened. And sending all those damned pictures directly to him."

Henderson nodded. "The call you received this morning. We all agree it sounds like Mr. Adelman's voice, but the idea that Adelman, even if he were involved, would make the call himself is ridiculous. We've already got the lab doing an analysis to determine if it's composed of edited sound bites, perhaps from yesterday's press conference. If it is, the perpetrator spent some serious time making that tape—just to make it more of a game, to mess with everyone's minds that much more."

"Even the delivery this morning to Chief Mancini," Hopkins said, "was made in a Dunhill box, the only cigars he smokes."

Continuing to look at Henderson rather than acknowledging Hopkins, Jones-Walker said, "But you used the word *symbol*? The call, the box, the Jeep, Bert's bills, you think that's all symbolic?"

Henderson took a deep breath, looked at the others, and then stared into her eyes. "I believe so, ma'am," he said. "I think he's acting out some sort of a bizarre psycho-drama in his mind. I think maybe . . . ."

"Does that make Tonya some prop?" she interrupted, her tone becoming strident. "Some symbol?"

"Yes, ma'am," Henderson answered. "I'm afraid so. At least, as I see it now." His tone was deferential, but a vein in his neck began pulsing.

"Most likely, Mrs. Walker," Hopkins said, leaning forward, his forearms on the table, "you're the star of his play, the critical symbol. He's gone to the most trouble with props directly related to you."

"And what exactly am I a symbol of, Mr. Hopkins?" Her eyes bore into him.

Hopkins looked out for a moment at the lawn, where the automatic sprinklers had just come on. A line of small rainbows played in the sun. He then turned and met her gaze. "When we know that," he said, "we'll have a better idea of who the guy is."

"That, Mr. Hopkins," she snapped, "isn't much help, is it?"

"It's a start," Hopkins said.

She continued to glare at Hopkins. "But my daughter doesn't have much time, does she?"

"No," Hopkins admitted. "Probably not."

They were all silent for a moment, and then Walker, who had been draped in his chair watching the other three talk, leaned forward and rubbed his hands together. "So one thing you're tellin' us is that you don't think any of this has anythin' to do with my comeback and the Bulls makin' the Finals."

Bert Adelman strode into the kitchen and stopped by the cooking island to whisper Spanish to the maid who was brewing more coffee.

"The timing does, yes," Hopkins answered. "And the use of your number, the forty-eight million in forty-eight hours, as Carl mentioned, that's all part of it. But this guy's been working on this, planning it for a long time, and he couldn't have been sure you'd even make the Finals."

As Adelman came up to the table, Jones-Walker, without saying anything, handed him a copy of the ransom demand and gestured to the empty chair to her right. Adelman looked at the e-mail printout but did not sit down.

"Your comeback," Hopkins went on, "and the Bulls reaching the Finals are just getting him that much more notoriety—something he apparently craves."

" 'Morning, Mr. Adelman," Henderson said. "Will you join us?" He pointed to the empty chair.

Adelman put his hand on Jones-Walker's shoulder, looked first at her and then at her husband, and said, "I'm truly sorry about this morning's development. We're doing everything possible to ensure that nothing worse happens."

Jones-Walker glanced up at him, patted his hand, half-brushing it from her shoulder, and said, "Thanks, Bert." As Adelman took his seat, she turned back to Hopkins, and asked, "If this sicko's been doing all this planning, how long would you say he's been invading my e-mail?"

"How long have you had it?" Hopkins asked.

"That's not funny, Mr. Hopkins," she retorted.

He shook his head. "I didn't mean it to be funny," he said, his tone conciliatory. "You'd better assume that this guy's been electronically eavesdropping on you for a long time, Mrs. Walker."

Jones-Walker's face became even tighter, and her eyes betrayed a momentary hint of anxiety.

Walker gazed at his wife for a moment, waved to the maid, and said, "Now that Bert's here, can we talk about how we're gonna pay the ransom?"

Adelman opened his briefcase, took out a manila folder, and snapped the briefcase shut. The maid placed a mug of hot coffee, a small crystal sugar bowl, and a spoon in front of him. "There are complex, interwoven issues here," he said, "but the first, Sky, is *whether* the ransom should be paid at all."

Walker seized the edge of the table. "What do you mean? If that's what it's gonna take to get Tonya back, I'm gonna pay."

"It's not that simple, Sky," Adelman said. "Payment of the ransom in no way guarantees Tonya will be freed."

His eyes wide, Walker looked from Adelman to Hopkins.

"Mr. Walker," Henderson said, "I think what Mr. Adelman is saying is that, historically speaking, paying the ransom in kidnapping cases hasn't necessarily resulted in the victim's safe return."

Adelman added a half teaspoon of sugar to his coffee, stirred it, took a napkin from the tray of bagels, and placed the spoon neatly on the napkin.

"What if we don't pay?" Walker asked.

Henderson shrugged. "Unless we can solve the case very quickly, it would almost certainly be . . . negative."

"Then we pay." Walker folded his hands on the table.

"Two further issues, Sky, Monique," Adelman said, gazing at both parents. "First, I just spoke with Cameron Bransfield. That's why I was late." He glanced at his watch. "I apologize, but it was crucial to our meeting here. He and his team are taking the most auspicious approach to this problem, and he assures me that he'll have information on the subjects today. Twenty-four hours at the outside, and we'll have their tails in a sling. Cam's pretty much guaranteed it."

Shaking his head, Hopkins stared out the French doors but could find no more rainbows.

"Excuse me, Mr. Adelman," Henderson said, "you're telling these people . . . What the . . . What, sir, are you saying?"

Adelman sipped his coffee before answering, "I'm saying, Carl, that I expect this problem to be satisfactorily resolved in twenty-four hours or less. I'm also providing my friends, the Walkers, with hope and a realistic expectation, commodities that, given the nature of this tragedy, have been lacking." He took another sip of coffee and added, "And I promise you that the information gathered will be shared with the FBI."

Henderson shook his head and smiled wryly. "Mr. Adelman," he said, "you're trying to stomp a rattler with your boots off."

"Carl," Adelman answered, his tone condescending, "Tom,

here, and now you have spent a good deal of energy trying to convince us that we're dealing with a single person." He picked up a copy of the ransom demand and waved it at Hopkins and Henderson. "Some weirdo, acting alone, out to get Monique and the rest of us. If that's the case, our resources are necessarily superior to his."

Hopkins bit his lip and again studied the sprinklers.

"And if my technical team is right, you're grossly underestimating this guy, Mr. Adelman," Henderson said.

"Perhaps." Adelman shrugged, as if to dismiss that possibility.

"I hope whatever you've got Bransfield doing doesn't impede our investigation," Henderson said. "And I hope, for these people's sake, you know what you're doing."

"I do," Adelman answered.

Her head cocked, Jones-Walker stared at the copy of the ransom demand Adelman still held.

Walker slammed the heel of his hand on the table, which shook but did not break. "Boys," he said, "My daughter's life is the only *real* issue." His voice was even deeper than it had been before. "So if you're done with your squabblin', can we get back to the ransom?" He looked across the table at Hopkins and Henderson, then leaned forward and glanced sideways at Adelman. "Good. Now, I hope what you're tellin' us is right, Bert. But we've still gotta get the ransom money together. Just in case."

Adelman nodded thoughtfully. He put down the copy of the ransom demand, opened the manila folder, and took out a packet of paper. "That's the other bit of complexity, Sky," he said. "I've gone back over your assets very carefully." He tapped the packet. "I've brought with me an updated summary of your holdings. And frankly, raising that kind of cash in the time frame is problematic, if not impossible. I'm not saying it can't be done, but . . ."

"What am I worth, Bert?" Walker wore his famous game face, a scowl that lit his dark eyes.

Adelman took an alligator glass-case from the inside pocket of his suitcoat, put on a pair of gold-rimmed glasses, and flipped to the last page of the packet. "As of the first of this month," he answered, glancing over the top of the glasses at Hopkins and Henderson as if to remind them that the figures should never become public knowledge, "you have assets of one hundred fifty-eight million and change."

"So, what's the problem?"

"The problem, as I know you're aware, Sky, is that only ten, maybe twenty, percent of that sum can be made liquid quickly, much less overnight." He looked to Jones-Walker for support, but she seemed to have begun her own search for rainbows in the yard. "Anything more than twenty-five million will cause serious repercussions." He took off his glasses. "You may well jeopardize a majority of your investments."

"None of that matters to me. Just get it done." Walker still had his game face in place. "Am I bein' clear, Bert?"

chapter 21

Hopkins had just enough time to shower and shave before the 8:00 A.M. press briefing, again held outside on the lawn near the department's front entrance. Three officers had been assigned to traffic control along the road, and the parking lot had been cleared of all North Ridge vehicles to accommodate the hundreds of reporters from around the world. Australian and Japanese television crews jostled for space with the Europeans and Americans. Jack Bollinger was granting so many interviews himself that he was ensconced under an elm tree on the lawn on the other side of the lot. As Hopkins stepped out of the station, Sergeant Banks, who was guarding the front door, said, "Look at that dipshit holding court over there." The day was too warm for even Bollinger to wear his trenchcoat, but he had turned up the collar of his sport coat and had adopted a grim, war-weary pose for the occasion. "What an asshole," Banks rumbled. "A buddy of mine at WLN was tellin' me he's been camping out at his desk every night. Doesn't even leave the office he's so afraid he'll miss a fax or somethin' comin' in from the perp."

"I believe it," Hopkins said, shaking his head. He moved toward the platform and podium set up with microphones and power cables for the press briefing.

During the briefing's first twenty minutes, when most questions focused on the delivery of the child's finger, Hopkins had to speak only once, to state that Chief Mancini was busy working on the case and would not be available for comment, at least until afternoon. In fact, Mancini, vacillating between fitful diatribes about the kidnapper and sullen silence, had holed himself up alone in his office. While Henderson answered questions, Hopkins stood behind him on his right, hands at his sides, mentally organizing his day, listing the people he needed to talk with, and trying to make sense of the information he had. He knew that his lack of sleep was catching up with him; though he felt so much nervous energy it was difficult to stand still, he wasn't thinking as clearly as he should be.

Gradually, as reporters' questions began going over old ground, Henderson's answers became a litany of curt responses: No, the Jeep had still not been located. No, none of those already interviewed was considered a suspect. No, the FBI did not have any information about whether Sky Walker would play in that night's championship game. Yes, the Walkers were understandably quite upset about what had happened that morning. Yes, there had been a witness to the delivery of the finger, but no further information could be disseminated at present. Yes, the Walkers had apparently hired a private investigator, but, no, that should not be taken as a sign of their lack of confidence in either the North Ridge police or the FBI. Yes, there had finally been a ransom demand, but, no, the details were not going to be made public at this time.

Immediately after that last answer, Jack Bollinger, who had

been unable to join his camera crew in the front row until the briefing had already begun, raised a folded white sheet of paper in the air as though he had been waiting all his life for the moment. The reporters huddled near him lowered their hands so that Henderson had no choice but to call on him. Keeping the paper raised, Bollinger shook it until it unfolded. His nose was sunburned, but the rest of his face, made-up for the camera, looked pallid. Dark circles puffed under his eyes. "Two questions, Mr. Henderson," he began once everyone had quieted down. "Given the exorbitant amount of the ransom demand . . ." He paused as the throng began to murmur. ". . . and the incredibly short amount of time to raise the money . . ." He waited as more cameras were turned toward him. ". . . how can the kidnapper possibly expect the Walkers to pay?"

"I have no comment on your supposition, Mr. Bollinger," Henderson answered. The collar of his shirt was soaked with sweat, but his drawl only became slower and more calm.

"But you do *know* the amount of the demand and the time frame," Bollinger sneered, turning slightly away from Henderson and toward the phalanx of cameras.

Banks' assessment of Bollinger is far too kind, Hopkins thought. And, as he stared at the sheet of paper Bollinger gripped, he became aware of something he knew he should have realized sooner. Mentally kicking himself, he glanced over his shoulder at Banks, who still stood in front of the station's main entrance, arms folded across his thick chest, looking ready to clothesline anyone who tried to enter.

"Yes, sir," Henderson replied, "I'm familiar with the ransom demand, but—and, perhaps I need to reiterate this point— the specifics of the demand are not a topic I'm at liberty to discuss at this briefing." He stared steadily down at Bollinger. "Now, do you have a question I may answer?"

Smirking, Bollinger growled, "Mr. Henderson, don't you think forty-eight million dollars in forty-eight hours is an impossible demand, even for our Number 48?"

When the mass of reporters erupted, Hopkins was already making his way from the platform to the door. As he came up to Banks, the Sergeant asked, "What the hell just happened over there?"

Hopkins looked back at the melee, which, with cameras swinging and microphone booms swaying, was taking on the air of a medieval joust. "As soon as you can, haul that dildo Bollinger into my office. If he refuses, and the bastard'll probably grandstand on you with all those cameras focused on him, inform him that I'm already processing a search warrant that'll cover *all* his computer records."

"You got it, Hoop." Banks grinned. "Glad to."

Hopkins started to open the door, turned, and said, "Hey, Dave, after you've got him, make sure that warrant's ready fast."

Hopkins met Ross coming down the corridor cradling a thick stack of paper in her arms. "Thank God," she said. "I was afraid I'd get out there with these before I ran into you." She gestured with her chin for him to take a sheet.

The press release, printed on department letterhead, read:

The North Ridge Police Department apologizes to the Sky Walker family for any trauma due to the comments made by Chief Peter Mancini at the June 7th press conference. The North Ridge Police Department further states that the perpetrator will be apprehended soon and punished to the full extent of the law.

"The Chief typed it up himself," Ross said. "Had me run off two hundred copies. Told me to distribute them to the media. We can't . . ."

Hopkins took the stack of paper from her. "I'll take care of it, Meghan," he said.

Touching his arm for a moment, she asked, "How're you doing?"

He shrugged his shoulders.

"You had to inform the Walkers about the . . . about what happened this morning?"

"Yeah."

"How'd they take it?"

"The mother went into instant denial but later started asking tough, pertinent questions. And the father . . ." He shifted the stack of papers so that he could carry them under one arm. "He wants to fry the bastard *personally.*"

"The Chief," she said, "would gladly light the fire." She bit her lip. "It's not exactly the break we were hoping for last night."

"No." He exhaled slowly. "And I didn't think things could get much worse."

"What can I do?" she asked, touching his arm again. "Anything I can do?"

He looked up the corridor toward the Investigations Unit office. "Yeah," he said. "Will you find Paul Kim for me? Tell him I want to ask him some questions about computers. And contact Ken Culhane, the guy from the gymnastics center. I need to ask him about the call he got from Monique Jones-Walker." He patted the stack of papers. "I'll talk to Mancini, tell him the briefing turned into a zoo, and I wouldn't let you distribute these."

A tense clamor pervaded the Investigations Unit office. One of the FBI teams had moved in, causing some of the North Ridge officers to double up at desks. With the delivery of the severed finger and the ransom note, there was an even more acute sense of urgency among the investigators following up leads on the phones. Hopkins tossed the press releases into the wastebasket, shuffled the pile of phone messages on his cluttered desk, grabbed a legal pad, selected a dozen files, and headed for Interview Room B, where he'd be better able to concentrate. He sat on the far side of the table, facing the doorway and office, and read the detectives' reports on their canvass of Chief Mancini's neighborhood. A neighbor, up early to go perch fishing at the lake, had noticed an off-white delivery van slowing in front of Mancini's house. The van hadn't stopped, perhaps because the driver, a middle-aged, bearded man in a dark cowboy hat, had seen the neighbor pulling out of his garage. The neighbor had tried to get the van's license plate number, but it had been smudged with dirt.

As Hopkins leaned back in the chair, wondering about the beard and cowboy hat, Paul Kim stuck his head in the doorway and said, "You wanted to see me, Commander?" Kim, a civilian who ran the day-to-day operations of the records office and managed the entire department's computer system, was almost forty but looked younger. His long black hair, parted in the middle, framed his thin face. His eyes blinked behind wire-rimmed glasses.

"Yeah, Paul," Hopkins answered, "I need to understand how the perp we're dealing with is operating. Getting into all these systems. And . . ." Looking over Kim's shoulder, he saw Banks and Bollinger approaching. "Can you hold on a minute?" he asked Kim. "I've got to deal with this jerk. It shouldn't take long."

As Kim stepped back, Bollinger stormed through the door. "What is this shit, Hopkins?" he grumbled. "You can't touch my computer records!"

Hopkins closed the file he had just read. "Shut the door and take a seat," he said, his voice formal and distant.

Bollinger shut the door but did not sit. His scalp was damp; sweat ran among the pockmarks on his face.

"Who was your source for that ransom demand you were waving around outside?" Hopkins asked.

Bollinger put his hands on the table, leaned over toward Hopkins, and said in a low voice, "Have you ever heard of the First Amendment?" He smelled as though he hadn't showered.

"Yeah, Bollinger, I have," Hopkins answered as he stood up. "But you're not protected if you're interfering with a criminal investigation."

"What the hell are you talking about?"

"Where'd you get that copy of the ransom demand?" Hopkins leaned forward, his height enabling him to look down at the reporter.

"I don't have to reveal my sources, and you know it!" Bollinger scoffed. He leaned back away from the table.

"The perp e-mailed that ransom demand directly to Monique Jones-Walker." Hopkins' voice rose almost to a shout. "And I doubt, even though you apparently have some weird relationship with the guy, he'd fax it to you immediately. He seems to like to keep you begging."

Bollinger hesitated, wiping the sweat from his face. "Fuck you, Hopkins! You don't know shit."

Hopkins lowered his voice as he said, "I know you've been hacking Jones-Walker's e-mail."

Bollinger glowered at Hopkins and mumbled, "I've got work to do." He turned, flung open the door, and stomped out, stumbling a moment as he brushed by Henderson who was walking toward the interview room with a manila folder in his hand.

"Looks like you yanked his chain pretty hard," Henderson said as he entered the room. "What was that about?"

"The bastard's been hacking Monique Jones-Walker's e-mail."

A hint of a smile passed over Henderson's face. "The ransom demand?"

Hopkins nodded. "And maybe his knowing about the phone call and her polygraph results."

Henderson slapped the folder against the palm of his hand. "Maybe he's been putting his hands in her electronic drawers for a long time. It's even possible he's crossed the perp's tracks. No telling what we'd find in his records. Sounds like we've got probable cause."

Kim poked his head in the doorway again.

"Sorry, Paul," Hopkins said to him. "Come on in." He turned back to Henderson. "I'm already processing the search warrant."

Henderson nodded slowly. "Good," he said. "I'd like to stick it to that jackass for that stunt he pulled outside."

Kim sat down quietly in a chair.

"My thought exactly," Hopkins said. "I was just about to ask Paul about the perp's use of computers. Want to join us?"

Henderson nodded to Kim but said, "No. Thanks." He hesitated and then raised the folder. "This morning before the shit hit the fan . . ." He laid the folder on the table. ". . . my guys came across two loans Walker Management made to AIA Development. Ten million last December, and another five million the first of May." He'd taken off his suit-coat, and he rolled up the sleeves of his white shirt as he spoke. "There's nothing illegal, and payments are being made on schedule, but Adelman's ethics in loaning himself Walker's money are pretty dubious. And it's got me thinking about why Adelman was so insistent this morning that raising the money for the ransom demand would be impossible." He shrugged. "It may not get us any closer to finding Tonya Walker, but I'm going to have another conversation with your buddy, Bert."

Hopkins pointed to the folder. "Can I take a look at it later?"

Henderson picked up the folder. "Yeah. Sure. Of course." As he backed out of the room, he held the door handle and asked, "Want this closed?"

Flipping to a blank sheet of the legal pad, Hopkins nodded. He then jotted a note to himself to check out Adelman's finances. When he and Kim were alone in the quiet of the interview room, he rubbed his face, took a breath, and said, "I was trying to get into the perp's mind this morning. And I kept getting stuck on the idea that the guy seems to've invaded Mrs. Walker's life through her computer."

Kim nodded, unsure about answering.

"What do you think?" Hopkins asked.

Kim blinked. "I only know what I've heard around the office."

"And?"

"I think you're dealing with a cracker."

"A cracker?"

"A hacker who's . . . who gets off not just on breaking into systems but on destroying them, planting viruses or logic bombs." Kim paused. "And I'm out there on this one, Commander, but he seems to've crossed over from cyberspace into the Walkers' lives."

Hopkins, who had started to take notes, put down his pen. "What do you mean?"

Kim raised his hands, as if in surrender, and said, "This really isn't my area of expertise, Commander."

"I know, Paul," Hopkins answered. "But keep talking. You're making sense."

"He was able to invade WLN's system to reach Mrs. Walker. And we know he had no trouble invading Walker Management and the AIA files, without, one of the FBI agents told me, leaving any tracks at all." He hesitated. "But rather than plant a virus or a bomb, he's destroying them all by kidnapping the girl. She's . . . her kidnapping's the virus that's wiping them all out. Does that make any sense, Commander?"

"Yeah, Paul, it kind of does." Hopkins scratched his scalp with the pen cap. "What about our systems here?"

Kim did not answer immediately. He looked around at the bare walls and the viewing port's mirror. "I, ah, wondered about that, too. So I spent four hours last night looking for evidence of tampering in our system. And I didn't find a thing."

Hopkins picked up his pen and started to write notes again.

"Ah, Commander," Kim said, interrupting him.

Hopkins looked up.

"That, ah, doesn't mean our system's secure. It only means he's very good at covering his tracks."

"What?"

"Our system's not secure against any really skilled hacker." Kim wrung his hands. "With our links to PIMS and NCIC and the State Police, there's got to be holes, ways in from the outside."

"And?" Hopkins asked.

"It would be most sensible to assume that our security's been breached." Kim's tone was apologetic. "The likelihood is that he's read every e-mail message that you and Chief Mancini and . . . basically every message he's wanted to read."

"Christ." Hopkins tossed his pen onto the pad. "And the FBI files?"

Kim grimaced. "Their defenses would be stronger, of course, but their files aren't encrypted. And they're connected to the Net. They may be secure, but they're probably not as impregnable as Mr. Henderson would like to . . ."

"Should we shut down our system?" Hopkins asked.

"That's not really feasible, Commander," Kim answered.

"But?" Hopkins prodded him again.

"But if you have any really sensitive information, anything that might break open the case, I would definitely not log it into the system. Don't even refer to it on the system. Hand-deliver it, and make a checklist of whoever sees it. But, ah, be careful. If he saw a sudden stoppage in the flow of information in the system, he'd know immediately that something was up. And he'd run to cover."

"Could we catch him? Trace him through the network?"

"Not likely, Commander."

Hopkins waited for him to elaborate.

"You can catch hackers that way. But if he's skilled, and it looks like he's very skilled, he's probably entering these systems through the Web. Probably routing himself around the world to prevent a trace. You'd need permission from foreign governments and a great deal of time."

"Neither of which we have," Hopkins murmured. "Is there anything we could do?"

"Well . . ." Kim hesitated again. "I could set up a printer to print out the commands of anybody hacking your computer. It wouldn't tell us where he's coming from. Or even if it's the guy you're after. But it would let us know what files the hacker's reading and maybe even how he's entering. See, Commander, a hacker tries to erase all his tracks before he leaves, but the printer'd mark his tracks as he made them . . ."

"What if I disconnect my computer from the system?"

"Hu—uh?" Kim stuttered. "What? It won't work if you're off-line."

Hopkins leaned forward. "You can set the printer up for another computer, for Chief Mancini's. But this guy thinks he knows everything. That's his edge—invading systems, stealing information. If I disconnect my computer, what's he going to do?"

Kim smiled at the mirrored viewing port. "He's going to wonder why you went off-line. He's going to try to find you. And he's probably going to get frustrated and angry."

chapter 23

The newsroom was an absolute zoo, the frenzy to feed the tube consuming the plebeians and patricians alike. Immune to the bedlam, Jack Bollinger emptied the trash on his computer screen, the cleansing and scouring finally finished, the last files sloughed. He sat back, scratched his crotch, furtively slid open his desk's lower drawer, slipped out the flask of Jack Daniel's Old No. 7, and tipped a healthy dollop into his mug of coffee (it was almost noon, and, in any case, *purely celebratory*). He'd leapt out of the pack forever that morning, first with the scoop about the finger in the Dunhill box and then with the ransom demand. There'd been high-fives and hugs galore when he'd returned to the station. He'd take his pick of the litter tonight, no question about it. The briefing, *his briefing*, was running around the world, viewed globally by every petty potentate and sumptuous princess.

He smiled as the coffee and Jack burned his throat. His dogged determination, staying on top of the story constantly for over forty hours, had paid off phenomenally. No one, not the Ratherses or the Jenningses or the Brokaws, with their highly placed sources, or any of the other pretty boys or lispy fems could touch him. The world was now a place where everyone knew his name.

It had not been without cost, however. He didn't really *need* any of the files he'd deep-sixed. He should have tossed the WLN files anyway, and the communiqués from the Snatcher, though of historical value, might have caused sticky legal problems. But his collection was quite another matter. He had most of it backed-up on disks at home, safely hidden, but the convenience, the *serviceability*, of being able to to browse through it whenever he got the urge would definitely be missed. The station had blocked the initial search warrant, but even the shiftiest of the station's shysters had suggested that they were skating on thin ice and he'd better Zamboni the files fast. It was all Hopkins' fault. The lame jock was hopelessly overmatched, as the retired watch commander had so smugly pointed out, but he was going to break a lot of china and upset a lot of apple carts in his bungling search for the Snatcher.

And continuing was not without its risks, either. Being dependent on the Snatcher aggravated him. True, the lunatic hadn't been exaggerating about the story of the century, the scoop of a lifetime, the media mayhem out there outstripping anything anybody'd ever witnessed. But the Snatcher, whatever else he was, was a megalomaniac—sending all those communiqués as though he was nothing more than the guy's personal lapdog. And the morning's communiqués had been progressively more presumptuous. Informing him just after 4:00 A.M. that a gift had been delivered to the North Ridge Chief, stating that it was not a bomb, but failing to mention what it was. Waiting until almost 6:30 to explain that the Dunhill box contained the girl's finger. And finally, before that scoop had even aired, suggesting that the ransom demand was being delivered, but forbidding him yet again—a categorical prohibition, this time—from obtaining the specifics the whole world would want to know. He'd solved that problem expeditiously enough, having undressed Monique for months, but the Snatcher had still had the temerity to proscribe his actions. He was a reporter, and the lunatic had to've known he'd nose around until he found the facts. That was his job, his life.

But that was it exactly: the Snatcher knew too much, far too much. What did the guy know about him? And how might he use that information? He'd never really trusted any of his sources. They always had agendas, and this lunatic's was certainly the most bizarre yet. And what part he ultimately was supposed to play in that grandiose scheme certainly hadn't been clarified. He swallowed the rest of the coffee and Jack, felt acid rising, the old esophagitus rearing up, and rooted through his desk for a Zantac.

James Robert Saville slid into his seat in front of the Command Center's console and glanced up at the clock. Sixteen-fifteen. He'd been away too long. But the sorties had, as always, been highly successful. The van was ready. The Safe House was set up. Bransfield's Big Surprise was waiting. And the shrine! The shrine was yet another elegant touch. It'd drive all those morons right out of their skulls. He'd lose some equipment, a cheap clone, a modem, a timer, and a tape recorder—but there were costs in any operation. And the payback here was huge, a whole new level of the game. Anyway, he had backups. You always needed backup systems. Always.

He grabbed the super-remote and began to surf the channels. He was everywhere, not merely ubiquitous, but omnipresent! Too much really to keep up with, this media circus he'd created. And, hell, events were just going to keep accel-

erating. They'd skyrocket, until all those morons toasted their
synapses! Even he couldn't keep up anymore. And that bothered him a lot. He'd have to be highly selective when he reviewed his tapes. All those news breaks and noon news
programs and special reports! And Phil and Oprah and Mon-
tel and Jenny and Sally and Ricki and fucking Geraldo and all
their wretched pretenders. On every one of those gabfests,
dawn to dusk, local and national, he was *it*, the only show
around! And it was all great theater!

This called for tunes! The Stones! "Jumpin' Jack Flash"!
"Sympathy for the Devil"! As he turned to his CD player, he
realized the kid was silent. Did he need to feed her? He wasn't
sure. He'd doused her light before his sorties, and she'd been
asleep then—knocked out by the Tylenol #3, another item
procured ever so easily with an ersatz prescription. What time
had that been? Oh-nine-forty. He should look in on her, but
he needed to check his sources first. Priorities were priorities.
His sources were critical. The kid could wait. Anyway, in the
final analysis, it was unavoidable that the kid suffered. It wasn't
fair, but it couldn't be helped. That's just the way it was. And
as he knew only too well, it'd been going on for years. His
mother'd seldom touched him again after that horrific night
when she'd mangled his hand with the heel of her shoe. But in
a way, he'd wished she had. It was almost as though she'd disappeared, too. The constant neglect, the incessant loneliness,
the tedious days and interminable nights, they were in a way
even more excruciating. And all without Sarah, without so
much as a visit, without even a single word—ever. There were
rumors, of course, taunts at school, and his mother's intermittent rants with big words like *prostitute* and, later, *pornographic*, words he didn't immediately understand.

He caught himself, eyes welling, daunted by the turn his
thoughts had taken. All these years, and it was still so fucking
present, more real than fucking real. Nothing was going to

change it. Nothing. Ever. And dwelling on it was counterproductive. Worse than useless! He had work to do, goddamn it.
Important work. Work no one else in the world could do. He
typed maniacally at the keyboard, striking the thoughts away,
scoping the activity, checking his sources. And there had been
a shitload of activity while he was off on his sorties!

Bertie was working hard, moving huge chunks of change.
Handicapped, of course, by that sinkhole AIA. Major blunder,
that one. But Bertie might get the gold together anyway. A
man of wealth and taste, all right. Commendable, really. No
mean feat. Four point eight billion centavos. The lucre didn't
really matter in the least, of course. He could lift bits of dough
from any number of banks any time he wished. But it was part
of the game, part of the show, and he had his coffers, strategi-
cally placed worldwide, ready to be filled. Brimming with
shekels, they'd be. And then empty, and others would fill.
Gravy boats overflowing! Major scratch, bread like you
wouldn't believe. The magic, the marvels of modern banking!
They ought to be called Jiffy-Launder shops. He'd move all
that moolah, shuffle it, deal it to the loonies left and right.
Tender prestidigitation, that's what it would be! Now you see
it, now you don't! Truly elegant sleight of hand! And laughs
galore—all at Monique-the-Media-Babe's expense!

And Cam, there he was, too, that dud from California,
about to make the discovery of his life. He was still logged on,
but not for long. The bait was far too juicy to resist. Fame,
stardom and celebrity, kudos and accolades from the rich and
famous. The dude who surfed in from La-La Land and snared
the Walker kidnapper. He'd swallow it whole! The fool. Any
minute now. Any minute.

Old Pit Bull was up to something. He'd already dumped a
bunch of files. Not that it would do him any good. Bull had
leapt right out of the goddamned Pit that morning. Anything
for attention, that dingo. Overstepped all boundaries with that

ransom demand exposé. Sure, it had been one delectable moment, that FBI Hottentot swinging in the breeze. But it was beyond Pit Bull's run. He had no business hacking around again in Monique's files. It had been expressly forbidden. And he would have to be punished, too, of course. A muzzle, at the very least. Probably the Dog House for that mutt. Maybe even the Big Stick. The inevitability of it all. And Pit Bull thinking that dumping his files would save his sorry ass. What fools these mongrels be!

Saville abruptly stopped keyboarding, stared at the main screen, cross-checked the other screens. The Hoopmeister was gone. Vamoose. Vanished. What was the local hero up to? Hiding? Why? Or had he been given the boot? No, his files'd still be on-line. The Hoopmeister was balking. Refusing to play. That wasn't nice. Not nice at all. Saville scratched at the adhesive from the beard he'd left on because he'd been in such a rush to get back to his sources. He quickly checked the other NRPD files, and everything was copacetic. What gave? What was the Hoopmeister up to?

chapter 24

Cameron Bransfield waited in his rented Mustang across the street and halfway down the block from the two-flat in Chicago's Olsonville neighborhood. The tops of the spruces and elms held last light, and he wasn't prepared to move until after dark. The block was quiet, the brown and red brick two-flats ranked in a nondescript row. The few people that had passed the Mustang in the forty-five minutes he had been there were young professionals, mostly single, whose salaries apparently did not enable them to live in more fashionable neighborhoods closer to the lake and Loop. He'd seen two mothers pushing babies in umbrella strollers earlier but no older children at all. It was the perfect spot, he figured, for the kidnapper's lair—nothing that would draw anyone's attention, and young, self-absorbed neighbors who might wave but would never pry. The building itself was perfect, too. The brick facade, more orange than red, was in need of tuckpointing. The front porch roof was a little ramshackle, the gutter a bit askew. The small rectangle of weed-infested front yard held as much dirt as grass. It wasn't exactly an eyesore, but it wasn't the least bit memorable either. A person could live there for years and never be noticed.

A light went on behind the drawn shades in the front room of the upstairs apartment. Bransfield ran the back of his hand across his mouth. Someone was up there, all right. He waited for a young woman walking her golden retriever to pass, slipped off his Ray-Bans, rolled up the window, stepped out of the Mustang, locked the door, and stretched. He was a large man, broad-shouldered, thickly muscled, well over two hundred pounds, and sitting so long in the car had tightened him up. The evening was warm, but he wore his blue linen sport jacket to conceal the Smith & Wesson .45 in his shoulder holster. Wearing jeans and black sneakers, he was dressed to move easily in the gathering darkness. Only the thick wave of blond hair falling across his forehead might draw a second glance from someone. He was a transplant from Oklahoma, had never even ridden a surfboard, but he relished his reputation as, in *People Weekly*'s phrase, *one cool California hunk.*

He rolled his neck, moved to the sidewalk, and sauntered away from the building toward the corner. He paused at the corner for a moment and then headed to the alley behind the building. He counted the back porches along the alley until he found his target. There was a large window to the right of the back door, and a small window to the left. An outside light illuminated the wooden porch. Cross braces had been added to support the dilapidated deck and stairs. He had hoped to make his approach from the back, but he realized that the light and the porch's apparent creakiness would put him at serious risk.

The garage, a wood frame structure listing to starboard and covered with peeling brown paint, stood on a cracked concrete slab. The bases of the two doors showed signs of rot, but a new padlock hung from the latch. He could see nothing through the vertical slit between the doors, but the grimy side window offered a glimpse, once his eyes adjusted to the dim interior, of a plain, off-white van similar to the description of the vehicle used that morning to deliver the girl's finger. He slinked around the corner of the garage and, hidden from the second story's view by the deck and stairs, tried the garage's rear door, but it, too, was locked. He stood quietly for a moment, gazing up through the deck's slats at the back of the apartment. Only scant light came from the large window, no light at all from the small window. Whoever was inside could see out far better than he could see in, and as soon as he reached the level of the deck, he would be completely vulnerable.

His mind made up, he sidled up the alley. A calm alertness, a readiness for battle, came over him as he turned the corner and headed down the street. Energy surged with each step. He walked up to the building's front door as if he owned the place. Inside the vestibule, he noted that there was no name on either mailbox. Both of the oak and glass inner doors were locked, but his Gold Card remedied that. He slowly opened the door on the right.

Looking up the narrow, carpeted stairwell, he mused about how the electronic trace had led his team around the world to a spot less than twelve miles from the Walker mansion. The trail had been convoluted, but the kidnapper had doomed himself by hacking too long in the AIA system and then daring to invade the Baker and Bransfield system. The kidnapper might be a brilliant hacker, but he had failed to realize that private enterprises had no need for either search warrants or the rules of international law. Promises of six-figure rewards had led his team to New York, then across the Atlantic to London, through a hub in Sweden, back to Toronto, and finally to Atlanta before ending right here in Chicago.

He crept up the stairs, testing each one before putting his full weight on it. The air was close, and the carpet smelled musty. Halfway up, he stopped and listened. There was faint music but no other sound. He drew the .45 from his holster. The decision to bring the kidnapper in himself had not been made lightly. He had thought about contacting the police, but the kidnapper had likely compromised their systems as well, and the crucial element of surprise would have been lost. He had also considered bringing his own backup, but the team he had brought to Chicago included computer experts, not field personnel, and, time being of the essence, he had not been willing to wait while someone flew in. He had finally settled for a quick call to Bert Adelman and a solitary drive to this unremarkable neighborhood and building.

As he slowly worked his way up the rest of the stairs, the adrenaline pulsed in his temples. It had been four years since he had smashed in a door, and he was starting to sweat. On the small upstairs landing he shifted the .45 to his left hand, wiped his right hand on his jeans, and switched the gun back. There were two locks on the door but no dead bolt, which was a break. He listened again, the music more distinct, a Beatles song.

He took three deep breaths, waited again for any sound of danger, and stepped back to the edge of the landing. For a fleeting moment as he raised his foot, he sensed that something wasn't right. But his adrenaline was pumping, and he kicked hard under the doorknob and sprang forward. The jamb around the lock splintered, a chain snapped, and the door flew open. Swinging his .45 up in front of him, he gaped at the opposite wall, covered from floor to ceiling with photographs of Monique Jones-Walker. In the next second, he remembered the name of the song, "Happiness Is a Warm Gun," and registered a beeping just above his head.

The explosion decapitated him. His body, hurled out of the doorway, tumbled backward down the stairs and sprawled against the shattered oak and glass door. His right arm was gone; his left, an almost unrecognizable mass of bone and tissue dislocated at the shoulder and elbow, pointed bizarrely at the mailboxes in the vestibule. Blood spurted from his severed carotid artery. Smoke choked the stairwell and billowed from the building's entrance.

chapter 25

His pager beeped as Hopkins climbed
the stairs to his apartment at 10:15 P.M. He carried a paper bag
containing the Italian beef and sausage combo sandwich and
french fries he had picked up on the way home. His day had
been hectic—a surfeit of leads that ultimately provided no
real information. The FBI crime lab had found blood samples
that matched Tonya Walker's type, but there had been no fin-
gerprints or fibers on the cotton or cigar box. A clerk at a
Loop tobacconist had remembered the stooped, bearded, elderly man who had purchased the last nine Dunhill cigars and
pointedly insisted on obtaining the empty box. The man had
worn a Panama hat and dark glasses; a cast covered his right
hand and wrist. The police artist's rendering of the old man
had shown no identifiable features. The line of the face had
been similar to the description of the middle-aged man seen
in the van at Chief Mancini's house, but it took a serious leap
of imagination to conclude that both men were the same
person.

The voice on the phone at the Walkers' had been Bert Adelman's, but every syllable had been electronically lifted and meticulously edited from the previous day's press conference. Ken Culhane had confirmed Hopkins' suspicion that the call from Monique Jones-Walker just prior to the kidnapping had been a curt demand that he have Tonya ready to be picked up; Culhane hadn't really gotten involved in a conversation with her at all, and, looking back, admitted that the call might have been a tape-recording. During Hopkins' interview with Culhane, his daughter Cari had called to see how he was and to tell him that she thought she had done well on her Physics final. He had promised to call her back but hadn't had the chance. When he had informed Monique Jones-Walker that Bollinger had most likely stolen the ransom demand and the earlier information about the polygraph from her e-mail, she had thanked him for letting her know that her other colleagues at WLN hadn't betrayed her. As he was leaving the office, more than seventeen hours after he had arrived at Chief Mancini's house, Hopkins heard that the Chicago Bulls, without Sky Walker, had just lost the first game of the NBA Finals 101–92.

Hopkins called the number on his pager as soon as he reached the phone in the kitchenette. He slipped a couple of french fries from the bag and was pulling a long neck Rolling Rock from the refrigerator when Carl Henderson answered.

Hopkins popped the beer's cap against the edge of the counter. "Carl," he said, "Tom Hopkins. I got your page." They had left a meeting together only forty-five minutes before, and he couldn't imagine what Henderson wanted.

"Are you watching the news?" Henderson asked.

"What? No. I just got home." He cradled the receiver between his shoulder and ear, swigged the beer, took the sandwich from the bag, and began to unwrap it.

"There's been a bombing in Chicago," Henderson said. "An apartment building on the north side." The cellular connection made his drawl seem even slower. "One victim, male Caucasian, apparently FUBAR." He paused. "The media ghouls don't know it yet, but the victim is Adelman's friend, Cameron Bransfield."

"Oh, shit!" Hopkins said, looking down at the sandwich. "Are you sure?"

"The Chicago police reached me just as I was leaving the office. There was a driver's license, credit cards, and an investigator's I.D. in the victim's wallet. They told me there's not much else left of the guy. And, they said I had to see the apartment ASAP. I'm on my way there now."

Hopkins took out his pen and small black pocket-planner. "What's the address?" he asked. When he finished writing, he said, "I'll meet you there."

When Hopkins arrived at the scene of the bombing, he parked his Taurus next to the police barricade at the street's corner, showed his badge to a uniformed officer, and hurried down the block to the building. The fire was out, but an ambulance, two fire trucks, and three squad cars jammed the street. The smell of smoke lingered in the trees, and the flashing lights played across the yards and buildings. Four television crews mingled with bystanders behind the police cordon. Firefighers milled about, and two paramedics wheeled a gurney carrying a body bag toward the ambulance. Carl Henderson stood with a lanky police captain near the two-flat's smoke-stained front entrance.

After waving Hopkins over, Henderson said, "Hoop, this is Captain Andy Domalski, Chicago PD." He gestured toward Domalski. "Andy, Tom Hopkins from North Ridge."

Domalski, taller and thinner than Hopkins, had an aquiline nose and dark eyes. He nodded to Hopkins and said, "I was just tellin' Agent Henderson that the device was not very sophisticated but extremely lethal. It looks like it was set just above the door and triggered to go off when the lock was broken." He shook his head. "The victim had no chance. No chance whatever." Still shaking his head, he looked over at the entrance. "The back door and windows were locked, but we were able to gain access, no problem. It seems like the bomber knew the victim would approach through the front stairwell and force entry."

Hopkins looked over at Henderson and then asked Domalski, "Any witnesses?"

"No. Unh-unh. We're still canvassing the neighborhood. A number of people noticed the victim sitting in a new Mustang down the street, but nobody saw anything else. Nobody seems to even have a clue who lives here. We're in the process of tracking down the landlord."

"Okay," Henderson said. "Can we go up?"

When Domalski led them around the back of the building to the wooden stairs, Henderson asked, "What's in the garage?"

"Something else you'll want to look at," Domalski answered. "A white van with a message on the dash."

"That figures," Hopkins muttered as they started up the stairs.

Splintered glass from the windows the firefighters had broken crunched under their feet as they crossed the deck and entered the back door. The odor of smoke permeated the kitchen, but there was no damage other than the glass shards that littered the counters and floor. The first bedroom along the narrow hallway leading toward the front of the apartment held only a futon and a cheap ceramic lamp with an orange shade. In the second bedroom, an IBM clone stood on a card table. A telephone and modem had toppled onto the floor next to a folding chair, and a bright yellow portable CD player lay near the wall.

"This door was shut," Domalski said. "And with the direction of the blast, nothing much was destroyed except near the front door and stairs." He pointed to the card table. "There's a note over there that I, uh, think is for you, Agent Henderson."

Without touching anything, Henderson and Hopkins peered at the note, printed in boldface type, which said:

Hey, FBI BOOGIE, buddy of mine!
BRANSFIELD'S signed quite terminally off-line!
A wannabe hip California dude!
His trace was too rude and pathetically crude!
Trying to BYTE a little too much, he's now DEAD!!!
Blown all to pieces—Find the BITS of his HEAD?

"Jesus!" Hopkins said.

Henderson's face remained impassive, but the vein in his neck throbbed visibly.

"The note's only part of it," Domalski, who had waited in the doorway, said. "You gotta see what's up front."

An emptiness gnawing at his stomach, Hopkins asked, "What's in the CD player?"

"The Beatles," Domalski answered. The *White Album*'s second disk, if that means anything to you. It was set to play continuously. Was still going when I got here."

As they left the room, Hopkins said to Henderson, "He's been here, but he's never worked here. Never lived here. It's got some other purpose for him." When they entered the living room, he watched the evidence technicians working around the obliterated doorway. In the hallway outside, a tiny tuft of seared blond hair was smeared on the charred wall. Turning, he froze. An upholstered church kneeler, apparently knocked over by the blast, lay against the opposite wall. Above it, from floor to ceiling, photographs of Monique Jones-Walker papered the entire wall and most of the two other walls. Some of the photos had burned completely, some were scorched, and some had curled from the heat, but the sheer number of nine-by-eleven-inch images, each one different from the others, was staggering.

"They've all been scanned from other sources," Domalski said. "And printed, as far as I can tell, on the same printer."

"My, my, my," Henderson murmured as he stepped closer to the wall, studying each of the images. "Hoop," he said over his shoulder. "Help me out here. I'm guessing each of these is from a different day, a different news program."

Domalski went over to talk to his evidence technicians as Hopkins worked his way along the wall, inspecting every photograph. Jones-Walker seemed to wear a different outfit in each of the hundreds of shots, and though many of the images showed her at the WLN anchor desk, some had been taken of her out on location. The perp seemed to have collected at least a daily photo from each of her television newscasts, apparently *every* day, for God knew how long. He was at the corner when, crouching low by a series of unburned photographs near the floor, he said, "This one's at the Boone School fire. I recognize the building behind her." He stood and, looking at Henderson, added, "That was over two years ago."

Henderson gave a low whistle and said, "This guy's been building up to this for one long goddamned time."

Lost in thought, Hopkins walked to the front window and gazed down through the tattered shade and shattered glass at the street. The ambulance and the hook and ladder were gone, but the lights of the other fire truck and the squad cars still swam in the darkness. The crowd had grown, and he counted five television crews among the onlookers. At the edge of the police cordon, Bert Adelman stood talking to a uniformed officer.

"I'll be back," Hopkins said to Henderson. He hurried along the hall, across the deck, and down the stairs. When he rounded the front of the building, he saw Adelman pointing impatiently up at the windows of the second-story apartment.

As Hopkins approached them, the policeman, a heavy man whose belly bulged over his belt, was saying, "I don't give a flyin' fuck who you are. If you was Jesus H. Christ himself, I wouldn't let you in that building."

When Adelman saw Hopkins, he called, "Tom, will you tell this officer who I am so I can go up there?" He wore a clean blue suit; his shirt collar was open, revealing a finely wrought gold rope chain around his neck.

Turning toward Hopkins, the policeman said, "And who are you?"

As Hopkins showed his badge to the officer, he said, "It's not my call, Mr. Adelman. I'm out of my jurisdiction." Then, to the policeman, he added, "I'll take care of this gentleman."

The officer stood there for a moment between them and then ambled fifteen feet away.

Twisting his University of Chicago ring, Adelman said, "It's Cam, isn't it?"

"Apparently," Hopkins answered. "The body was bagged before I got here. The word is there wasn't much left that was recognizable."

"Damn it," Adelman muttered. He rubbed the back of his neck and looked off down the street for a moment. "What happened?" he asked when he finally looked back.

"The door was booby-trapped. Bransfield walked right into it."

Adelman looked away again.

"What was he working on?" Hopkins asked. "What was he doing down here?"

"He'd traced the kidnapper's trail through the Web . . . over to Europe and back," Adelman answered, still looking away. "The trail ended here."

"That it did, Mr. Adelman," Hopkins said.

"What do you mean by that?" Adelman snapped.

"I need the information Bransfield gathered," Hopkins said. "*All* of it. Files, disks, printouts, hard copies, names of those he was working with, names of contacts, informants, everything. On my desk by seven A.M. tomorrow."

As if he had not heard a word, Adelman stared past Hopkins at the building's facade.

"Is that clear, Mr. Adelman?" Hopkins felt the emptiness in his stomach filling with anger.

Adelman focused on Hopkins. "It was a mistake," he said. "I realize now that I underestimated my adversary. It was a mistake to send Cam here alone."

"A mistake?" Hopkins asked, the anger boiling. "A mistake, you arrogant asshole, is when you shank a drive at your country club. Bits of a guy you called your close personal friend are splattered across that staircase in there. And your client's only child is in even more danger than she was."

"Don't get tough with me, Tom," Adelman said, his voice cold. "I . . ."

"Just make sure that information, all of it, is on my desk at seven," Hopkins interrupted him.

As Hopkins turned to leave, Adelman sneered, "I have no idea why you're out to get me, but you'll fail, you . . ."

Hopkins spun around. "I don't give a shit about you, Mr. Adelman. All I'm trying to do is save Tonya Walker's life. And all your bullshit has made that job a whole lot harder." As he turned again, he saw that one of the television cameras was trained on him. When he took a step toward it, the cameraman stumbled backward into the crowd.

chapter 26

James Robert Saville munched a handful of Cheetos as he rewound the videotape. He'd come down a little from the incredible rush he'd had at the first news of the blast, but he was still flying high, soaring above the city, sky-writing his legacy in the minds of the masses. He hadn't liked the surgery on the kid. Not at all. It was too messy and too, well, *intimate*. But Bransfield's Big Surprise had been far different. He hadn't really expected to feel much more than he did when a particularly elegant logic bomb went off, but this was better, more powerful. Nothing virtual. Sometimes, amazingly enough, the world out there did have its advantages over cyberspace. And when the media morons found out it was Sky and Monique Walker's private dick, they'd go ballistic. This'd send the bastards into orbit. Rocket 'em into deep space!

"Bert Baby and the Hoopmeister—Instant Reply!" he shouted. It began with Hopkins calling that stale bagel an *arrogant bleep*! What had they been saying before that? he won-

dered. Had to've been some major flames that idiotic cameraman hadn't been quick enough to catch, goddamn it. But that
bit about the golf club was great. And then Bert whining that
the Hoopmeister was out to get him—and Hop flaming that
gold-chained bagel but good! Turning and burning! And another bleep—just for good measure. "Score!" he yelled. The
Hoopmeister was really into it. Showing some serious ire! And
starting to go after that cameraman! No score there, but an excellent pass. He'd have to be rewarded. He wasn't supposed to
take the lead in all this, at least not yet, but he was upstaging
everybody. And after this performance, the Hoopmeister deserved a free throw. No problem. It wasn't like he had any
real chance of winning the game anyway.

Where the hell was that Hottentot Henderson during all
this? The first poem hadn't aired, but this one just *had to.* The
occasion called for it! What was it anyway, eulogy or elegy? He
couldn't remember. Not his best effort, certainly. Hadn't had
time to get the rhythm right. Hell, he'd been improvising.
But the shrine, now that had taken real effort. Nothing im-
promptu about that. Over time, real time, major time. And the
kneeler! He'd never actually used the kneeler, but those morons couldn't know that. And they'd, no doubt, wax eloquent
about the religious symbolism. A Madonna cult, maybe! That
little gift in the van would fan that particular fire. Wouldn't
that be something! The media morons got positively orgasmic
over anything that smacked of a religious cult.

In a way, it *was* a mother and child reunion, but they'd
never get it. They'd fall for some of that good old-time reli-
gion instead. Turn the whole thing into a fucking Chautauqua
for an hour or two. Those media morons had the attention
span of a newt. They needed a revival, each and every day.
And they'd get their dose, their religious conversion, right
here and now! But only for a little while. And then they'd get
back to the real Americana, to the only thing more important

than instant, praise the Lord, no fuss, no muss, salvation—forty-eight mil, the long green, the magnificent patch of cabbage, the biggest head of lettuce ever, enough spinach to make your eyes pop!

No, he'd never knelt before the bitch. Never paid homage. He'd stalked around that shrine. Flaming the bitch, telling her off, ranting, screaming all those things he'd never been able to lay on his mother. He should've told her, of course, should've worked up the nerve. He'd tell her now. He'd do it now, for sure. Only he couldn't. Those breasts, those fulsome tits, that the city, the country, the world loved to ogle, lopped off. But not before the big C had spread. Metastasis, that was the word. And then she'd vanished. Not instantly, like Sarah, but slowly. All that voluptuousness all those morons had such constant hard-ons over withering away, drying up. And then gone altogether. Leaving him more alone than alone. No one even to despise. No target for all the fucking bile that just kept building. That never stopped. No matter what he did. No matter where he tried to channel it.

And, all the time he'd spent creating that shrine, all the time he'd spent there baring his every thought, sharing his deepest secrets, the bitch had listened every bit as well as his mother. Which was, of course, not at all. Nada. Just stood there, talking to the camera. Pretending she was speaking to real people. But there were never any real people. Just the camera. The electronic eye, but no brain. No heart. No soul.

A shiver passed through his body. He was having cold sweats again. He shook his head angrily, wiped his forehead with his sleeve, and punched the rewind button. He'd been caught in it again. Sinking fast. Couldn't get away from it even when awake, even for a day. Even when so much was going on and he had so much to do, there was no escape. No exit, as that existential Frog'd said. He'd watch the Hoopmeister flame Bagel Bert one more time, and then he'd send the dude to the

Charity Stripe. Just this once. And chain the Pit Bull in the dog house at the same time. Sending the Bull barking up the wrong tree'd been a real pisser. And cutting off his chow had been a good one, too. The Bull must be turning into one ornery cur right now. But it wasn't enough. It'd really been little more than a couple of raps with a rolled newspaper. There had to be some pain. Real pain. Meting it out and granting the Hoopmeister his freebie all at once—it was just another moment of fortuitous symmetry. Pure serendipity. Another instance of his shimmering elegance.

Tonya Walker had no idea how long she had been in darkness. Time and pain played tricks on her. She'd managed to get the vial open on her third try, and two tablets washed down with Evian had numbed the throbbing, transported her into a bizarre dreamscape inhabited by colors and shapes that spoke a language she'd never heard before. At some point, she wasn't sure when, she'd swallowed two more tablets. The constant darkness disoriented her but did not frighten her, for the Beast with her father's face came only in the light. Hunched against the wall so that her hands, as if in prayer, were braced upward to lessen the pain, she drifted in and out of consciousness. She no longer knew for sure when she was awake and when she was not. The pain never left, but it ebbed and flowed in a rhythm she did not understand. It had become part of her life, the focus of her life.

Although her throat and mouth were dry, she seldom drank from the water bottle she kept in her lap. The water was *hers*, and she needed to make it last. And anyway, the pain of moving was worse than the thirst. She never thought of food at all. She'd gone to a place beyond hunger, to some foreign shore far from the life she had known. Gymnastics, school, the house, the lake—all were distant in time and space. Her mother waking her each morning with a kiss and a glass of fresh orange juice, her father picking her up as though she were a pillow, spinning around, laughing with her, hugging her—these were things that had happened a long time ago in a very different life. The present, this life, was pure cyclical pain. Pain and heat and grogginess and a feeling like her head was a swollen balloon.

When the light flared, the pain shot through her body, and a whimper escaped before she could stop it. She pressed against the wall, buried her head between her upraised arms. She would not look up, would never look at the Beast. She shut her eyes tight until colors raced about, held her breath, gasped, held her breath again.

For his part, James Robert Saville was aghast despite himself. The room stank; a heavy, fetid closeness choked him. Cowering in the corner, sniveling, her head bowed, her hair snarled, her bandaged hand raised in surrender, she no longer reminded him of Sarah. He saw only himself. He'd turned her into the child he was. He wanted to explain, "I had to do it, had to show them I meant business," wanted to say, "it'll be over soon." But he knew it wouldn't be. Whatever happened in the next thirty hours, it would never end for her—just as it never ended for him.

chapter 27

At 7:15 A.M., **Hopkins** entered the North Ridge Police Department through the basement garage. He had left the crime scene shortly after 2:00 A.M. The absentee landlord, awakened by the Chicago Police detectives, informed them that both apartments of the two-flat had been rented to one tenant eight months before. He had never seen the tenant but had no complaints about him at all; he only wished that his tenants in other buildings were half as solid. The terms of the lease agreement had been reached over the telephone, the papers faxed and signed and returned without a hitch. The rent had been paid on time with a money order every month. The detectives had also discovered inside the van locked in the garage four Dunhill cigars, still wrapped, arranged on the dashboard in the shape of a capital **M**.

When Hopkins had finally gotten home, he had thrown out the Italian beef and sausage combo that still lay on the counter. Unable to sleep, he headed to the lake and sat on the rocks, breathing the air, staring at the distant red and green lights flashing at the harbor mouth, and trying to clear his mind of jumbled, disturbing thoughts. Each new incident—the photographs of Tonya Walker, the delivery of the finger in the cigar box, the ransom demand, Cameron Bransfield's murder, and the discovery of the van with the cigars on the dashboard—added an overlay of meaning and an abundance of leads that invariably circled back on themselves, producing nothing but illusions of progress. And the finger and the bomb both raised the ante without providing any clue to the perp's identity. The obsession with Monique Jones-Walker was the key, he knew, but that knowledge seemed to be no help at all.

When he'd finally become drowsy, he'd returned home and slept for two hours. Now, as he climbed the stairs and entered his office, he felt lightheaded. Henderson, who had remained at the crime scene after Hopkins left, was not in the office, but the North Ridge detectives and the FBI team were already at work. With the bombing, the sense of urgency had deepened almost to despair. He sat at his desk and turned to a clean page of a legal pad. Nothing had arrived yet from Bert Adelman, so he flipped through the copies of lead sheets stacked next to the telephone. After a while, aware of a presence near him, he looked up to find Paul Kim standing silently near his desk. Kim's hands were folded in front of him, and his head was cocked to his right. His eyes blinked rapidly behind his glasses.

"Ah, Commander," Kim said, "I didn't want to disturb you, but I, ah, think we've got something on the computer." He nodded repeatedly as he spoke.

"What?" Hopkins asked. "Already? Really?"

"Yes, Commander," Kim answered. "There was, ah, quite a bit of activity overnight."

Kim led Hopkins to Chief Mancini's office, a spacious room with windows that looked out through the trees at the road. One wall was covered with certificates of achievement,

awards, and plaques, another wall with photographs of Mancini shaking hands with various North Ridge mayors and
other local officials. Across from two dark Windsor chairs,
the large oak desk was uncluttered except for a telephone,
blotter, gold pen and pencil set, and a framed picture of
Mancini with his wife, his two sons and their wives, and his
five young grandchildren. The computer and printer were set
up on a rolling metal computer table to the right of the desk.

Picking up the thick printout next to the computer, Kim
said, "Four hackers invaded the system last night."

"Four?"

Kim frowned. "Well, four break-ins. The system was invaded four separate times from the outside. And it looks to me,
based on what the hackers examined each time . . ." He fanned
the printout, showing a long series of letters and numbers.
". . . that it was four different people. It could've been the
same person more than once, but it doesn't look like it."

Hopkins rubbed an eye that burned from lack of sleep.
"Can you trace them, the hackers?"

"No. Unh-unh," Kim answered. He raised the printouts.
"These only show us what commands the hackers used while
they were in the system. What files they looked at. And if they
made any changes." He gazed down at the printouts. "I
haven't had a chance to examine these as carefully as I should,
but it seems as though they were all just lurking. None of
them damaged the system."

"How'd they get in?"

"All of them came in through the Net, one through NCIC
and the other three through PIMS. Probably used stolen pass-
words." He looked at Hopkins. "But, as I told you yesterday,
the guy you're looking for wouldn't leave a trail we could follow anyway."

"Actually," Hopkins said, "he deliberately left a trail that
led a private investigator to his death."

"Cameron Bransfield, yes." Kim nodded solemnly. "I read about that this morning. And there are stories going around the office. But, Commander, that's the point I was making yesterday. He's a very skilled hacker, and following his trail through the Net would take weeks if not months. And . . ."

"Paul," Hopkins interrupted, "when the information from Adelman about Bransfield comes in, will you take a look at it? See if there's something that might help us?"

"Yes, of course." Kim went on nodding. "Anything I can do to help." He laid the printouts next to the printer. "But Commander, what I really wanted you to see is on the computer." He slid the mouse and clicked on an icon on the screen. "The second of the hackers last night left a file. I haven't read it, but I think it's for you."

"What?" Hopkins asked. "Why didn't you say so?"

Kim grimaced. "I was trying to explain."

Hopkins sat in Chief Mancini's swivel armchair. He took the mouse, looked at the file titled "HOP," began to click on the icon, and abruptly let go of the mouse. "Could it be a bomb or a virus?" he asked.

Kim leaned over his shoulder and looked at the screen. "Our defenses against viruses, our disinfectants are excellent," he said. "I am less confident about logic bombs." He straightened his glasses and blinked hard. "But actually, Commander, I am assuming that because you were off-line, it is an attempt to communicate with you. I assume also that if the hacker you are after wanted to destroy our system, he would have done so already."

"Or," Hopkins said, "he'll time it so that it happens when it's most crucial, when we need the system most." He clicked the mouse, opening the file. Inside, there was a document named "HOOPMEISTER" and another file marked "BULL-SHIT." When he clicked on the document's icon, it opened to reveal a note that said:

Where have you gone, HOP HOOPMEISTER?
A lonely hacker turns his eyes to you.

That away to FLAME Bagel Bert! SCORched
him! Nothing but NET! And here's your TROPHY:
all the FILES that PIT BULL dumped yesterday! It's
like finding his buried BONES! These'll be sent to
certain brethren of PIT BULL'S in the PRINT
MEDIA at HIGH NOON, but you get the first
chance to gnaw on 'em. KUDOS!

You've got yourself a good SHOT, HOP! Don't
blow it. No ILLEGAL DEFENSES, or you'll get a
TECHnical! Maybe even an EJECTION like that
dud Cam!

Get back on-line, HOP. We'll CHAT! Do lunch!
Maybe even TALK!

When he finished reading the note, Hopkins sat back. "It's
him, all right," he said as much to himself as to Kim. He took
a deep breath. "Here, take a look at this."

As Kim, who had moved back a step, leaned forward to
read the note, a sudden chill ran along Hopkins' neck. "Christ,"
he murmured, "the guy's talking to me."

When Kim finished reading, he stood up straight and
folded his hands. "The word *talk*, Commander," he said, "to
hackers means to speak of important or, ah, touchy issues." He
nodded toward the screen. "It looks like you got his attention."

Hopkins clicked on the BULLSHIT icon, which opened
to ten additional files. Two files, with the names "M. J-W."
and "T.W.," looked damning, but the other eight file names,
ranging from ".alt.arts.paraphillia" to ".alt.rec.sadomas," rang
no bells.

Eyes blinking, Kim stared at the screen. "Oh," he said,
"those are Net Newsgroup files. Pornographic. There's some
really strong stuff online." He pointed to two files named

".alt.sex.lolitas" and ".alt.art.pedophilia." "It looks like he's pretty heavily into some very, ah, salacious material involving children, ah, young girls."

Hopkins smiled ironically. "So the perp's delivery of the Tonya Walker photographs to Bollinger," he said, "was symbolic, too." His smile faded as he wondered what the kidnapper's agenda was for him.

As Hopkins slid the mouse over to click on the M. J-W. file, Chief Mancini opened the office door. He stopped when he saw Kim and Hopkins. Still holding the door handle, he asked, "Do . . . ? Has he made contact?" His face was ashen.

Kim stepped back from the desk and said, "We think so, sir. Yes."

Nodding, Mancini came into the office. "Good," he said. "It's about time something went right." He looked at Hopkins. "That scene of yours with Adelman on television last night isn't going to do the department any good, Hoop."

"Christ," Hopkins exclaimed, "that's it. *Hoop.*" His blood racing, he looked back at the icons on the screen. "The guy knows me."

"What . . . ?" Mancini said.

Hopkins closed the file and clicked on the document icon. "Take a look at this note I got from the perp," he said as he stood up.

"What note? The perp sent you a note . . . ?" Mancini asked. He sat down and squinted at the screen.

As Mancini read the note, Hopkins said, "He gets his information from invading systems, from stealing files, right?"

Mancini finished reading, looked up, and said, "Yes. So?"

Kim moved back closer to the desk.

"I doubt there's anything in any of our computer files that refers to me as *Hop.*"

"Maybe it was in the papers," Mancini said. "Or on television."

"Maybe *Hoop*. But not *Hop*. Nobody's called me Hop since high school." He pointed at the printing on the screen. "The guy's local. Or, he at least grew up around here." Blood pounded in his head. "And he can't be a whole lot older or younger than me."

chapter 28

At 8:40 A.M., Hopkins sat on the couch in Interview Room A jotting notes and trying to think of any possible connection between Monique Jones-Walker and anyone he'd known growing up. Carl Henderson, who had been up all night and had arrived in the office only ten minutes before the 8:00 A.M. press briefing, had suggested that Hopkins, after the previous night's televised argument with Bert Adelman, skip the briefing altogether so that Bollinger and his cronies had no obvious target. Hopkins had used the time to go through the T.W. and M. J-W. files, to reassign his detectives, and finally to catch up on reports from North Ridge and Chicago investigators and evaluate the updated FBI profile of the kidnapper. The T.W. file had contained background information about Tonya Walker as well as the kidnapping photographs that had been scanned back into the computer. More than a dozen additional photos showed the child performing in her leotard in the floor exercise and on the balance beam. The M. J-W. file included documents dating back almost a year. There were office memos and notes from meetings, but also a series of e-mail messages between Bert Adelman and Monique Jones-Walker about a lucrative network offer that would entail her leaving WLN and moving to CBS News in New York to act as substitute anchor for Dan Rather and to produce periodic news specials on minority and women's issues. The deal had apparently almost been finalized the Friday before the kidnapping.

The M. J-W. file had contained, finally, a series of e-mail postings in the kidnapper's characteristic manic prose. The first had instructed Bollinger to be by the telephone Sunday evening for a tip about the story of the century. A second had told him to be at his fax machine for a series of gifts every two hours that he'd find too enticing for words. A third, posted the night before the ransom demand had been received, castigated him for continuing to hack into Monique Jones-Walker's files and informed him that there would be dire consequences if he did not cease and desist. And the others ranted about the delivery to Mancini's house, the contents of the cigar box, and the impending release of the ransom demand.

From the Chicago investigative reports, Hopkins had learned that the van in the garage had been rented the previous week, charged to Jack Bollinger's WLN American Express card, and picked up by a youngish man who was a little overweight, bearded, and left-handed. He'd worn a WLN maintenance uniform, a well-worn WLN *News at Nine* baseball cap, reflective sunglasses, and an Ace bandage on his right hand. The phone number the two-flat's renter had given the landlord was Jack Bollinger's private line, and the fax number had been that of a public phone. Hopkins made a note to find out how someone used a public phone to send a fax, but he had already concluded that an adept hacker could pretty much do anything he wanted on the nation's computer systems.

Carl Henderson entered the interview room, shut the

164 ~ jay amberg

door, and slumped into the chair to Hopkins' right. The skin around his bloodshot eyes was puffy.

"How'd it go?" Hopkins asked him.

"That was about as much fun as cleaning a horse barn," Henderson said, speaking slowly, as though even his voice was exhausted. "The coyotes are closing in. They've lost all confidence in your department, think you're a bunch of rubes that can't stop shooting your mouths off. And I'm sinking the entire Bureau all by myself." He smiled wearily. "Everything just keeps going down the crapper. Half the goddamned questions were about the religious significance of the kneeler and the photographs and the cigars left in the shape of the **M**." He shook his head. "One of those dildos even asked if I thought Bransfield's death was symbolic of the beheading of John the Baptist."

"Who'd the perp notify this time?" Hopkins asked.

"Actually quite a few—local papers, *New York Times*. Maybe one or two others. From what I could tell, all faxes."

"Not Jack Bollinger, though?"

"No, he was uncharacteristically subdued." Henderson smiled again. "I gather he was in Milwaukee on a hot tip when the bomb went off. Seems pretty pissed about it." He laughed. "Think it was our boy's doing?"

"I'd bet on it," Hopkins said. "And Bollinger's going to be a lot more pissed when he finds out all the files he thought he trashed have been sent to newspapers around the country. He's about to become the bloodied shark in the feeding frenzy."

"Nothing the media does would surprise me," Henderson said.

"You know," Hopkins mused, "I get the distinct feeling that most of them'd be a little disappointed if we got the Walker girl back alive."

"No, that's not it," Henderson replied. "They'd be disappointed if the story ended today, but they want a happy ending, just like with that girl who fell down the well in Texas."

Hopkins did not say anything for a minute. He understood Henderson's point, but the media circus that surrounded the police department—the pure, amoral fervor of the press— disgusted him. A little girl's life was nothing more than a hot story to them. Finally, he slid the legal pad onto the table between them and asked, "Did you get a chance to look at that note the perp sent me?"

"Yeah." Henderson nodded. "And I sure as hell didn't mention during the briefing that the kidnapper congratulated you for reaming Bert Adelman on camera for the whole world to see."

"What did you think?" Hopkins asked.

"Truthfully?" Henderson sat back in his chair. "I think you're leaping too fast at the idea that the perp's local. Clutching at it because it's the only straw that makes any sense to you. Obviously, the note sounds like he's talking to you personally. But so did that little ditty he left me at that apartment in Chicago. The guy personalizes everything." He rubbed his hands along the arms of the chair. "You really think the guy knew you in high school?"

"Yeah," Hopkins answered. "Otherwise, he wouldn't have called me Hop." He leaned forward, his forearms on his knees. "Carl," he asked, "when you go home, back to your hometown, what do people think of you as? A Rhodes Scholar? An FBI agent?"

"A wrestler," Henderson answered. "A state champ. An NCAA champ." He nodded. "I see what you mean."

"And what do they expect you to talk about?"

"Wrestling. Or, as they say it, *wrasslin'*. Drives me nuts." Hopkins sat back.

Henderson shrugged. "Okay," he said. "I'm not going to fight you if you want to redirect some of your detectives.

We're being deep-fried by the media. Time's running out . . ."
He shook his head. ". . . And this angle's no worse than anything else we got."

Hopkins picked up the legal pad. "I've already assigned
teams to check the records over an eight-year period, three
ahead of me and four behind me, at my school and the five
closest high schools. Four are public, and one's a Catholic
boys' school. We've got to get to deans, guidance counselors,
assistant principals—anybody who's been in the school
twenty-five years. To simplify the initial interviews, I'm thinking of cross-referencing three, or at most, four traits."

"Agreed," Henderson answered.

"First, he must've been smart," Hopkins said. "A geek,
maybe, but very smart. We're checking who, in that eight-
year window, went to U of I in engineering or MIT, Cal Tech,
places like that."

"No," Henderson said. "This guy may be a genius, but he
didn't go to a prestigious college." His voice gained energy as
he began to warm to the idea. "This sort of guy only does the
work he likes. He probably flunked as many classes as he
passed. Hell, he may not even have graduated from high
school."

"Yeah, okay." Hopkins glanced at his notes. "Good point.
What else?"

"A single parent, a mother or grandmother at home. Almost certainly no father in the picture. He had a thing about
his mother, but that may not've been demonstrated in school.
What would've shown up is trouble with any kind of male authority figure. Couldn't handle authority at all."

"Got it," Hopkins said as he circled the item on his legal
pad. "What about a disability?"

"The right hand?" Henderson asked.

"Yeah. The couple of times he's been sighted, he looks different, but there's always a hat and a beard, which are obvi-

ously disguises. The hand's also covered, though. He's hiding something that'd be identifiable."

"I agree," Henderson said, finally tucking the handkerchief into his back pocket. "But it may simply be a tattoo or other mark. And even if it is a disability of some sort, we don't know if it dates back to his childhood." He loosened his tie and unbuttoned his collar. "Still, it might be worth . . ."

A knock on the door interrupted them.

Meghan Ross cracked the door and peeked in. "Excuse me," she said. "Mr. Adelman is here and would like a word with Agent Henderson." There was a glint in her eye, but her tone conveyed nothing.

Henderson looked at Hopkins, who said, "The man definitely does not like to be kept waiting."

"All right," Henderson said. "Ask him to come in here."

Ross pushed the door open and stepped back, saying, "Mr. Adelman."

Hopkins and Henderson started to stand as Adelman entered the room, but, his tone excessively cordial, he said, "Please, don't get up." He glanced from Hopkins to Henderson. "I will only take a moment of your time, Carl." He was immaculately dressed in a charcoal worsted wool suit, but his face was haggard. His tan seemed to have faded, and the skin around his temples was pinched. "The documentation Tom requested is being delivered to your Chicago field office. The material includes the names of Cain's associates and those they contacted." He tugged his gold and diamond cuff link as he spoke.

Hopkins glanced at his watch as Henderson said, "Thank you."

"I have also," Adelman said, still speaking only to Henderson, "mustered considerable financial resources, and it looks very much like the Walkers will be able to meet the ransom demand well ahead of schedule."

"Good," Henderson said, "that's something . . ."

"There is one caveat," Adelman said. "And the Walkers and I concur completely in this matter."

"What's that?" Henderson asked.

"There must be proof, unambiguous proof, that Tonya Walker is still alive before any funds are transferred to the kidnapper."

Henderson tapped the arms of the chair. "That's fair," he said, "perfectly reasonable. But you're dealing with an unstable, even volatile, person in this kidnapper, Mr. Adelman. And he might . . ."

"Mr. Henderson," Adelman said, "I'm preparing to deliver forty-eight million dollars to this maniac. Even he has got to see that there has to be some quid pro quo."

"That makes sense to me," Henderson said. "But he . . ."

"Mr. Henderson," Adelman interrupted again, "this ransom is, in essence, a business transaction. And each party is due . . ."

"Fine," Henderson said. "I understand your point, and we'll do everything possible . . ."

"Good," Adelman said. He yanked his cuff link again. "Tom," he added, looking down his nose at Hopkins, "I have a long memory. I did not have you removed from this case . . ." He waved his hand. ". . . solely because Sky Walker, for reasons that escape me, is adamant that you continue. But I do not take kindly to attempts at public humiliation. And when this is over, which it will be soon, I will deal with you."

Hopkins stood up, stared hard into Adelman's dark eyes, and called, "Officer Ross?" When she appeared in the doorway, he said, "Will you escort Mr. Adelman out?" He turned toward her. "And then would you join Agent Henderson and me? There are some communications issues we need to discuss."

chapter 29

Unable to sit, Sky Walker paced back and forth across the kitchen. The North Ridge trap-and-trace officer no longer perched by the telephone because no one expected any more calls from the kidnapper. If there was any further contact, it would be through his wife's computer system. The disheartening sense that the best shot he had had to save his daughter had exploded at an apartment in Chicago was driving him crazy. He was used to getting things done, and not only was there nothing he could do but he could never escape the awareness of his helplessness. Everything on television bellowed about his lost daughter and his devastated life, the most recent reports howling about the deal his agent had arranged for his wife behind his back, the deal that would've torn her from Tonya and him. Every call from the Bulls' front office or his entourage or his teammates or friends served only to remind him of his ineffectiveness.

When a gust of wind buffeted the French doors, he went over and closed them. He then abruptly reopened them, stepped out onto the patio, and listened to the rumble of the lake competing with the distant helicopters. Whitecaps formed under the rising wind, but the sky was clear except for an occasional cloud scudding in from the northeast. He took a deep breath, wiped his face and beard with his hands, tugged at the waistband of his light linen pants, shook his head, and gazed at his verdant lawn and shrubs. He crossed to the wooden steps that cut down the bluff to the beach. Below him an armed guard stood by the water ready to repel any more reporters like the camera crew that had tried to reach the house by boat earlier that morning. He wanted to shout at the sky and relentless waves, to plead with the world to return his daughter, to offer anything—his house and his holdings, his career, even his life—for her safety. But, as he stood there, the roar of the helicopters grew louder, the beating of the rotors stronger. He turned just as the first helicopter flew over the trees from the south. He strode back to the patio as the helicopter hovered over the lake just beyond his property, slowly lowering so that the cameraman could get a better shot.

He slammed the French doors, slumped into one of the chairs arranged around the glass table in the alcove, stood quickly, and retreated to the cooking island where he couldn't be seen from outside. Leaning against the island, he ground the heels of his hands into his eyes. When the doorbell rang, he didn't move. He stared at his hands, front and back, watching them shake as they never had before a game. He ran his hand along the back of his neck under the collar of his striped dashiki, squared his shoulders, and crossed his arms.

Monique Jones-Walker and Bert Adelman entered the kitchen together. She had a lit cigarette in one hand and a black Chicago Bulls ashtray in the other. "Robert," she said, "Bert has news for us."

Walker nodded but did not say anything.

She looked from her husband to Adelman, pointed to the table, and dragged on the cigarette. "Twenty-three rooms," she said, exhaling smoke, "and we live in the kitchen." She and Adelman sat down across from each other, but Walker remained where he was. As she set down the ashtray and ground out the cigarette, Adelman placed his briefcase on the table, opened it, and slipped out a glossy red Walker Management portfolio folder.

"Monique, Sky," Adelman said, "I've gotten the finances in order. We'll be able to meet the demand on schedule."

Walker, still silent, came over to the table but did not sit down.

Nodding, Jones-Walker said, "Good." She took a half-crushed pack of Virginia Slims and a gold lighter from the pocket of her blue jeans. Her hand trembled as she shook out a cigarette and tried unsuccessfully to light it.

Adelman took the lighter from her and lit her cigarette.

"I thought you weren't smokin' in the house," Walker said, his tone more perplexed than irritated.

"That's right, Robert," she snapped. "I wasn't. For Tonya's sake." She bit her lip. "But she's not   " She jammed out the cigarette, squashing it until it bent and broke.

"Sky," Adelman said, "you have to understand that you're going to lose a lot more than forty-eight million."

Jones-Walker ground the extinguished cigarette into the ashtray and stared out the French windows at a cloud-shadow passing over the lawn.

"Your investment portfolio," Adelman went on, "has been virtually . . ."

"Bert," Walker said, "I told you before it doesn't matter."

"I understand," Adelman said. He fingered a cuff link. "Of course, you can't put a price on . . ."

"Bert," Walker growled. He set his hands on the table and

leaned forward so that his bulk was above his agent. "I don't want to hear another word about the money. Not now or ever. You got that?"

Adelman looked across the table rather than up at Walker. He pursed his lips, nodded, and tapped the portfolio with his forefinger. "I understand perfectly," he said, still not looking up. "I have, however, taken one essential precaution." He cocked his head so that he seemed to be speaking to the portfolio. "I have insisted that the kidnapper provide proof that Tonya . . . is still alive . . . before the funds are transferred."

"I don't give . . ." Walker began.

"Robert," his wife interrupted, "it's only sensible." Her voice was choked. "We have to know."

Still leaning over, Walker turned toward her. He hesitated before saying, "Okay. Yeah. That's okay." He turned back to Adelman. "But you're not goin' to do nothin' that'd jeopardize Tonya." His game face set hard, he glanced at his wife. "No secret deals. Nothin' behind my back. I mean, nothing'. You got that?"

Adelman, who had still not looked at Walker, picked up the portfolio and shoved it back into the briefcase. "I would never," he said, his voice simmering, "do anything that would endanger Tonya's safety."

Jones-Walker stuffed her cigarettes and lighter back into her pocket.

Walker finally lifted his hands from the table, leaving marks on the glass. He straightened up and folded his arms across his chest. "What happened with Bransfield?" he asked.

Adelman snapped the clasp on his briefcase, exhaled, and looked up at Walker. "He made a tactical error . . . and unfortunately . . ." He waved his hand.

"Hopkins was right," Walker said. "What Hoop said to you on TV was right, Bert . . ."

Jones-Walker scraped back her chair and stood up. "Stop it, Robert," she said, her voice quavering. "Things are bad enough without the two of you . . ." She turned and stalked toward the door.

chapter 30

Knowing that the first thing he said would be crucial, Hopkins sat in Chief Mancini's chair staring at the computer screen. He had to play to the kidnapper's ego, but he couldn't seem patronizing. He had to be firm, but if he came off as another male authority figure the whole thing would go up in flames. Carl Henderson and Paul Kim stood on either side of the chair; Mancini paced the carpet between the desk and the closed door. It was shortly after noon, the time Hopkins and Henderson had assumed that the kidnapper, having sent the Bollinger files to the newspapers, would most likely check the file he had delivered to the North Ridge Police Department the previous night.

Although Kim had brought Hopkins' computer back on line, Henderson and Hopkins had agreed that the quiet and privacy of Mancini's office would enhance their chances of making contact. Hopkins had spent part of the morning with Meghan Ross devising a system so that the investigators checking the local high school records could report all information directly to her. Nothing was to be word-processed at all. She would act as a clearinghouse, bypassing the department's computer system completely. At Paul Kim's suggestion, Mancini had ordered the rest of the police department's computer use to continue as normally as possible so as not to spook the kidnapper. If necessary, bogus reports would be created to provide the appearance of routine activity in the computer system.

The printer began to hum. Kim scanned the printout, turned to Hopkins, and said, "We've got a visitor. Someone's invading the system." The printer stopped. "He's lurking. It could be your hacker."

They waited two minutes before the printer began again. "Okay," Kim said. "He's starting to check the files." His voice rose. "He's coming directly here." The document file the kidnapper had left was on the screen, and Kim had opened a chat box below the note to Hopkins. "It must be your guy."

Hopkins felt a deep calm settling over him. Any residual nervousness had dissipated. He finally had the ball, and the flow of the game was coming to him.

"He's here," Kim said. Mancini stopped pacing, came over, and stood behind the chair.

The Bollinger files were useful in tying up loose ends, Hopkins typed. **I'd like to take you up on your offer to talk.** Although he was not an especially fast typist, the words seemed to appear instantly on the screen.

Nothing happened at first. Henderson leaned over to look more closely at the screen. Mancini turned away.

Then, **That you, HOOPMEISTER?** appeared in the chat box.

Hopkins found himself almost smiling. He had made contact, finally. **Yes,** he typed, **it's Hop.** It was almost like going one-on-one.

Hey, newbie, what's up?
The ransom will be ready by midnight our time.

HOT DAMN! Bagel Bert did his thing. Knew he would.
Mancini turned back and stared at the screen.

Hopkins cracked his knuckles and began to type again. **We need instructions.**

No prob, Hop! They'll be faxed to you. Cancel that. To MONIQUE, BABY, at twenty-one hundred hours. Exactly.

"Watch," Kim said, blinking his eyes rapidly as he pointed at the screen. "His right hand is slow. The o's and p's especially. He's definitely slower with his right hand."

There is one issue, Hopkins typed, **that needs to be resolved.**

NO EXCUSES. NO TRICKS!

Hopkins glanced up at Henderson. **No trick.** He'd play the good cop to Adelman's bad cop. **Adelman needs verification that Tonya's alive before he'll transfer $.**

He wants her whole HAND! Is that it? He wants her EAR, too?!?

"Oh, no!" Mancini murmured. He slapped his hand against the back of the chair. "Hoop!"

No, Hopkins typed. **That isn't necessary. We know you're a player. That you're very serious about this. Adelman simply needs proof that Tonya's OK.**

What the hell does the Bagel want?

He wants one photograph, Hopkins typed. **The girl with the front page of today's** *Tribune.*

Trib Online?

"No," Henderson said, "too easy for him to fake it. Superimpose it." He glanced at Kim, who nodded. "The paper."

"He'll balk," Hopkins said.

"Maybe," Henderson answered. "And maybe he'll fuck up while he's out getting it."

Hopkins gazed at the plaques and awards on the wall, took a deep breath, and typed, **Not good enough for Adelman. It's got to be the paper.**

There was a pause, then the screen filled. **He'll get the EAR, GODDAMN IT! He'll get her WHOLE HEAD! Is that what YOU want?**

We want to deliver the $! Hopkins answered. **The $ for the safe return of the girl. That's it.**

There was no response.

After a minute, Henderson asked, "Think we lost him?"

Kim looked at the print out. "He's still there," he said. "He hasn't moved."

Hopkins glanced out the windows at the tree branches swaying in the wind that had risen with the sun that morning, and then he typed, **One photograph. That's all the verification we need. It's that simple.**

James Robert Saville tore off his glasses and rubbed his eyes. It wasn't that simple, goddamn it! Not that simple at all! Nobody who knew anything about anything bothered with newspapers anymore. Newspapers were practically snail-mail. He'd have to make a sortie out there to get the paper. And he'd made too many sorties already. It was fucking Catch 22, that's what it was. The risks were increasing exponentially. They had witnesses, composite sketches—true, none of the pics was even close, but he still didn't like it. Not at all.

And there was the feeling, a nagging, nauseating feeling that something was terribly wrong. Something was running amuck, and he couldn't tell what. The feeling had started the moment the Hoopmeister had signed on. And he couldn't place it. He was sweating badly, on the verge of hyperventilating, about to gag, and he had no idea why. He despised not knowing! Missing something irked him more than almost anything else! There was no time for any nice touches or clever turns or poetry. Hardly time even for a pun or two.

He grabbed his glasses and feverishly struck the keys. **OK,** he typed. **Photo faxed at fifteen hundred hours. NO GOD-DAMNED TRICKS—or SKY & MONIQUE-BABY will be served TONYA'S HEAD on a PLATTER! No KIDding! Oh, and Hop, say hello to your little friend for me!!!**

chapter 31

When Hopkins left Chief Mancini's office, Meghan Ross was waiting for him in the hallway. "Hoop," she said, "we've gotten calls from Jane Heckman at the *Trib* and Mark Weinstein at the *New York Times*. The perp . . ." She gestured toward the computer framed by the open door of the office. ". . . sent the Bollinger files to the newspapers with your name on an e-mail note. As though the files came from you."

"Shit," Hopkins muttered, closing the office door. "I should've known." The perp's final comment kept rushing through his mind. What had the guy meant? he wondered. Was it some cryptic message about Ross? Was she his next target? Rubbing the back of his neck, he said, "Meghan, I think . . ." He struggled to clear his mind.

She took hold of his arm. "Hoop," she asked, looking into his face, "you okay?"

He shook his head. "Yeah. I don't know. The guy . . . At the end of . . . He told me to say hi to my little friend."

She let go of his arm. "You mean me?" she asked, her eyes narrowing.

"I don't know. That's all he said."

"How could he know about that?" She looked off along the hallway, grimaced for a moment, and then gazed at the overhead lights. "Maybe he meant Dave Banks," she said, smiling ironically, "or the Chief." She touched his elbow. "What should I do about Heckman and Weinstein?"

Returning her smile, he answered, "Tell them, and any other reporters who call, that I also received a set of the files. Say that I can verify the files' authenticity, but stress that the files came directly from Tonya Walker's kidnapper. That neither I nor anyone else connected with the investigation had anything to do with the public release of the files." He took a breath, scratched the side of his nose, and exhaled. "Make sure they understand that, as far as we can ascertain at this time, it's *solely* the work of the kidnapper."

"Right," she said. "Got it." She tapped her temple with her forefinger. "I almost forgot, Cari's out in the lobby. She brought you lunch."

Hopkins nodded. "Okay," he said, glancing at his watch. "Has anybody gotten back from the high schools yet?"

"Maniatis and Downey so far," she answered. "I'm charting what they're coming up with."

"Good," he said. "I'm going to take fifteen minutes with Cari."

"Okay." She looked again along the hallway. "Hoop, there's more guys out there that fit the perp's profile than we'd want to think."

"Yeah," he said. "Be careful, Meghan."

As Hopkins entered the lobby, Cari rose from the molded plastic chair, smiled, and held up two white paper bags.

"Hi," she said. "Pastrami on rye with Swiss, light on the mustard."

He kissed her on the cheek and said, "Great! You're wonderful." He realized that for three days he had eaten nothing but cereal standing in his kitchenette and cheeseburgers at his desk.

"Is it okay?" she asked. "Do you have time?"

He looked out the front door to the parking lot where three television crews were camped out. "Yeah," he said. "Let's go around back." There wasn't another press briefing scheduled until four o'clock, and he figured the swarm wouldn't fully form again for a couple of hours. He led her down to the basement, out the garage door, and over to the lawn. They settled under an oak in shade dappled by sunshine. The wind was blowing from the northeast, gusting to over twenty miles an hour. The waving branches and rustling leaves caused the light to dance across the grass. From one bag, she took two wrapped sandwiches, a carton of cucumber salad, two plastic forks, and a small pile of napkins she tucked under her leg so that they wouldn't blow away. As she lifted two sixteen-ounce bottles of lemonade from the other bag, her hair blew back from her face in rippling waves.

"Looks good," he said as he took one of the bottles from her. "Excellent idea. Thanks."

He unwrapped his sandwich, took a bite, and said, "Mort's Deli?"

She smiled. "You bet. Only place for pastrami." She bit into her Swiss cheese, lettuce, and tomato sandwich, set it down, reached into the pocket of her khaki hiking shorts, and pulled out a scrunchie. As she gathered her hair in a long ponytail, she asked, "You all right, Dad?"

"Yeah, I'm getting by," he answered. Thinking again about the perp's message, he picked up a piece of pastrami that had fallen onto the wrapper and popped it into his mouth.

"Even Mom's worried," she said. She opened the carton of cucumber salad, stuck a fork into it, and passed it to him. "She saw you on TV last night. Told me when I got home that you looked like a rubber band about to snap."

"I haven't slept much since this Walker thing started," he said. He took a bite of the salad and passed the carton back to her. "Or eaten much, either." He looked into his daughter's green eyes shining in the sunlight. "This thing's getting to me, Cari. But I'm gonna be okay." He felt buoyed by making contact with the kidnapper and by having his investigators scouring the school records. There was no euphoria at all, but at least he finally felt that he was doing something. He was no longer back on his heels waiting for the next travesty. "I'll be okay," he repeated.

He picked up the second half of his sandwich and took a bite. They ate in silence for a minute. A cloud swept overhead, stealing the light from her eyes. She cocked her head and said, "My graduation's tomorrow night."

He looked closely at her. Her nose and cheekbones were slightly sunburnt. Wisps of hair, having come loose from the ponytail, purled around her face. The cloud passed, and the light returned to her eyes. He thought back to that Monday morning when he sat on the rocks by the lake wondering how he'd react if anything happened to her. It seemed a long time ago. He had been so preoccupied with Tonya Walker that his own daughter's graduation had slipped his mind. But whatever happened in the Walker case, he knew, would most likely occur in the next twenty-four hours. "I'll be there, Car," he said. "Promise."

"I knew you would." She smiled. "Mom said . . ." She lifted the fork without taking any salad. "I've got an extra ticket . . . if there's somebody you want to bring."

"Thanks, Car, but . . ." Glancing past her across the lawn, he saw Jack Bollinger marching toward them.

"Mom's having a few people back to the house afterward for cake and stuff," she added.

Bollinger was almost to them.

"Thanks," Hopkins said, "but one ticket'll be fine."

"Where the hell do you get off sending shit like that to the papers?" Bollinger shouted. His face was flushed, the pockmarks pink-gray.

Cari started, dropped the fork into the salad, and stared up at the reporter.

"If you have something to ask me," Hopkins said, "I'll be in my office in ten minutes." Anger welled and spread through his body, but he kept his voice calm. He turned back to his daughter. "I'm sorry, Car. I'd hoped we . . ."

Bollinger kicked the grass next to Hopkins. "*Now*, fucker!" he yelled, clenching his fists.

Hopkins sprang to his feet. "Look, you ignorant . . . ," he began. Then, noticing two of the television crews scampering across the lawn with their minicams, he muttered, "Damn it," took a breath, and looked up through the trees at a cloud about to cover the sun. "Walk away from the cameras," he said to Bollinger.

"Where the hell do you get off . . ."

Checking the anger in his throat, Hopkins said, "Do you really want this conversation on video, Mr. Bollinger?"

Bollinger glowered at the approaching crews, turned, and stomped away.

Hopkins stooped next to his daughter. "I'm sorry, Cari," he said. "Lunch was a great idea." As he rose, he said, "Don't say anything to the cameras. Smile, wave, and say nothing."

When he caught up with Bollinger, he said, "First of all, if you're ever that rude in front of my daughter again, I'll kick your ass back into whatever shit hole you crawled out of."

"Fuck you," Bollinger snarled. His breath smelled of sour mash.

"I had nothing to do with those files."

"Bullshit!" Bollinger burped, then hammered his chest with his fist and took a moment to catch his breath. "You tell me you're going after my fucking files, and the very next morning I'm getting calls from fucking reporters . . ."

"The perp sent those files!"

"Bullshit," Bollinger growled again, but his tone suggested he realized it was true.

"You fool," Hopkins said, still pacing next to the reporter. "You dumped the files when you got back to your office."

Bollinger stopped. "How the hell do you know that?"

Exhaling, Hopkins looked back at the tree where one of the camera crews had stopped to shoot his daughter waving at them. The other crew was still coming toward him. "Because the perp told me," he said.

"What the . . . ?"

"He sent your files to me, too. With a note saying they were the ones you'd dumped."

Bollinger stared wildly, silent for a change.

Hopkins shook his head. "C'mon Bollinger," he said, "you knew the perp'd been hacking your files before this. It's the way he operates."

"God fucking damn it!" Glaring at Hopkins, Bollinger raised his fist, unclenched it, and, his hand quavering, clenched it again.

The camera crew began shooting even before they stopped jogging.

"Look, Bollinger," Hopkins said, his voice even, "I personally don't give a damn how perverted your private life is. But it looks like the worm's turning. Your little hobby's about to become front-page material."

Bollinger's face was florid.

"I received the files illegally," Hopkins went on, his tone still calm, "so, even though I'd have a pretty strong obstruction case, I'm not going to do anything with 'em—except show them to Monique Jones-Walker and anybody else from WLN who wants to see the little games you've been playing with the station's computer system."

"Fuck you!" Bollinger reached up and shoved Hopkins' shoulder.

Hopkins set his feet. "That's battery," he said. "You touch me again and you're going to jail."

"Yeah?" Bollinger snarled. "Yeah?" He pushed Hopkins hard with both hands.

Hopkins took a step back. Feeling like he was on a schoolyard, he nearly laughed. "Okay," he said, "you're under arrest. You have the right to . . ."

Bollinger swung wildly at Hopkins, who ducked and planted his feet. Before Bollinger could throw another punch, Hopkins hurled himself at the reporter and, pinning his arms, wrestled him to the ground. The camera crew moved in for a better angle, and, across the lawn, Cari stood staring in astonishment at her father grappling with the thrashing reporter.

"You have the right to remain silent!" Hopkins shouted into Bollinger's face.

chapter 32

In full costume, James Robert Saville entered the washroom. The still-video Xap Shot camera hung from the strap around his neck. He carried the front section of that morning's *Chicago Tribune*, headlining,

Walker Kidnapper Strikes Again
Investigator Dead in Explosion

Getting the paper had been a hassle. The first three places he'd gone had sold out of it, and he'd had to head clear across town to find a copy at a convenience store. He was amazed really that he was such big news in print. It hadn't occurred to him that anybody but a few senile geezers would read about his exploits when they could see it all, live and in color, on the Videot Box. Another little epiphany, that. Live and learn. Apparently a lot of morons were still addicted to hard copy. A Stale Tale, that's what a newspaper should be called. Anyway, he was glad he'd thrown Bollinger's bone the columnists' way.

The fact that he was even selling fast in print was a compliment, of course, another tribute to his work. But obtaining the paper had still been a surreal nuisance. All that time out there in harm's way for a fucking Stale Tale. It was another goddamned annoyance he didn't need, didn't have time for, shouldn't have to put up with. More than an annoyance, an imposition—and, to be candid, an egregious error—by that slick bastard, Bertie Bagel Adelman. Did Bertie think he'd already played all his cards? The Bagel was still going to get chewed up and spewed out, all right! Chomped and stomped! Munched, crunched, and punched! Masticated in a major way! Expectorated with a vengeance! He'd be lucky to have a dime by the time the last crumb was scarfed from the country's plate.

And here she was, the kid, cringing in the corner, whimpering, her bandaged hand raised like a goddamned white flag. "Okay, young lady," he said. Stepping over the line of wrapped Twinkies, he pulverized one of the Tylenol #3 strewn across the floor like some downer archipelago. "Now, do as you're told, and you won't get hurt. Look up here. Take this newspaper." She didn't move, went on cowering. Exasperated, he stepped forward, crunching another Tylenol, and raised his voice. "Take this paper. Hold it up for the camera. Do it! Now! Do you hear me, young lady?" Except for her wretched trembling, she still didn't move. "Listen to me, young lady! You'll do this *now*, or you'll really regret it."

She despised the Voice, so unlike her father's. With all the pain and darkness, the hunger and thirst, she was no longer sure where she was. The Evian was gone, and she'd spilled the painkillers when, trying to get a couple more from the vial, she'd bumped her hand against the floor. Even this foul-smelling room, too dark and then, suddenly, too bright, seemed somehow distant, as though she weren't here, but somewhere else, nowhere in particular. Not even the burning spray of the showers could infuse this world of glare and midnight with reality. She had never really known what had happened to her or why. And now she was unsure about almost everything, even who she really was. But she knew that Voice, always starting high and rising higher. And she loathed it.

The Voice began coaxing her. "Be a good girl. Do this now, and you'll get to go home. You do want to go home, don't you?" She wondered where home was. She remembered a large house and a pink and white room with stuffed animals, but that was no longer her home. A small, stinking, stark white room with a shackle in the wall was her home, and she could not stand being there. She dug her legs into the floor tiles, pressed her shoulder against the wall. She would never be cajoled by the Voice.

The Voice grew shrill, began to screech. "If you ever want to go home, you'll do exactly as I say. Right now!" A rolled newspaper struck her head repeatedly. "Do it, now! If you don't . . . You'll regret . . ."

It didn't hurt, not like her hand, but it made her want to hide, to retreat anywhere away from the Voice. Her hair, mussed by the flailing paper, kicked and bounded about her shoulders. Inside her, a voice was rising, a voice she hadn't known she still possessed. "Stop it!" she screamed.

Five more blows struck her, and then there was just the light and the ventilation fan and the Beast sucking air through the mask of her father's face. She'd sworn she'd never look at the the Beast again, but she turned and raised her hand for the paper. The Beast unrolled it and flattened it against his overalls.

"That's better, young lady," the Beast said, his voice not quite so shrill. "You're finally figuring out what's good for you." The Beast leaned over and handed her the newspaper.

Pain shooting up her arm, she took the paper.

"Hold it so the front page is up," the Beast said, fumbling with the camera, pointing it so that its silver-black eye was on her. "Not that way. So that the headline shows."

She tilted the paper.

"Up more," the Beast said. "No, not like that." He crouched close by, raising the camera until it flashed, far brighter than the white walls. "One more, just in case," he said as he bent nearer to her. "That's better!"

As the Beast began to step away, his boot slipped on one of the Twinkies, and he sprawled forward, his head cracking the tiles next to the newspaper. Without thinking, as though she were another person watching herself, she seized her father's face, tore it from the Beast, and clung to it.

The white walls swam. Unsure at first what had happened, James Robert Saville looked over at the kid. She was curled, her face turned toward him, one eye gaping through tangled hair at him as though he was diseased. And then he saw the mask clutched against her chest. He raised his left hand and touched his chin with his glove. *His chin!* No mask. No beard. He rubbed his face, got to his knees, and shrieked, "No! You didn't . . . That was bad. Very, very bad!" He stepped back away from her unblinking gaze.

She lifted the mask, pulled it over her bandaged hand, and twisted away from him, pressing against the wall.

"Keep it!" he screamed. "Keep the goddamned mask!" He held up the camera and, stepping back, smashed another Twinkie under his boot. He stared down at the white cream oozing from beneath the sole. "Goddamn you!" His head pounding uncontrollably, he yanked the strap from around his neck and flicked the video disk from the Xap Shot. "You're dead, you . . . little . . . bitch!"

She turned away, curled tighter into a ball, and, cradling the mask over her maimed hand, rocked back and forth.

"You sealed your fate, young lady," he hissed. Scraping his boot on the tiles, he retreated to the doorway. "You're going to regret . . . You'll never . . . ," he sputtered as he switched off the light. He slammed the door and, safely back in the Command Center, slumped against the wall, his mind racing.

His boot was a mess. The washroom was a mess. Everything was a mess. He'd been so meticulous. Adapted to every new situation. But this was too much. She'd ruined everything. All that trouble he'd gone to with the costume every goddamned time he'd gone in there. And now she'd seen his face! He tore off his gloves and wiped the sweat from his eyes. She had to be deleted. He had no choice. It wasn't supposed to happen this way. She should've gotten back. Should've made it home. But not now. She'd messed up everything.

He stripped off his boots and paced the Command Center carpet in his socks. Maybe it'd been inevitable. Children *were* always victims. It wasn't like he didn't know that. It was a fact of life, every day, every fucking minute. But deleting her wasn't part of the master plan. He didn't want to do it. But she left him no choice. No choice at all. And it meant more work. Letting her go would've been easier. Simpler. In its own way, more elegant. But it might actually be cleaner this way. Cleaner and better.

Still, even before she'd messed things up, he'd had so much more work to do, goddamn it. And now, rearranging the setup was going to take some thought. Reconfiguring angles. Adjusting trajectory. Fastidious planning he just didn't have time for. And complex procedures. And more procurement. That meant another fucking sortie! A long one. He'd have to be flying, of course. And he'd really be tempting fate, the possibility—hell, the probability—of serious flak erupting at any goddamned moment. Flak mushrooming all around him!

He stopped pacing, glared at the clock. Almost fifteen hundred hours already! He slipped the video disk into the computer's external drive, tapped the instructions on the keyboard, and gazed at the screen. The shot was poor, artless even. The kid was cowering, peaking through an avalanche of hair. And only part of the headline, bent at an angle, was readable:

> ### r Kidnapper
> ### tor Dead in Ex

Shivers ran up his back, and his shoulders quaked. It read like he was dead! Was it an omen? A portent? His breath caught in his throat. He was so close to pulling it all off. The Crime of the Century! A crime so astounding, so brilliant that no one would ever be able to forget him. No one! And everything was suddenly on the verge of flying apart! It was all that little bitch's fault!

chapter 33

Hopkins stood next to Meghan Ross in the fishbowl, scanning the chart on his desk. As Cari and the camera crews had looked on, he'd handcuffed Bollinger and then taken him into the station, where Bollinger had been booked and released. The tape of the altercation had already aired more than a dozen times in the two and a half hours since Bollinger had confronted him on the lawn. And, each time the clip was shown, it was shortened. He'd heard just a minute before that the three o'clock *Newsbreak* had presented only his tackling of Bollinger—so that it appeared as though the hotheaded Walker kidnapping investigator had assaulted an innocent reporter.

Hopkins was neither pleased with nor angry at himself. As he'd replayed what had happened in his mind, it seemed that the incident had been unavoidable, that Bollinger had intended all along to provoke him. It was inevitable, too, that there would be repercussions. Calls for his suspension had already inundated the department, and Chief Mancini had been summoned to the North Ridge mayor's office to explain this latest police gaffe. Because the whole thing was on tape, Hopkins wasn't worried about disciplinary action or lawsuits, but he was concerned that his ability to lead the investigation had been further eroded.

The handwritten chart he and Ross studied was made with marking pens on white posterboard. The vertical axis of the chart listed the names of thirty-seven men who had attended local high schools and who might, according to those interviewed, fit the kidnapper's profile. The horizontal axis included columns for the name of the school, year of graduation, family background, standardized test scores, academic performance, disciplinary problems, and any disability. Some of the spaces for current addresses had been filled in as detectives made follow-up calls, but almost two-thirds were still blank.

"Nobody's jumping off the chart at me," he said. His shirtsleeves were rolled up, and his tie was loosened at his collar.

Ross continued to stare at the chart. "What about number fifteen?" she asked, pointing to the names of James Patrick McGinty, who had graduated from Hopkins' high school three years behind him. McGinty's was one of only four names that had anything marked in the disability column on the chart; there, she had printed, WITHERED RIGHT ARM.

"Yeah," he said, "He doesn't ring any bells, but he's a possibility."

She pulled a folder from the plastic file case she had set next to the chart on the desk. "Beltram is working on him," she said, opening the folder. "The dean of students had no trouble remembering the guy. Apparently he was a real loner, had only one close friend. And that kid dropped out." She glanced at a photocopied sheet. "Spectacular test scores but mediocre grades except in math and physics. Almost no involvement in school. The radio club when he was a freshman, and then no other extracurriculars in four years."

"You've got DISCIPLINARY PROBLEMS checked," he said.

"Yeah," she answered, "but nothing major." She brushed her hair back from her face. "Mostly run-ins during math classes where he seemed to think he knew more than his teachers."

"And a single mother," he said, glancing again at the chart.

"The only child of an overprotective mother. A divorce sometime before high school." She handed him the file folder. "There's nothing current on him that Beltram's been able to dig up locally so we're checking in the computer."

He opened the file folder. The photocopied yearbook picture showed a long-haired, thin-faced boy who did not look at all familiar. "You're using the computer to trace this guy?" he asked.

"Not ours or PIMS'," she said. "Henderson called the Bureau's Chicago field office and had all the names put into the Feds' computer from there."

Scanning the information sheet in the file, Hopkins stopped at the name of the person interviewed. "Stephen Glass is the dean now?" he asked. "He was my Trig . . ."

The phone rang, and Ross, who was screening calls, picked up the receiver and said, "Investigations Unit, Commander Hopkins' office." She listened for a moment, murmured, "Yes, right away," and hung up. Anxiety showed in her eyes as she turned to him and said, "That was Henderson. He needs you in the Chief's office ASAP."

Standing in the doorway of Chief Mancini's office, Henderson said to Hopkins, "The bastard won't talk to me—only you." As they crossed the office, he added, "This guy's not too anal. He logged on at three exactly—to the second."

Paul Kim stood next to a fax machine he'd wheeled in on another cart and patched into the system. He nodded deferentially as Hopkins swung Mancini's chair around and sat in front of the computer. Hopkins looked up at the two men, took a deep breath, and typed, **This is Tom Hopkins.**

Without speaking, the three men waited almost a minute before the first message appeared on the screen: **Hey, HOOP-MEISTER, you got tossed from the game, huh, dude?**

No, Hopkins typed. **I'm still here.** He looked across at Kim, who had taken off his glasses and was rubbing his eye.

Hey, excellent! the next message on the screen read. **Bertie couldn't get you benched, but that take-down on the Pit Bull might get you BOOTED yet! That old dog's still got some new tricks, huh! Taking the CHARGE so you'd FOUL OUT! And you PLAYED right into it! Not smart, HOOPMEISTER, but a great show! The FANS just got to gotta love it!**

Looking over Hopkins' shoulder at the screen, Henderson muttered, "The bastard knows everything."

Hopkins wiped his face, stifled the anger rising again, and then typed, **We're just waiting for the verification Adelman needs.**

So, Hop, did you say hello to the little woman for me?!? Give her my BEST!!!

Although he felt his breath catch as though he'd just been hit, Hopkins did not respond.

"What's that about?" Henderson asked.

"Not sure," Hopkins answered. Hesitating, he scratched the side of his nose. "Might be a reference to Ross and me."

"You and Ross an item?"

"Used to be. For a while last . . . two years ago." Hopkins glanced up at Kim, who, eyes blinking, was gazing at Mancini's awards and plaques as though he hadn't heard anything. "I guess I'm next on his hit list," he said.

Henderson smiled sardonically. "Damn," he said, his drawl exaggerated, "and I assumed I'd have that particular honor."

The fax'll be passed to you in thirty seconds. SHOOT it on over to MONIQUE-the-MEDIA-BABE & the Skywalker.

They waited again. For Hopkins, time seemed almost to stop. He looked first at the fax machine and then at the computer screen. Henderson walked over to the windows and gazed out at the building clouds. Finally, when the fax machine purred, Kim took out the cover sheet and then bent back the next sheet so he could see it as it came out. Henderson returned from the windows.

"Oh, my goodness!" Kim murmured, lifting the sheet so that Henderson could see it.

Henderson took the sheet from him, stared at it for a moment, and then passed it to Hopkins, saying, "It sure as hell isn't faked."

Hopkins was taken by the girl's eyes, which seemed alive with alarm and hostility even on the faxed copy of the print. "Yeah," he said, "he couldn't have created that look." He had difficulty turning his gaze from the photograph. Finally, he gave the fax to Kim and typed, **Received the photo. Will pass on to Adelman.** "Can you Xerox five copies," he asked Kim, "and put two in separate envelopes?"

Kim nodded, folded the fax without creasing it, and left the office.

Do that, Hoop! appeared on the screen. **And tell Bagel Bertie no funny business with the $$$! Nothing like those moronic illegal pranks he's trying to pull with AIA Development. The IRS, if there was a single fucking brain cell in the entire agency, would already have the Bagel by his sesame seeds! Twisted his sesame seeds right off, goddamn it! Absolutely!**

"What the hell?" Henderson said as he leaned closer to the computer and stared at the words streaming onto the screen.

That is, if Bertie's still got his seeds after the Vegas books and their greaseball paisanos get through with him! If he's not real careful, he's gonna show up as puppy chow. Bertie in a can! Can ya see it?!? I can!!!

"Now I know why they're called rants," Henderson said.

Ask Bertie who ANGEL is! Ask him about his HABIT!!! It makes Pete Rose and Michael Jordan's action look like penny-ante stuff! Ask him about all that AIA $$$ he's laid on Angel's line! No nickels and dimes for the old Bagel! No way!

"He's giving us Adelman," Hopkins murmured, shaking his head.

Ask him about the 500K he's dropped on the Bulls to win the championship! Seems like one dumb fucking way to try to recoup your losses, huh! And we all know Bertie's not stupid, not old Bertie! He's ADDICTED! Hopelessly! Hell, he's probably laid money on whether the kid ever gets back to Walkerville on the Lake!

"No wonder Adelman kept insisting the Mafia was involved," Henderson said.

If you want some fun, ask Bertie what Angel's promised to do to him when the Bulls lose and he doesn't come up with the cash FAST!

"Yeah," Hopkins said. "He must've thought it was some Mafia conspiracy to ruin him. To keep Walker from playing so the Bulls would lose." He typed, **We need instructions for the ransom money.**

Never interrupt ME!!! appeared on the screen. **It's not polite at all, Hop!!! And what the fuck's wrong with your memory?!? Don't you ever pay any attention? Didn't I already say you'd get perfect instructions at 21:00 exactly?!? You pay attention to me, Hop—or you'll be riding the bench forever!!! Got that, Hop?!?**

"Jesus, shit," Henderson muttered. He stood up straight and brushed his hand through his hair. "This guy's got no fuse at all."

Hopkins wiped his mouth with the back of his hand and typed, **Yes.**

Nothing appeared on the screen for a minute. Hopkins rolled his neck and took a deep breath.

That's better! Now, make sure Bertie the Bagel gets this right! No subterfuge with the $$$! No secret deals like he's been cooking for MONIQUE-the-MEDIA-BABE in the BIG APPLE without that gargantuan chump Skywalker knowing! Everything's got to be up FRONT, Hoopmeister—or the kid never gets BACK!!!

chapter 34

Walker opened the front door himself. "Come on in, Hoop," he said, his sonorous voice weary. "I was sorta expectin' you." He shut out the drone of the helicopters and led Hopkins through the living room. As he passed the grand piano, he let his fingers play gently across the keys, the soft sound lingering even as they entered the library. He pointed to the couch and then wedged himself into the leather armchair.

Hopkins handed him one of the two brown manila envelopes he held. He could smell the vellum-bound books and, remembering that Jones-Walker had called the room a shrine, had a sense that he had entered a place that represented some distant past—an antiquated, even arcane place. It seemed to him much more a museum than it had the first time he'd been there.

Walker's hand trembled as he opened the envelope and slipped out the copy of the photograph. Shaking his head, he stared at the photograph for a long time without saying a word.

Hopkins sat down on the couch, laid the second envelope next to him, leaned forward with his elbows on his knees, and said, "It's a good sign, I think." He waved at the sheet. "Look at her eyes. There's a lot of life there."

Walker did not look up. The paper quivered in his hand until he slid it back into the envelope and set the envelope against the ottoman by his feet. He lowered his head and covered his face with his hands, the edges of the Band-Aids showing above the cuff of his striped dashiki. His massive shoulders heaved once, and then he was still for a minute. When he finally looked up, his eyes glistened. "I'm gonna get that fucker, Hoop," he said. "I ain't never gonna rest till I see him dead." He clutched his beard and sucked in his breath. "He's taken Tonya and messed with my life." Rubbing his hands on his beige linen pants, he paused again before adding, "That deal Bert cut with Monique, I didn't know shit about it. He was arranging for her to be in New York, away from me and Tonya more than half the time." He looked over at the trophy case as if trying to discern some truth there. "The two people I count on most . . ." He turned toward Hopkins. "I don't know who to trust now, Hoop."

Hopkins had no easy answer for him. He made an X with the heel of his shoe in the deep burgundy carpet. Fame and fortune were no protection from life's vicissitudes—no protection at all.

They sat quietly for a couple of minutes, and then Walker asked, "You've been talkin' to him, the kidnapper?"

"Not talking exactly," Hopkins answered. "I've been communicating with him on the computer through the Net."

"And?" Walker pulled on the sleeves of his dashiki.

Hopkins shrugged. "The guy's crazy, a lunatic, but there's a sort of pattern in everything he does. Everything's an attempt to show he's better . . . no, smarter and more clever than everybody else. He's trying to get the world's attention. Maybe somehow get even with the world for something."

Walker gazed at the trophy case again. "He's *got* the world's attention, Hoop."

Hopkins thought of Sirhan Sirhan's comment, after he had shot Robert Kennedy, to the effect that it had taken Kennedy his whole life to become famous, and he, Sirhan, had become famous instantly. "Yeah," Hopkins said, "and maybe, with luck, that'll be enough for him, and we'll be able to get Tonya back."

Outside the window, the American flag snapped in the brisk wind.

His voice a whisper, Walker asked, "Do you really think so, Hoop?" He stared at Hopkins. "Don't bullshit me like Bert did."

Hopkins took a deep breath. "Yeah," he said, realizing he actually believed it himself. "I can't promise you anything, but I'm definitely not convinced he plans to kill her. We'll have to see how the ransom goes down." He picked up the envelope next to him on the couch. "Here's a copy of the photograph for Mr. Adelman. I wasn't sure if he'd be here . . ."

Walker sat back in the chair, squeezed the arms, and said, "I don't think Bert's . . . Maybe you better fax it to his office."

Hopkins nodded. "But the ransom's all set, right?"

"I don't know what else Bert's been doin' behind my back, but he's gonna have that cash ready." Walker's features began to harden again into his game face. "I've made sure. It may be the last thing he ever does for me, but he'll come through with the money."

Hopkins tapped the envelope against his thigh. "Is it possible," he asked, "that Mr. Adelman has a gambling problem?"

Walker's eyes narrowed. "Bert's bet a lot on games over the years. Always on the Bulls, as far as I know. Why?"

"Does he have money riding on the Finals?"

"You mean, on the game, to . . ." Walker shook his head as if to clear it. "I don't even know what day it is anymore. On tomorrow night's game?"

Hopkins nodded.

"Maybe. Probably." Walker gazed at the Band-Aids on his hand. "Bert's got a competition problem, Hoop. I love to win. But I love the game more. Just playin' it, bein' parta it." He shook his head again. "Bert, he *needs* to win. That's why he's been such a good agent. He keeps score on everything. The deals, especially. He's got to always come out on top, or it eats away at him." He ran his hand through his beard. "Maybe that's why he felt he had to do that New York deal for Monique." He raised the palm of his hand. "Does that answer your question?"

"Yeah, it does," Hopkins said. "And there's just one more thing."

"Shoot."

"Is your wife home?"

"She's upstairs." Walker rubbed his hands together. "But I don't think she's gonna want to talk to you."

"That's okay. What I want is a bathrobe or something for Tonya." He held up the envelope. "When we do find her, I want her to be able to put on something of her own. Something from home that she feels safe with."

Walker lifted himself from the chair, leaving the envelope leaning against the ottoman. "I'll get one for you." The thought of the bathrobe, something tangible he could do for his daughter, seemed to energize him. His frame practically filling the library doorway, he added, "It'll just take me a minute."

Hopkins stood, gazed out the window at the flapping flag, turned, and looked over at the trophies in the case. He retained the sense, irrational as it was, that Tonya Walker would somehow return to her life in the house.

chapter 35

James Robert Saville set the large shopping bag on the Command Center's floor, shut the door, and tried to catch his breath. His hands shook, and sweat poured down his chest and back. A cop had been parked across from the hardware store, and another had been idling in the grocery store lot. But most troubling had been the unmarked pig out in front of North Ridge High School. What the hell had he been doing there at four o'clock on a June afternoon? Something was wrong. Very wrong.

He wasn't afraid. It wasn't precisely fear—but a persistent unease, a sickening gnawing at his insides that had begun at noon and would not go away. Maybe sleeping would've helped, but there'd been too much to do. There simply hadn't been enough time. And there was no way he was going to risk having that goddamned nightmare. Not now. Not at this point. But he couldn't shake the feeling that something was radically wrong—and he had to find out what. He despised not knowing.

As he sat in his Command Chair, he heard the yelling. The kid had begun her fucking yawping again, more of a wail now and even more brain-numbing. He didn't know if he could take it. Nausea was billowing in his stomach, and he had far too much to do. There was no way he was going to get the ransom directions out on time. He hated being late. Truly loathed it! And he needed to check his tape of the FBI's afternoon press briefing. He glanced at the wall clock—16:32. The briefing was probably just ending. What pile of crap had that Hottentot Henderson laid on the media morons this time? Everything was under investigation, being looked into, checked out. All of which meant that they still didn't know shit! He'd be okay—if only he could concentrate. He grabbed the wastebasket and leaned over it. Sweat beaded on his forehead as he gagged. But he didn't puke. If only he could puke, he might feel better. Needing air, he lifted his head and glared at the washroom door. That goddamned yawping had to stop. The kid needed to shut up, or he'd shut her up but good!

Gulping air, he pulled the warm liter bottle of Mountain Dew from the shopping bag and twisted off the cap. He guzzled half the bottle, belched tumultuously, set the bottle in the air-cooled bottle dolly, put on his headphones, and jacked the sound on the *White Album*. Raising his hands, he stared at them, trying to force them to stop quivering so he could keyboard. He didn't have time for this shit, but he'd root through the Net until he found out what the hell was happening. They couldn't keep everything hidden from him. The ransom and the Big Surprise for Tonya's guests would have to wait. He abhorred falling off his timetable, but it couldn't be helped at this point. The world was just going to have to wait a little longer for his next move. He was the one in control of everything, goddamn it, and they could hold their breath until he was good and ready! Nothing was going to happen until he said so anyway! He held all the cards, and they knew it!

Finally, his hands were steady enough, and he began by checking his armor and trip-wires, routing himself untraceably around the world, and then entering the North Ridge Police Department system. The kid's yelping didn't stop, but he caught only intermittent chunks of it between songs. As he worked his way through the files, he checked everything methodically, merely lurking, not disturbing anything. And there was absolutely nothing wrong at NRPD.

But maybe that was *exactly* the problem! With the ransom deadline approaching, there should be a flurry of activity. And there wasn't. If anything, there was *less* activity, goddamn it! He quickly covered his tracks, left NRPD and entered PIMS through the gaping backdoor he'd discovered months before. There was nothing interesting there either, except that there'd been little more than a trickle of information coming out of North Ridge. And that wasn't right either. There should've been a goddamned flood! NCIC provided no new leads at all. The FBI field-office system took a little longer to hack into, but there he finally discovered a new folder titled WALKER LIST. The morons had less than no imagination! Why not just advertise it on the Net?

He found in the folder a list of names and birthdates. All were males around his age or a little older. A couple of the first dozen names seemed vaguely familiar. And then he froze. He lurched to his feet, gagging, a cold sweat breaking. He tore off the headphones, grabbed the wastebasket and, barely having time to lean over, spewed the Mountain Dew into it. He coughed and choked, swept off his glasses, and wiped his mouth and chin with his forearm. Rinsing his mouth with more Mountain Dew, he could hear the kid's wailing. He tried to ignore it, squinted at the list, put his glasses back on, and hunched close to the screen. The name and birthdate were correct, all right—and it couldn't be much worse if his own name were there emblazoned in forty-eight point boldface!

They'd get to J.P., maybe even that night, and he'd tell them! It'd been years, but he knew more than enough. He'd make the connection instantaneously—even if the FBI morons didn't! He was every bit as smart as they were stupid. Off the charts J.P. was, the absolute end of the bell curve's tail! And he wouldn't be able to fake it once he made the connection! They'd know he knew. And they'd wring it out of him in no time at all! Hell, J.P.'d spill it even before they asked! The simple irrevocable fact was that J.P. was a blabbermouth. Couldn't keep a secret to save his skinny ass! He'd babble and jabber, all right! Prattle and tattle, goddamn it!

He thought of that afternoon just before Thanksgiving of his sophomore year. He and J.P. were home alone as usual, gorging on Snowballs and HoHos and Orange Crush they'd picked up at the 7-Eleven after school. J.P.'d been pestering him again about getting into his mother's drawers. He'd refused as he always did. It wasn't that the room was sacred, but rather that it was his private domain, too. In her extended absences, he'd gone through every drawer, explored every shelf, reconnoitered every nook and cranny of her room and closet. He'd even slept for awhile with a satin slip of hers—until she'd found out and swore that if he ever did anything that sick again she'd send him away for good.

J.P.'d run upstairs into her room, slamming the door behind him. By the time he got there, J.P.'d already had her panties around his neck and was whipping a bra in the air like a lasso. They'd started laughing, couldn't stop! Then they were strewing her underwear around! Wearing the frilliest items! And getting positively petrified boners!

And then she'd loomed in the doorway, home early for the first time in more than a month. She hadn't screamed or shrieked. She'd turned to ice, her gelid voice saying, "So this is what you do. While I work. This, this perversion." Her cold, dispassionate voice was terrifying, far worse than her raging violence.

He'd been unable to speak, of course, but it wouldn't have mattered anyway. She'd glanced at the bulge in J.P.'s pants, and a savage smile crept over her face. That smile! Angry, furiously angry, but insidious, triumphant, too! She laughed, a short, vicious titter, gestured with her thumb toward the door, and said, "Get out. Now."

She hadn't beaten him afterward. Hadn't even spoken to him. She'd simply shipped him off to the Concentration Camp by the Monday after Thanksgiving. To the Gulag, where the other inmates had harassed him unmercifully and the guards had been exponentially meaner than those at Deerbrook. And where he'd not had a single friend, no friend at all. And she hadn't let him out except for brief visits during which he was never allowed to see J.P. She'd only brought him home finally to witness the goddamned double mastectomy and to watch her melt into nothingness before his eyes. And even then she hadn't given a flying fuck for him . . .

But why had they honed in on J.P.'s name? How'd they get it? What the hell was this list? He slumped back into his chair and, still unable to regulate his breathing, glowered at the screen. Who'd latched onto the nexus, finally got the right link? And why? That Hottentot Henderson? He was the obvious choice, but he was a newbie in every way. No way Monique-the-Media-Babe or the Skywalker could either. Or Bagel Bertie—he was so egomaniacally blind he'd never see beyond the Mafia bookmakers! The Hoopmeister? Not that idiotic jock . . .

When the truth hit him, he seized the wastebasket, smelled the sweetly vile vomit, and retched again. He'd done it to himself! It was his own fucking fault! No wonder he'd been nauseous since noon. Irony of ironies, his body had known all along! He'd been too clever for his own goddamn good—just like that dud Bransfield. And, if he wasn't careful, the results could be just as catastrophic! He slapped the side of his head. Making contact had been an unnecessary risk to begin with, and then calling the pig *Hop*! He was too shrewd to do anything as witless as that. It was the lack of sleep. But that was no excuse. He'd flown for days without sleep before. Calling the guy *Hop*, that had been almost unforgivably dense! Apparently that musclehead wasn't quite as dumb as he'd looked all those years ago out there on the court exhorting his teammates and punching the air with his fist every time he hit a shot from downtown. How quickly had the Hoopmeister picked up on it? Too quickly, goddamn it!

And then the Hoopmeister had strung him along! Pretending that all he cared about was the ransom and getting the kid back—and all the time having his dicks hanging out at the schools. Culling names of all the local dweebs and geeks! No doubt, already crunching them through the government computers! Trying to gather all the info needed to nail him! It'd be too little, too late, of course. He'd already have skipped across the pond by the time the morons got it right.

The Hoopmeister would fail miserably, but that wasn't the point. Betrayal, yet again, that was the *real* point. That Hop'd have to be ejected from the game had always been inevitable. But now he'd have to be punished, too—unendurable psychological pain followed by ultimate physical pain. He began to keyboard furiously, sorting through files until he found the photo. He stared at it on the monitors for a long moment. Yeah, he knew just how to do it. The resemblance to Sarah was there, all right. Maybe not all that much, but still something in the eyes and hair. He printed the photograph. It meant even more work, a lot more, but the Hoopmeister was going to pay *dearly*!

He suddenly felt better. He could breathe. The sweating

had stopped, and his hands barely trembled. Maybe puking had helped, but more likely it was finally *knowing*! Now that he knew what he had to do, he could deal with it. It was not knowing, as always, that got to him. Now he could prioritize. Put everything in order! Get everything accomplished! He'd never get back on schedule with all the work he was adding, but he'd get it all done. After he checked the tape of the afternoon briefing, he'd toss one last bone Bollinger's way. Even now, the Pit Bull, he knew, would still fetch for him. The cur couldn't help himself. His career was buried in dung, but he'd still dig up that one last bone. The morons hadn't been able to bust Monique-the-Media-Babe's cherry Cherokee on their own, so he'd have the Pit Bull put his paws on it for them. It would keep them all busy while he attended to more important matters like the Big Surprise and the moolah and Hoop-meister's ejection and his own final glorious soaring flight above the whole sordid mess.

But first that demonic yawping had to be dealt with. He couldn't get anything done until that fiendish yammering ceased.

Tonya Walker held her father's face over the bandaged hand. She couldn't see it in the dark, but the mask and her safety yell took her mind off the pain. She didn't know when she'd started to yell again. Earlier, without water or more painkillers, she'd still escaped for a while into sleep. And then she'd spoken to her father's face, telling him she was hidden in a white room, chained up in darkness, without her leotard or anything else. Her hand hurt a lot, and sometimes her whole body hurt—and she couldn't wait for him to come for her. He needed to come get her right away. And then the keening had simply begun, something within her but separate from her that continued, involuntarily, like breathing, as a way of keeping the attention of her father's face held close to her in the endless darkness.

As the door swung open and the light again immersed her, she covered her eyes with her father's face and kept yelling. She heard the Beast scrape across the tiles toward her. When the mask was yanked from her, she squinted into the light. Without the mask on, the Beast's face looked like oatmeal, soft and gray-white. He was mean and weird but not all that scary.

"Shut up!" the Beast shouted. "Shut up, or you'll be sorry, young lady!"

She stared into his mushy face and went on yelling.

He flung the mask back at her. His hands shaking, he stood over her and screamed, "All right! Fine! If that's the way you want it!" He stalked out of the white room and, for the first time, left the door open. She wondered what was out there in the Beast's cave. Periodically she had thought she'd heard voices from television talking about her. And once she'd been sure she'd heard Mr. Adelman saying the same words over and over again, sometimes fast and sometimes very slowly. But she was no longer certain what had happened and what she had imagined. She straightened out the mask and hung it over the bandages. The mask, she knew, was real—and the pain.

The Beast returned with a roll of shiny silver-gray tape. "Okay!" he screeched. "You asked for it, young lady!" As he yanked the end of the tape, it unrolled with a ripping sound. "You're going to shut up once and for all!"

He tried to set the tape over her mouth, but she got her hands up in front of her face. When he swatted them away, pain lit her whole body. He grabbed her hair, pulled her head down, and stuck the tape to the back of her neck. Gasping in a bright fog of pain, she heard the tape tearing from the roll, felt it go across her ear and mouth and around to the back of

her head again, binding her hair much too tightly. The tearing continued, and the tape looped around again, catching the
base of her nose so that she could barely breathe through one
nostril. While the tape circled a third time, she raised her head
just enough so that the tape crossed her chin.

The tape next went around her bare arms, pinning them to
her sides, once, twice, then a third and fourth time. "There!"
the Beast howled. "See how you like that, young lady!" There
was a final tearing of tape, and he let go.

She collapsed on the tiles, sniffing for air, almost suffocat-
ing as the room plunged into darkness. When the door
slammed, she reached up and, the pain still pulsing through
her, clawed the tape from her nose. She might, if she really
worked at it, eventually be able to drag the tape from her
mouth, too, but all she cared about at the moment was the air
flowing into her nostrils.

chapter 36

When Hopkins got back to the North Ridge police station, the dispatcher told him to report directly to Chief Mancini's office. After leaving the photograph to be faxed to Bert Adelman, he found Mancini sitting at his desk massaging his temples with the tips of his fingers. Paul Kim stood by the computer leafing through a printout.

Mancini looked up at Hopkins and said, "The perp's been in the system again."

"He invaded the system," Kim said, holding up the printout, "but didn't alter anything or leave any messages." He handed the sheets of paper to Hopkins.

Hopkins fanned the paper, trying to focus on the numbers and letters that seemed to waver on the pages. Lightheaded, exhaustion suddenly rolling over him, he looked out the window. The sky had clouded over, lowering into a dull, uniform gray. The tree branches bent under a stiffening northeaster. "What's all this mean?" he asked, looking back at the printout.

Kim pushed his glasses up his nose. "He was very thorough, Commander, very relentless." His eyes blinked rapidly. "I don't think, however, that he discovered anything."

"But he must be suspicious," Hopkins said.

"Yes, Commander," Kim answered, "or he would not have taken the time . . ." He pointed to the printout. ". . . to be so meticulous."

Hopkins nodded. "How long was he in the system?"

"Almost twenty-five minutes—long enough to check everything carefully," Kim said.

Mancini straightened his tie. "Do you think he knows something?" he asked.

"I believe he does, sir." Kim's eyes continued to blink repeatedly. "Not discovering anything may have been as useful to him as discovering something."

Mancini looked askance at Kim, as though he felt Kim invariably spoke in Zen conundrums.

"Did the FBI team let you look through the Bransfield materials?" Hopkins asked Kim.

"Yes, Commander." Kim patted the edges of the computer paper so that the stack was perfectly uniform. "And I spoke with two of Mr. Bransfield's investigators."

"And?" Hopkins rubbed his eyes. He needed a cup of coffee or a large Coke badly.

"The error Mr. Bransfield made was *stopping* when the trail returned to the private residence in Chicago."

Hopkins nodded. "And?"

"He made the erroneous assumption that it must be the end of the trail. But the trail next leads to Singapore."

"Singapore?" Hopkins asked.

"Yes, Commander. I went no farther because it is illegal for us to pursue the matter without permission."

"Singapore, Saskatchewan, it doesn't matter." Mancini ran his tongue along his teeth. "It might as well be Mars."

"There's no time anyway," Hopkins said. He stared at the first few drops of rain streaking the window. "Can you stay on tonight, Paul?" he asked. "We're probably going to need you at some point before this is over."

"Yes, of course," Kim said, glancing at Mancini. "I was already planning to continue monitoring activity in the system."

"Good. Thanks," Hopkins said. He took a deep breath and exhaled slowly.

"Uh, Mr. Kim," Mancini said, "could you excuse us for a minute?"

"Certainly." Half bowing his head, Kim placed the printout on the cart. "Of course."

When Kim had closed the door behind him, Mancini folded his hands on his desk. "Have a seat, Hoop," he said, nodding toward one of the Windsor chairs.

Hopkins stayed standing. "I sort of need some coffee, sir," he said. "Can I get you a cup?"

"That sludge in your office? My stomach couldn't take it." Mancini cocked his head, stared into Hopkins eyes, and asked. "Are you all right, Hoop? You're not usually a coffee drinker."

"Yeah. I was just fading a little there for a minute."

"Have you gotten any sleep at all?"

Hopkins shrugged. "Some." He didn't want to think about how little he'd had in the last three days.

Mancini unfolded his hands and ran a finger under his starched collar. "The perp's getting to you, huh?"

"You could say that." He hadn't thought about the kidnapper except in terms of how he might trip him up, but he knew it had become personal even before the contact through the computer. And with every passing hour, it was becoming more personal. Perhaps, he realized, *too* personal.

"What's this crap," Mancini asked, "about the perp talking to you about Ross?"

Hopkins looked out at the waving branches. "He's referred to 'my little friend' a couple of times. Nothing specific. No direct references to anyone."

"It's gonna look bad if it gets out that you're diddling . . ."

"Officer Ross and I," Hopkins interrupted, trying to keep the emotion out of his voice, "have had a purely professional relationship since I became I.U. commander. And for a long time before that, sir."

Mancini inspected his fingernails. "I'm under a great deal of pressure to remove you, Hoop," he said. "I'm not going to do it. It's your investigation." He picked at a cuticle. "But with that Adelman confrontation last night and the scene with Bollinger today and now the perp bringing up this crap . . ." He looked at Hopkins. "You've got to understand that if this thing blows up on us, it's your head that's going to r . . ." He stopped suddenly, seemingly aware that he was describing Cameron Bransfield's death.

"Damn it," Hopkins said, "the guy's talking to me. It's all we've got right now."

"Okay, Hoop. All right," Mancini said, shaking his head slowly. "Like I said, you've got the ball." He looked over at the computer, printer, and fax machine. "But I want you to realize what's at stake for you."

"I wouldn't have it any other way."

"Fine," Mancini said, gesturing toward the computer. "And you're okay about putting all your eggs in one basket?"

"Yeah, I guess I am."

Mancini put his hands flat on the desk, gazed at them for a moment, and then looked up again and asked, "And you're sure you're right?"

"No," Hopkins admitted. The more fatigued he became, the more doubts he had. He'd based everything on the kidnapper's reference to his old nickname. And the kidnapper had pet names for everyone. If the kidnapper had come across *Hop* in some records somewhere, then everything being done with that list of thirty-seven names was completely misguided. "No," he repeated. "But I think it's our best shot."

chapter 37

Hopkins gazed at the steam rising from the coffee in the mug he'd borrowed. As he raised the mug and inhaled the steam, Ross came into the fishbowl and said, "Ready for an update?"

He sipped the strong, bitter coffee. "Yeah," he said. "Thanks." Putting the mug on his desk, he added, "Meghan, the perp asked if I'd said hello to the little woman yet."

She bit her lip, stared at the steaming coffee, shrugged, and said, "So he probably wasn't referring to Dave Banks, huh." She waved her hand as if to brush the thought from her mind. "I've got a lot of stuff to show you."

They entered Interview Room B where she had been debriefing the detectives. "Henderson," she said, "is down at the FBI field office. He'll bring the info from the Feds' computer back with him. But we've been able to locate twenty-one of the guys on our own." She ran her finger down the CURRENT STATUS column on the chart. "And all of them check out okay.

They've got families or jobs or something that precludes them from the kind of activity we're looking for."

Drinking the coffee, Hopkins scanned the column. A half-dozen of the men were involved with computers in some way, but none of them lived in the area. Two others were doctors, and the rest had occupations ranging from educational consultant to NASA engineer in Houston. He wondered again if he had somehow made the wrong connection. "Can I take a look at the files of the sixteen guys that haven't been located yet?" he asked.

"Sure." Cross-checking the chart, she began to pull file folders from the plastic case. Her hair fell across her cheek as she leaned over so she tucked it behind her ear. Her tan seemed to have faded, and there were dark rings under her eyes. "You want to work here or at your desk?"

"This is fine." He finished the coffee in one long draught.

"Here you go," she said, handing him the stack of folders.

"Thanks," he said as he opened the first one. There was no photograph of Samuel Wallace Wilson, who had begun North Ridge High School the same year Hopkins had started Deerbrook. He nodded his head slowly as he read the report. Although they were the same age and had lived in adjacent communities, their high school experiences had been different enough to be foreign. Because Wilson had refused to hand in assignments, he had been moved from his honors classes into a special program second semester of his freshman year. He had been truant most of that March and run away from his stepfather's house in May. His sophomore year, he had been suspended when school officials found three ounces of marijuana in his locker. Later that year, he'd been transferred to the district's alternative high school, from which he'd dropped out as soon as he turned sixteen. The summer after his class graduated, he'd earned a General Education Diploma, scoring in the top one percent of the country on the exam.

As he closed the folder, Ross, who had been transferring information from a note pad to the chart, said, "I'm going to see if our guys've come up with anything new. Can I get you anything?"

He shook his head and reached for the next folder.

As she stood up, she touched his shoulder and asked, "You sure?"

"Yeah, thanks anyway, Meghan." He watched her walk away for a moment before opening the file. The following four files did nothing but remind him once more how different people's lives could be. The caffeine coursing through him, he started to sweat. The sixth file was James Patrick McGinty's. After reading it, he sat back and looked again at the Xeroxed photograph. Something he could not pinpoint bothered him, so he carried the file to the fishbowl, looked up the number for Stephen and Lenore Glass, and called the dean's house.

A woman's voice said, "Hello."

"Is Stephen Glass there?" Hopkins asked. He cradled the phone with his shoulder and reached for a legal pad.

"Yes," she answered. "Who may I say is calling?"

"Commander Hopkins from the North Ridge Police Department." He flipped to a clean page in the pad and reopened the file.

"Tom Hopkins?" a man's voice asked.

"Mr. Glass."

"How're you doing . . ." The voice became more somber. "You're calling about the Walker case, aren't you?"

"Yes," Hopkins said. He scrawled JAMES PATRICK MCGINTY at the top of the page. "May I ask you about one of the names you gave Detective Beltram?"

"Of course."

"James Patrick McGinty. What do you remember about him?"

"J.P.? Well, the obvious—the boy's disability. His hand was practically useless."

"His right hand?" Hopkins wrote J.P. under the name.

"Yes. But J.P. was a truly gifted student. I had him in accelerated geometry his freshman year. He was one of only four freshman in the class."

"What was he like?" Hopkins jotted notes on paper.

"Squirrelly might be the kindest way to put it. More often than not, he failed to apply himself. He got A's on tests but seldom did his homework . . ."

Sergeant Banks stood in the fishbowl's doorway and said, "Hey, Hoop, you gotta see what's on the tube."

"Just a second, Mr. Glass," Hopkins said. He held the receiver against his chest and asked, "What's happening?"

"WLN just ran a promo saying that Pit Bull's gonna report live on a major break in the Walker case in two minutes." Banks spoke so fast that it came out almost like one long word.

"Oh, shit," Hopkins mumbled. "I'll be there. Just a sec." He waved his pen at the sergeant, raised the receiver, and said, "Sorry, Mr. Glass. You were telling me about J.P. McGinty."

"Ah, yes, as I said, he was different. Spent most of his time reading sci-fi novels in the back of class."

Hopkins glanced at the report and asked, "You told Detective Beltram that he was a loner?"

"Yes. Exactly." He paused as though trying to recollect his memories. "J.P.'s mother smothered him, I think. And he was starved for friendship. Used to come into the office sometimes and just talk my ear off. Mercifully, the other students didn't pick on him much. But I'd have to say he was pretty much friendless. He attended Deerbrook for four years, but he wandered through the halls in his own private little world."

"You mentioned he had one friend his freshman year?"

"Yes. Yes, I suppose I did. Another boy in my geometry class. Almost as bright as J.P. but even more out of touch with the school. His mother withdrew him abruptly first semester sophomore year. Sent him to Calvert Military Academy down near Indianapolis, if I remember correctly. J.P never really . . ."

An uncanny feeling rose along Hopkins' spine. "What was the boy's name, Mr. Glass?" he asked.

"Jimmy Saville," Glass answered.

"Saville?"

"Yes, you remember. His mother was that reporter for WNDR . . ."

As Glass continued to speak, Hopkins twirled the pen and stared at the name he had just written.

". . . that got breast cancer. Did a series of specials on women and cancer before she lost her battle. Powerful stuff. I'm not sure she was much of a mother, though . . ."

Hopkins remembered an early season basketball game his senior year. During warm-ups, one of his teammates pointed out the two boys, one with a withered arm and the other with his wrist in a brown brace, sitting in the half-empty stands. Laughing, his teammate asked, "Hey, Hop, how the fuck do they shake hands?" Hopkins had never been sure if the boys had heard, thought they probably hadn't. But he'd never seen either of them at another game.

". . . I'd call to talk about Jimmy's lack of homework and his belligerence. An angry boy. Always thought he was right and everybody else was wrong. But she didn't return my calls . . ."

Sergeant Banks stuck his head in the door. "Hoop," he shouted, "Pit Bull's found the Cherokee!"

Hopkins did not even hear him. He knew. He had no hard evidence, but he knew. It all made perfect sense, everything from the obsession with computers and cyberspace to the choice of Tonya Walker. In the programmers' phrase, it was elegant. Despite the caffeine, he felt himself becoming deeply calm. He was absolutely sure.

". . . Didn't show up for parent night," Glass went on. "Never really acknowledged the boy at all."

Sergeant Banks stood in front of his desk, almost blocking out the light, asking, "You okay, Hoop?"

Hopkins looked up and nodded.

"It's Pit Bull. He's found the Cherokee!"

Hopkins lifted his hand and mouthed, "Wait a minute, Dave." Then, he asked Glass, "What happened to him, to Jimmy Saville?"

"Not sure." There was a pause on the line. "I really don't know."

"Would the school still have any records on him?"

"We might. We keep records on all students in the vault. But because he didn't graduate . . ."

"What about his family?"

"There was definitely no father around when I had Jimmy in class. I'm not sure there ever was one."

"Any siblings that might still be in the area?"

"He had a sister. Or a half-sister, anyway." There was another pause. "She would've been, uh, three or four years older than you. But there were problems there, too."

"Can I get copies of whatever records are available?"

"Of course."

"I mean, right away, Mr. Glass." He looked up at Banks. "If I send someone to meet you at the school."

"Well, yes. If it's that important, I can. Yes."

"Mr. Glass," he said, "it's critically important."

chapter 38

Jack Bollinger stood under the garage's eaves in front of the graffiti-splattered green door. His face and microphone were dry, but rain spotted his trenchcoat. "The elusive red Skywalker Grand Cherokee authorities have been searching for in vain since Sunday," he said, "has been parked right here in suburban North Ridge all along." His voice sounded like it was coming from the bottom of a steel drum. "This garage is located less than a mile from the town's police station and only two miles from the gymnastics center where Tonya Walker was last seen."

He glanced down at his rain-soaked spiral notebook, stepped to his right along the building's windowless, red brick facade, and looked into the camera, his dark eyes intense. "This is the perfect spot to ditch a getaway vehicle." He pointed his notebook to his right. "To the north is the cement wall and cyclone fence of All Souls Catholic Cemetery." He stopped by a black and yellow sign that said NO PARKING— POLICE ORDER. "Across Ridge Road here, the El tracks' twenty-foot-high concrete embankment forms an impregnable barrier, isolating this spot from the neighborhood beyond." He paced back to his left. "And to the south, across the border in Chicago less than one hundred yards away, is the Chicago Transit Authority rail yard surrounded by a twelve-foot wall topped with concertina wire."

Bollinger stopped in front of the green door again and paused to stare into the camera. "Yes, the kidnapper chose this site with care, knowing full well that no witnesses would be here on a Sunday night to see the Skywalker Grand Cherokee—perhaps with small, terrified Tonya Walker aboard." He reached down, turned the lock handle, and with a grunt yanked up the door. Inside the dark cavity of the garage, the red liftgate of the Jeep Grand Cherokee gleamed in the minicam's light.

"Haul that son of a bitch in!" Mancini fumed. "I don't care if the whole world sees it." His face was florid as he shouted into his hand-held radio. "He's obstructing justice. Tampering with evidence. And he damn well knows it." He pulled his handkerchief from his pocket and wiped his sweating forehead. "Send backup. Cordon off that whole damn block. Don't let any other TV crews anywhere near that garage. Over." Static crackled for a second as he slammed the radio onto the lunch table in front of him.

"What the hell's Pit Bull doing?" Ross whispered to Hopkins as he came up beside her in the lunchroom. Fifteen others, officers and civilian employees, stood with Mancini around the tables staring at the television set high in the corner of the room.

"Exactly what the perp wants him to," Hopkins answered, his voice low and impassive.

She gazed quizzically up at him, her eyes in the overhead

light the startling blue-green of the lake on a bright winter morning.

Hopkins pointed at the television screen. "The perp's trying to draw our attention from him to another of his media circuses. It's his idea of a red herring."

"What are you . . . ?

"Watch," he said. "Finding the Jeep's not going to do us any good now. But Pit Bull's going to have the whole world hanging on his every word one last time before the papers point out that he's a pedophile who's been using the station's Internet connections not only to collect child pornography but to steal information from colleagues and maybe even aid and abet in a Class A felony. The perp's set him up perfectly."

Mancini twisted the handkerchief around his hand.

Ross gazed at the screen for a moment and then said, "It does look like Pit Bull's rehearsed the whole thing."

"Yeah, Meghan," Hopkins said. "He's probably been at the site an hour, picked the garage's lock, checked everything out. Even choreographed all his moves with his cameraman."

"Pit Bull's such scum," she said. "He's . . ."

"It doesn't matter," he said. "The Jeep's inconsequential." When she looked at him again, he asked, "Has Carl Henderson gotten back yet?"

"No." She shook her head. "Not as of five minutes ago."

"I've got to talk to the Chief, get him alone, if possible," he said. "I know who the perp is. I know his name."

As Jack Bollinger walked slowly back toward the Cherokee, he said over his shoulder to the following camera, "Given the serious criticism leveled at North Ridge for the police department's questionable handling—some would say, inept bungling—of the Walker case, it should be no surprise really that they failed to locate a vehicle that had been virtually under their noses all the time." He stopped next to the Grand Cherokee and looked around the dark interior of the garage. "North Ridge patrol cars routinely pass this place. And, ironically, Ridge Road runs directly from the NRPD station to the Chicago neighborhood where Cameron Bransfield died so gruesomely last night. Investigations Unit Commander Thomas Hopkins must have driven right by here less than twenty hours ago as he rushed to the sight of the bombing—and a murder that many believe could have been prevented had North Ridge authorities properly supervised the private investigator's actions." A distant siren wailed as he slapped the Jeep's rear window with his notebook and then, leering at the camera, added, "Is it any wonder, then, that the kidnapper left the vehicle here, just within North Ridge's borders, confident, no doubt, that it would not be discovered by the local gendarmes?"

James Robert Saville put down the soldering iron, sniffled, wiped his nostrils with the back of the carpal-tunnel brace, gazed at the Videot Box tuned to the WLN News Special Report, and snickered. The Pit Bull was rabid! Starting to fucking foam at the mouth! The mutt had one mega-doggie-boner over this one, all right. Even farther gone than he'd expected him to be. Approaching the edge of the envelope! Might even fly right through it and get his chain instantly yanked by the station. But probably not. Definitely not! No matter how frenzied the Pit Bull got, the station gurus would never pull the plug with the whole world tuned in and turned on.

Glancing down at the wires and other materials he'd been working on, he wished he had time to really savor Pit Bull's show. And what a show it was going to be when the North Ridge pigs finally wallowed onto the scene! They'd be hog-wild! Maybe Pit Bull finally got what was happening. Or, more likely, he didn't. That was probably asking too much of the mongrel. But he did at least grasp the concept that if you were being sent to the pound, you might as well make the biggest stink possible. Shit on the finest carpet. Piss all over everything. Make those sons of bitches remember your scent forever—and a day!

He'd, of course, learned that particular lesson, like so much else, at a tender age. But he couldn't expect Pit Bull or any of those other peabrains to pick up anything very quickly. Perspicacity was his special forte, and he'd known it even before he escaped the Gulag in such spectacular fashion. Busted out with a major bang. No more whimpering for him. Shook the yoke for good, took it on the lam forever, broke fucking loose big time! It'd been the beginning, really. His first flight! His first fleeting solo! And it had all led to this moment. To his soaring so unimaginably high! To his skywriting his name so indelibly in the minds of all the morons everywhere.

Jack Bollinger swung open the Grand Cherokee's rear liftgate. "In here, certainly," he said, "Tonya Walker rode from the gymnastics center to her fate." He stepped back so that the camera could zoom in for a close-up of the black interior. The sound of sirens rose in the background. "What she thought was happening to her at that moment, we cannot imagine. But surely she could not have foreseen being trussed naked to a wall like an animal and having her ring finger cut off by the demon that abducted her."

After shutting the liftgate, he moved around to the driver's door, the cameraman following close behind. Flashing blue and silver lights wove around him on the walls as he flung open the door. "And it was here, in this driver's seat, that the demon perched as he made his getaway, watching, perhaps, for North Ridge squad cars, but knowing, too, that he had the authorities hopelessly outwitted."

"Hey, you," a male voice called, "step away from that vehicle immediately." The cameraman turned to shoot the two uniformed officers, one a lanky man with a mustache, and the other a stout, dark woman. Both had their guns holstered. Another siren stopped as the lights crisscrossing the walls doubled.

"Over here," Bollinger shouted, and the camera panned toward him again as he climbed into the Jeep. "On the passenger's seat, where you can't see it, the kidnapper left a message—a capital **M** formed with four small, elongated oval cakes—cakes commonly known as *ladyfingers*."

"Mr. Bollinger," a woman's voice yelled, "you're under arrest. Leave that vehicle *now*, or you'll be forcibly removed. This is the only warning you'll receive."

Bollinger smiled at the camera. His eyes narrowed. "What does the **M** mean?" he asked. "Monique? Mom? Mary, Mother of God?" His upper lip curled. "Murder? Mayhem?"

The lanky officer jostled the cameraman, reached into the Grand Cherokee, and grabbed the trenchcoat's sleeve. Bollinger pulled himself free, pivoted on the seat, and, still grinning, kicked the officer in the stomach. The female officer pulled her gun and leveled it at Bollinger; the two backup officers entering the garage drew their guns. As the lanky officer reached in a second time, Bollinger slammed the door on his hand. The camera caught the officer screaming and sinking to the floor, clutching his smashed fingers. Behind the Jeep's tinted glass, the door's lock snapped home.

chapter 39

As Hopkins and Mancini headed toward the Chief's office, Sergeant Banks hailed them, strode up the hallway, and handed Hopkins two file folders and a brown yearbook. "These are the originals, Hoop," he said. "None of the Xerox machines at the school were turned on."

"Thanks, Dave," Hopkins said. "I'll get copies made."

Banks pointed to the yellow strip of paper sticking out of the yearbook. "Mr. Glass found a picture of the guy. He sure doesn't look like much."

"That may be part of the problem," Hopkins said.

Banks nodded. "Pit Bull's gone and locked himself in the Cherokee?"

His face and neck still flushed, Mancini grimaced. "We can't get him out without destroying evidence, and the son of a bitch knows it."

"You want, I'll take the SWAT team over there and pull him out through the windshield," Banks said.

Mancini ran his index finger inside his collar. "It might

come to that. Beltram's over there now trying to negotiate with him."

Banks removed his uniform cap, wiped his shaved head, grinned, and said, "I could maybe rearrange his bones a little while I do it."

"We've stopped him from broadcasting, gotten the TV cameraman out of there," Mancini said. "Without the world watching, he may leave peacefully."

Hopkins smiled wryly. "But we'll keep your offer in mind, Dave."

"Damn straight! I might kinda enjoy it."

As Banks turned to leave, Hopkins said, "As soon as Carl Henderson gets back, ask him to meet us in the Chief's office, okay?"

"He's back, Hoop. He was comin' in when I was," Banks said over his shoulder. "I'll tell him."

As he entered Mancini's office, Hopkins scanned James Robert Saville's file, which held only a transcript, a doctor's letter excusing him from physical education, and a withdrawal form. The transcript showed B's in geometry his freshman year, C's in Biology, and D's in English, Spanish, and World History. The typed doctor's letter mentioned, "severe childhood trauma to the right hand that has resulted in a 30% incapacitation." The withdrawal form, filled out in a tight feminine script and signed by Margaret Saville, gave as the reason for the withdrawal "a personal family matter."

Mancini settled heavily in his chair and steepled his fingers in front of his mouth. When Hopkins handed him the folder, he asked, "So this is the guy you think is the perp?"

Nodding, Hopkins sat in one of the Windsor chairs. He opened the yearbook from his senior year to the page marked by the slip. The black and white freshman homeroom photo of Saville and his classmates had been taken outdoors by the school's bus entrance. Saville, a little shorter and chubbier than most of his classmates, stood at the left end of the front row. His round, blemished face, the size of a dime in the photograph, scowled at the camera. Still, except for his dour expression, he did not look significantly different from the others.

Mancini looked up from the folder, slapped the papers with the back of his hand, and said, "This sure isn't much to go on, Hoop."

Hopkins slipped the yearbook onto the desk. "No," he admitted. "But it's a start."

"I don't know, Hoop." Mancini shook his head. "I've got a bad feeling about this. It's too much of a longshot."

Hopkins turned the yearbook and slid it across the desk. As Mancini stared at the photograph, Hopkins leafed through the second folder. Kathleen Sarah Saville, four years older than Hopkins, had been a better student than her younger brother, but she, too, had been abruptly withdrawn from school in May of her sophomore year. And the reason had again been, "personal family matter." In her case, however, there were follow-up truancy and missing-person reports, the last dated on her sixteenth birthday.

"He looks pretty damned harmless," Mancini said.

Carl Henderson knocked, came into the office, and said, "I hear you got the name of a guy you think might be a suspect." He handed Hopkins a thick accordion file he'd been carrying under his arm.

Mancini spun the yearbook and tapped Saville's picture.

As he sat down in the other Windsor chair, Henderson studied the photograph and the names under it. Then, turning to Hopkins he said, "This guy's not even on your list. What makes you think he's the one?"

"He was a friend of one of the guys, but he didn't show up on the list because he left school his sophomore year." Hopkins drummed the accordion file with his fingers. "But he fits the profile. He's got a maimed right hand. And his mother was the hot local news reporter twenty-five years ago."

Mancini sat back in his chair, took out his handkerchief, wiped his face and neck, and balled up the handkerchief in his palm.

Henderson nodded. "You mean the Monique Jones-Walker of her time."

"Exactly," Hopkins said.

"You think he's getting even with his mother for something?" Mancini asked.

"With his mom, the media, the world." Shrugging, Hopkins turned toward Henderson. "Carl, you're the behavioralist."

"Let's see what you got on him."

"Not a lot," Mancini said as he gave Henderson the folder.

While the FBI agent looked over the records, Hopkins glanced for a moment at the rain streaking the office windows and then went through the accordion file until he found the information on James Patrick McGinty.

Henderson stared at Hopkins. "This is nothing, Hoop," he said. "It leads nowhere."

Squeezing the handkerchief, Mancini leaned forward. "Thank you. I was hoping someone else would see that point." He ran his tongue along his teeth. "Time's wasting here, and we've got that bastard in the Jeep already taking too much of our attention away from the investigation."

"Hear me out," Hopkins said. "It won't take long to find out if I'm on target." His voice was calm and authoritative, as though the Chief of Police and the FBI agent heading the investigation were already compelled to follow his plan. "We've got five initial moves. While Carl runs Saville through the Feds' computer, I'll call J.P. McGinty. If anybody still knows Saville, he will." He waved his thumb at the file folder. "We've got the doctor to contact, Calvert Military Academy where Mr. Glass thinks Saville went after his mother withdrew him from Deerbrook, and his sister, if we can track her down."

"What about the mother?" Henderson asked.

"She's dead. Breast cancer." Hopkins shook his head. "But you're right. Her doctors might provide leads, too."

"Okay," Mancini said. He began to fold the wrinkled handkerchief. "But if we're deciding to run with this, why not go public? Put out an all-points. Use PIMS and NCIC, everything. Make the Net work for us."

Flipping the folder shut, Henderson said, "There's nothing to put out. No description or anything. All you've got is a name he's probably no longer using."

Hopkins shook his head. "Anyway," he said, "the damage'd outweigh whatever information we came up with. He monitors everything, and it'd drive him instantly to ground. We need to keep him thinking he's still in control."

chapter 40

⟋⟍⟍⟍⟍⟍⟍⟍⟍⟍⟍) **The federal government's** computer information on James Patrick McGinty included date and place of birth, Social Security and driver's license numbers, credit history, marital status, automobile titles, income and real estate tax data, and current home and business addresses and telephones. McGinty was single, living in Palo Alto, California, driving a Mercedes, and making $148,000 plus stock options as the design vice-president of Omnitech, a Silicon Valley software company. Looking up from the information sheet, Hopkins wished he could see McGinty to get a better feel for what tack to take during the interview. He glanced at his watch, noting that it was only 4:15 P.M. in California, moved a folder from on top of his desk phone, and dialed McGinty's Omnitech extension.

"J.P. McGinty's office," a high, nasal male voice said.

"May I speak with Mr. McGinty?" Hopkins asked.

"He's in a meeting right now," the voice said. "May I have him return your call?"

"This is Commander Thomas Hopkins of the North Ridge, Illinois, Police Department. I need to speak to Mr. McGinty. It's urgent." He pulled out the legal pad on which he had written Stephen Glass's information about McGinty.

There was a long pause, and then the voice said peevishly, "I'll see what I can do. Please hold, Mr. Hopkins."

Hopkins reviewed the computer information and his earlier notes, turned to a blank page, and wrote the date and time.

"This is J.P. McGinty," he heard a minute later. The voice was soft and reserved.

"Mr. McGinty," Hopkins said, "this is Thomas Hopkins from North Ridge. I'm investigating . . ."

"North Ridge, Illinois? Near Deerbrook?"

"Yes," Hopkins answered. "I'm calling because . . ."

"It's about James, isn't it?"

Hopkins started. "James Robert Saville, yes."

"I thought as much." The voice was sad, even softer, almost a whisper. "When my executive assistant told me it was someone from the North Ridge police, I realized immediately it had to be about James."

Hopkins wrote the initials JRS on the legal pad. "Mr. McGinty," he said, his voice firm, "do you know something about Saville's involvement in Tonya Walker's kidnapping?"

"You can call me J.P. Everybody does." McGinty paused for a moment. "I don't really *know* anything. I haven't really been following the story very carefully. I almost never watch TV or read newspapers. But when I heard North Ridge, something just clicked." He hesitated, then asked, "Are you Hop Hopkins who played basketball at Deerbrook?"

"Yes, J.P." He shook his head ironically. Steering the conversation back to the topic, he asked, "Do you have any contact with Saville?"

"No. Not for over two . . . for almost three years."

"J.P., do you know where Saville is, where he's living now?"

"Yeah. I mean, no." The voice sounded more vulnerable than reserved. "Three years ago last April, he moved back to Chicago. Somewhere in the Chicago area, but I don't know exactly where."

"So you haven't seen him in three years?"

"I haven't actually *seen* him since high school. We always used the Net, communicated through e-mail."

"But you kept in touch with him?"

"No. Not really. After he ran away from that military school in Indiana, I never saw him. Never heard from him." McGinty paused again. "Then one day about six years ago, a message just appeared in my e-mail. We started chatting. I was into the Net, but I'm not very fast on the keyboard. I get flamed a lot. It was good for me to have an old friend. Eventually, James did some consulting for my firm . . ." His voice trailed off.

"And?" Hopkins stopped his note-taking for a moment.

"I'm a designer, Mr. . . . Can I call you 'Hop'?"

"Yeah, sure, J.P." His tone softened. McGinty, he realized, wanted to talk, perhaps even needed to talk.

"I'm really good at design, Hop. I have sort of a gift for it. And, it's lucrative. The firm takes care of me, rewards me very well. James is different. He's a hacker. And brilliant. Maybe the best Omnitech ever used. He created some elegant defenses for our systems. And did some other stuff for us later. He did very nicely financially by us, too. But James isn't very good at taking directions."

"He didn't get along with your boss?"

"No. And things gradually got worse. Finally, about two and a half years ago, my boss terminated him. I don't think James blamed me, but that was it. No more e-mail. No more chats."

"Did he do anything to get even with Omnitech?"

"How did you know?"

"Just a guess."

"Three months after James was terminated, part of our system crashed. Not the design section, the financial part. It was an incredible mess. And though we never knew who caused it, I've thought all along it was him."

"J.P., you said something clicked when you heard North Ridge."

"A couple of things, really." McGinty hesitated again. "James moved back because he was planning something. THE BIG OPERATION, he called it. Always keyboarded it all in caps."

"What was it, this big operation?" Hopkins scratched his temple with the top of his pen.

"He never said. He always had secrets, even when we were kids. He insisted on absolute secrecy in his dealings with the firm. And he became more secretive with me after he moved back—the last couple of months we chatted."

"Is he paranoid, J.P.?"

"I don't know." Another note of sadness crept into McGinty's voice. "But you could say that. When he consulted for us, I never knew where he lived. All his payments were made to numbered accounts in foreign banks. And those were different every time. He changed the accounts with each payment." McGinty sighed. "The whole time we chatted, he never said where he was. He could've been a mile away—or on another planet. It was like he wasn't really anywhere in the real world. He lived in cyberspace. Does that make sense?"

"Yeah, J.P., it does." It made too much sense to Hopkins. "But you're sure he moved back here?"

"That's one thing he did say. But probably only because we both grew up there. He told me he needed to move back for the big operation."

Henderson crossed the Investigations Unit office toward the fishbowl, knocked on the partition, and came in.

"You mentioned there were a couple of things that clicked?" Hopkins asked.

"Yeah. James bragged a lot about building himself something he called the Command Center." The sadness in McGinty's voice deepened. "A state-of-the-art electronic . . ."

His expression perplexed, Henderson stood next to the desk.

"J.P.," Hopkins interrupted. "You're being very helpful. Can you hold the line? Your information is vital, but I've got someone at my desk. I'll be right back." He cupped his hand over the receiver and looked up at Henderson.

Shaking his head, Henderson said, "Saville's not in the computer."

"What?"

"James Robert Saville doesn't exist. He no longer exists." Anger and frustration rose in Henderson's voice. "Hell, as far as the government knows, he never existed."

"Is that possible?"

"Theoretically, of course not. Nobody can crack that whole computer system. But there's definitely no record of him anywhere in the system. Nothing." He raised his hands. "Zip."

Confused, Hopkins lifted the receiver. "J.P.," he asked, "you still there?"

McGinty seemed to sense a change in Hopkins. "Yes, Hop," he said hesitantly.

"Could Sav . . ." Hopkins began. "Would Saville be capable of hacking into the federal government's computer system and wiping out all the evidence of his own existence?"

McGinty did not answer.

Looking at Henderson, Hopkins said, "J.P.?"

"Yes, he's that capable." McGinty's voice seemed diminished. "He's that skilled. And he's that relentless."

Hopkins nodded to Henderson, who frowned and turned away.

"Thanks, J.P.," Hopkins said. "You've been a great help."

"You don't want to hear about his command center?" McGinty asked, his voice sounding hurt.

"I'm sorry. Yes, I do." He wrote **Command Center** in block letters on the legal pad.

Henderson turned back and whispered, "I'll call that military school in Indiana."

"James envisioned the ultimate electronic environment," McGinty said. "Not just with computers and modems and scanners and printers. But with fax machines and top-of-the-line audio and video equipment. All top-notch stuff. And all his own, at only his disposal all the time."

"Including tape editors?"

"Yes. Of course. And eventually his own virtual reality headsets and gloves. He was going to home-brew it all, put it all together himself. Make it more sophisticated, he'd say, than anything Omnitech or any other company had."

"This command center, it'd be up and running by now?"

"In three years? Definitely. Maybe not all of it, but easily everything except the virtual reality stuff. Oh, and he was going to have one mega sound system. That was a must for him. The Beatles played in Comiskey Park on his birthday when he was four. His sister convinced him they'd played there especially for him. He had this thing for the Beatles and the Stones. He'd play the *White Album* over and over again. His favorite song was "Blackbird." He told me once it was a song for us. A song for people like us. I haven't listened to it in years . . ." His voice drifted off again.

Hopkins grabbed the other folder, scribbled KSS on the notepad, and asked, "What was his sister like?"

"I never met her. She and his mom always fought, I guess. Really bad fights, physical stuff. One night it apparently got worse than usual, and Sarah ran away. He wouldn't ever tell me exactly what happened, but he definitely thought it was his fault."

"She went by Sarah, not Kathleen?"

"Kathleen? James always called her Sarah. He worshipped her—or at least her memory. When he was little, she took care of him a lot, was really more of a mom to him. I saw a picture of her and him taken when he was about eight. He had it hidden in a book in his room. His mother wouldn't allow any pictures of her in the house. Sarah was kind of pretty, long blond hair and stuff. But he thought she was the most beautiful thing in the world."

Hopkins jotted LONG BLOND HAIR/PRETTY and then stared for a moment at what he had written. Shaking his head, he asked, "What about his mother?"

McGinty cleared his throat. He seemed almost to be choking as he said, "I'm probably the wrong person to ask about Margaret Saville."

Hopkins jotted THE MOM on the pad. Trying to sound matter of fact, he asked, "Why is that, J.P.?"

"She hated me."

Waiting for McGinty to go on, Hopkins didn't say anything.

"I'm, uh, not sure why, but she couldn't stand James ever being around me." McGinty's voice still sounded choked. "She was the meanest, coldest person I've ever known. She acted like he didn't exist. Most of the time she didn't even come home. Just left him there. But then she'd appear and get on his case about how hard she worked for him and what a miserable excuse for a son he was. You could tell in school the next day after she'd been home and gone into one of her rants."

Hopkins waited for a moment and then asked, "What about his father?"

"James never mentioned his father. I'm pretty sure he didn't know who he was."

Hopkins wrote a final note. "J.P.," he said, "I can't thank you enough for taking the time to talk to me."

"That's okay, Hop," McGinty said, his voice again a sad whisper. "Do you want to give me your number in case I think of anything else?"

"Yes. Good idea." Hopkins silently swore at himself for not having already done so. He gave McGinty the number and then said, his voice low, "You think Saville is Tonya Walker's kidnapper, don't you?"

"I wish I could tell you he wasn't." McGinty's voice grew smaller, more distant. "You never really know anybody, Hop. You think you know, but you don't really."

chapter 41

Wearing a rain slicker, Hopkins entered the Walkers' kitchen at 7:25 that evening. Rain drummed against the French windows and streamed down the glass. Bert Adelman sat across the table from Monique Jones-Walker. His gray Italian suit was impeccable as always, but the skin of his face looked aged, loose, as though his body were slowly deflating inside. His briefcase lay open on the table, and he was pointing to a printed spreadsheet with his gold pen. As he spoke in a low voice, Jones-Walker sat back and crossed her leg away from him. Her hair was pulled back from her face, and she wore no lipstick or other makeup. A cigarette hung between her index and middle fingers, the smoke swirling toward the storm outside.

Adelman turned to Hopkins and, his voice acerbic, said, "The messenger returneth."

"Evening," Hopkins said. He nodded to Jones-Walker. "Is Mr. Walker here?"

"He's in the gym working out," she answered.

Hopkins nodded again, looking into Jones-Walker's eyes, glimpsing for the first time the depth of her pain and anxiety.

She stared at him for a moment before shouting, "Consuela!" When the diminutive maid in the black uniform appeared, she said, "Consuela, get Señor Walker, *por favor.*" As the maid scurried from the room, Jones-Walker dragged on her cigarette, tapped the ash into the Chicago Bulls ashtray, gazed at the beating rain, and exhaled smoke through her nose. "What's Jack Bollinger up to now?" she asked. She slid her burgundy fingernails along the gold lighter on the table in front of her.

"He was still locked in the Cherokee ten minutes ago," he answered. Water dripping from his slicker puddled on the floor. He slipped off the hood, shook his head, and brushed rain from his face. "We know who the kidnapper is."

"You've positively identified him?" Adelman said, his expression dour. "Or is this another one of your hunches?"

"Oh, I'd *bet* on this one, Mr. Adelman," Hopkins said.

Adelman's eyes narrowed as he spun his pen.

Robert Walker, followed by the maid, strode into the kitchen, wiping his neck with a white towel. Another towel was draped over his head. His blue and gray Georgetown sweatshirt, with its sleeves cut off at the arm pits, was drenched with sweat, and the tatooed **S** glistened darkly—but he was not breathing hard at all.

Jamming out her cigarette, Jones-Walker said, "Mr. Hopkins thinks he's identified the kidnapper."

Walker held the towel under his chin and, glancing from his wife to Hopkins, said, "Consuela, please take Mr. Hopkins' coat." He did not acknowledge Adelman's presence.

As Hopkins took off his slicker and gave it to the maid, Walker turned a chair around, set it away from the others, and straddled it. He then gestured to the chair next to Adelman and said, "Tell us what you got, Hoop."

Hopkins sat down and looked across the table at Jones-Walker. "The kidnapper is James Robert Saville," he said, leaning forward, his forearms on the table. "Does that name mean anything to you?"

She raised her eyebrows, glanced at Adelman, and asked, "Any relation to Margaret Saville?"

Hopkins nodded. "Her only son."

The maid used a paper towel to wipe the wet floor where Hopkins had stood.

"Margaret Saville," Jones-Walker said to her husband, "was the first woman news anchor at WNBR. Very smart. And very tough."

Adelman hooked his elbow around the back of his chair, turned toward Hopkins, and, his tone sardonic, asked, "You think this guy's the kidnapper, Tom, just because he's related to a female news anchor?"

"Hear the man out, Bert," Walker said. He took the towel from his head and looped it around the back of his neck.

The corner of Adelman's right eye twitched for a second before he turned and sat back.

"I talked earlier today to a guy who may be Saville's only friend," Hopkins said. "The guy told me that Saville moved back to the Chicago area about three years ago for what he, Saville, always referred to as the *big operation.*"

"But the guy didn't know what this *big operation* was?" Adelman asked, his voice still scornful.

"No."

"And you're assuming that this *big operation* has to be the kidnapping?" Adelman asked.

"Yes."

"Then why the hell haven't you simply picked the guy up?"

"I'll get to that, Mr. Adelman."

Walker hung the second towel over the back of the chair and scowled at Adelman.

"According to his pediatrician," Hopkins went on, "Saville was physically abused by his mother. On one occasion, she maimed his right hand with some hard, fairly sharp object."

"Is that public record?" Adelman asked. "Or merely your surmise, Tom?"

"I spoke with the doctor half an hour ago. The injury was never a matter of public record because both the mother and the boy insisted he had just closed the garage door on it. They came to the office in the morning, but from the swelling and discoloration it was clear to the doctor that the injury had occurred sometime earlier. And, the bones were crushed in four different areas rather than along a line."

Jones-Walker turned the lighter in her hand, set it on her pack of cigarettes, and said, "Go on."

"His sophomore year, Mrs. Saville abruptly withdrew the boy from Deerbrook High School and sent him away to Calvert Military Academy outside Indianapolis." Hopkins glanced at his watch. "An hour ago, Carl Henderson spoke to Calvert's headmaster, who'd been a teacher at the school when Saville was there. According to him, Saville couldn't get along with anyone, loathed everything about the place except for the school's new computer lab. He spent all of his time haunting the lab and the school's computer programmer. Near the end of his junior year, after his mother died, he stole the cash from the school's refreshments fund and bolted. The next day, the school's mainframe crashed. The system was apparently so badly damaged that it had to be replaced. Saville vanished, disappeared completely."

The maid brought Walker a liter mug of iced lemonade. "Can I get you anythin'?" he asked Hopkins.

Hopkins shook his head and said, "Saville didn't surface again for seventeen years. Then he contacted that guy I mentioned, his friend from here, who was working for a software firm in California."

Walker drank half the mug of lemonade.

"Are you trying to tell us, Tom," Adelman interrupted, "that you haven't been able to come up with any records on this Saville character in all that time?"

"Mr. Adelman, I'm telling you there are no records of James Robert Saville anywhere in the government's computers."

Walker wiped his mouth and asked, "Anywhere?"

"Pardon me, Tom," Adelman said, his voice condescending, "but that's pretty difficult to believe."

"It is," Hopkins answered, his voice even. His pager beeped, and he unclipped it and looked at the department's emergency call-in number. "And personally, Mr. Adelman, I'd be more than happy if you hired a private investigator to check on the FBI's conclusion."

As Adelman fingered his gold and diamond tie clasp and glared at Hopkins, Walker finished the lemonade, a smile passing fleetingly over his lips.

"Saville doesn't exist," Hopkins said, "as far as the federal government knows. Apparently obliterating any record of himself is part of his plan, part of his defenses." He looked around the kitchen, noticed the fax machine plugged in over by the telephone on the counter, turned to Walker, and asked, "May I use a phone for a second?"

"So you don't really know anything about him now— where is he or what he looks like?" Adelman said as he took his flip phone from his suit coat pocket and handed it to Hopkins. "You don't really have any leads at all?"

"We know he's in the area," Hopkins said, punching in the emergency number. "We know he's Caucasian, his age, and his physical disability."

"That's nothing," Adelman scoffed.

Sergeant Banks answered on the first ring. "Hey, Hoop?" he asked.

"Yeah, Dave," he said. "What's up?"

"Pit Bull's got a key. He's started the Cherokee. He's been yellin' your name and your friend Monique's."

chapter 42

Jack Bollinger squeezed the steering wheel. The key had been under the floor mat just as the e-mail message had said it would be. There had been no instructions in the message, just the location of the unlocked Cherokee and the fact that the ignition key would be waiting. He gunned the engine. The Snatcher had to have known he wouldn't take directions anyway, that he was well beyond instructions—and recriminations.

The news that he was a pedophile had already been leaked by the newspaper queers, and when those self-righteous faggots and dykes came out with their columns in the morning, excoriating him for pillaging Jones-Walker's files as well as for his sexual proclivities, his career would be finished. Coupled with that bogus battery arrest Hopkins had nailed him with, he'd be lucky if he wasn't fired outright. He'd probably be "offered" early retirement. The best-case scenario was that he'd be censured and then booted into some excruciatingly invisible desk job, completely removed from the public eye. He wasn't going to let that happen—he was a newsman, a reporter, pure and simple. The real thrill of the job all those years had been cutting people down to size, knocking people's butts off their high horses, taking down the pompous politicians and arrogant athletes and supercilious socialites. And he had been good at it, the best.

He gazed in the rearview mirror through the rain outside at the police cruisers, parked at angles, blocking the garage's entrance. He wasn't going to slink away. There was enough blame to spread around, but most of it was that cocksucker Hopkins' fault. If Hopkins hadn't made contact with the Snatcher, the Snatcher would still be dependent on him to make things happen—just as in the case of the Cherokee now. And then there was the degradation of the arrest caught on video by that CNN imbecile. He took his flask from his raincoat pocket, swigged the Jack, felt the slow, eye-watering burn, and grinned malevolently. "Tom Hopkins and Monique Jones-Walker and the Skyjacker himself can all go to hell!" he shouted into the remote microphone he had kept hot even after his cameraman had been removed from the garage.

Hopkins, he had been told by the North Ridge negotiator, was out of the office, unavailable to speak to him. But there was only one place the cocksucker might have gone, and he'd tear a chunk out of his ass yet. A gaggle of his news brethren had certainly congregated nearby. He'd even heard a few minutes before the thwacking of a helicopter's blades (if the weather were any better, there'd be a *fleet* of hovering choppers). He checked the rearview mirror again. Although it was not yet night, the Northeaster's deep, blustering gloom had extinguished the day. Sheets of rain slanted across the entrance, but no one stood between him and the police cruisers.

Revving the engine, he shouted in his gravelly on-air voice, "Ready, folks! Here we go!" He popped the automatic gear shift into reverse and stomped on the accelerator. The Grand

Cherokee shot backward past the gawking negotiator and the loitering cops, across the garage, and into the police cruisers. Metal and chrome screamed and glass shattered as the vehicles lurched sideways. The Jeep skidded across the road on the wet pavement, smashed into the Chicago Transit Authority embankment, and recoiled into the center of the street. He shifted into four-wheel drive while the cops scrambled to their cruisers. Television lights lit the rain.

The wheels spun for a second, and he was off, speeding north, tearing through the police cordon, shooting past the cemetery in the downpour. "Tom Hopkins' parents are six feet under over here at All Souls," he shouted, "along with all those thousands of other mackerel snappers!" He had no idea if it were true, but that wasn't the point anymore. He downed another belt of Jack and smacked his chest twice before he caught his breath. He had a clear destination; he was racing toward one amazingly dramatic climax, not some lame surrender brokered by shysters. He fumbled around until he found the switch on the steering column and set the wipers beating. The police cars' flashers pulsed in the dusk behind him, and overhead the chopper skimmed above the trees and electrical wires, its pilot, no doubt, instructed to keep the Jeep on camera at any cost. The trees lining the cemetery's fence waved him on.

North of the cemetery, he swung the Jeep hydroplaning around the corner and sheared the mirrors off a line of cars parked in front of the brick two-flats. Sirens wailed in the dimness, and people were already peering out of the apartments' lighted windows. He spun around another corner, ran the traffic light without glancing either way, and sent the Jeep zigzagging north through the traffic that had slowed for the sirens and flashers. The squad cars and TV vans snaked behind, and the helicopter skirted the tops of the trees.

It was all an incredible rush now, as he worked the wheel

to the wipers' beat, turning into each potential skid and darting by the gapers in their station wagons and minivans. Intermittently he caught a glimpse of the roistering lake to his right
between the increasingly larger houses. Three of the four
ladyfingers flipped onto the floor. His low guttural laugh
rolled on as he raced north.

chapter 43

Hopkins and the Walkers stood by the kitchen counter staring at the Sony's screen. Adelman remained at the table going over his spreadsheets one last time before the kidnapper's fax was due to arrive. The sound on the television was breaking up, only bits of Bollinger's words audible in the static, and the image of the Grand Cherokee and the trailing light show, viewed from above, undulated. The Jeep seemed to have a sparkling, bejeweled train as it cruised through traffic, the trees on either side bowing in the wind like courtiers.

Hopkins rolled his neck and scratched the side of his nose. "He's heading this way," he murmured. "He's coming here."

Walker took the towel from his neck and wrapped it around his fist. Jones-Walker glanced at her husband, moved to her left, pressed the intercom button, and said, "Anthony, meet Mr. Walker and me at the front door."

As Hopkins reached for the flip phone on the table, Adelman put down his pen and turned toward the television. Hopkins punched the NRPD inside emergency number again and said to the dispatcher who answered, "This is Commander Hopkins. Send any available patrol cars to the Walker residence." He looked at the TV. "Yes, I know there's a vehicular chase in progress." His voice rose. "It's heading here, damn it."

When they reached the foyer, the maid handed Hopkins his slicker. Ignacio stood under the crystal chandelier, his hands folded in front of him, rocking back and forth on the balls of his feet. "I was watching TV," he said. "He's comin' here, ain't he?"

"That's what Mr. Hopkins thinks," Jones-Walker said. "Will you position yourself out front to greet Mr. Bollinger should he get this far?"

Ignacio nodded, pulled at the sleeves of his black uniform coat, and said, "Sure thing. No way he gets by me."

When Ignacio opened the door, Hopkins could hear the sound of sirens through the wind and rain. As Ignacio began to close the door, Hopkins stepped across the marble floor and, putting on the slicker, followed him onto the porch. The wind shook the evergreens and rattled the flagpole's line, but facing west they were shielded from the Northeaster by the mansion. Although the rain continued to blow across the lawn, the porch tiles were dry.

Walker came out onto the porch and, looping the towel forward and backward over his wrist, stood next to Hopkins. Ignacio unbuttoned his coat and ran his hand along his belt. Adelman and Jones-Walker remained in the doorway. Rain pounded the walk and driveway, sluiced along the blacktop, and swamped the lawn. The beating of the helicopter's rotors echoed around the porch, but it was nowhere in sight. The sirens' pitch changed as the squad cars approached. No one said anything.

Lights probed the rain pelting the road, and five seconds later the Grand Cherokee swerved toward the fence, smashed through the iron gates, and careened across the driveway. Plowing mud and turf, it skidded across the lawn and clipped the flagpole, toppling it. As the pole crashed onto the pavement, blocking the squad cars pulling into the driveway, its gold globe snapped off and bounced into the garden.

"Get back inside the house," Hopkins shouted over the din. "All of you. Now!"

Its front end and driver's side battered, the Grand Cherokee finally stalled fifteen yards from the porch. The helicopter thundered overhead, its lights sweeping the driveway and lawn. Walker twisted the towel over the knuckles of his right hand as the Jeep's door swung open. Bollinger stumbled out of the Cherokee, his trenchcoat disheveled, looked behind him at the police officers leaping from their cars, and then tramped through the soaked grass toward the porch.

"Halt!" Hopkins yelled as he stepped forward. The other police officers' shouts were drowned by the uproar.

Rain pouring down his face, Bollinger grinned maniacally. "Fuck yourself, cocksucker!" he screamed as he reached into his trenchcoat pocket.

"Halt, now!" Hopkins shouted.

Still grinning, Bollinger began to pull a dark metallic object from his pocket.

As Walker started down the steps toward the reporter, Hopkins grabbed his elbow. "No!" he said. "I'll handle . . ." Out of the corner of his eye, he saw Ignacio, feet spread and left hand bracing his right wrist, leveling his .357 Magnum. Turning, he yelled, "Don't!"

Ignacio fired twice.

The first shot snapped Bollinger's head back. His expression startled, he opened his mouth as if to call into the driving rain. The second seemed to have no effect for a moment, except that a dark hole appeared near the trenchcoat's lapel. Then he collapsed slowly onto the bottom steps.

* * *

Awestruck, James Robert Saville licked his lips and gazed up at the monitor. The figure in the trenchcoat stood for one fleeting moment at the foot of the steps and then slumped into a heap on the ground, as if kissing the wet walkway.

He was stunned. Truly goddamned stunned! The Hoopmeister had shot the Pit Bull! Gunned him down just like Atticus Finch'd plugged that rabid dog—what the hell was its name?—in that last book he'd ever read for school. It was amazing—absolute bullshot! And Hop rubbing out Pit Bull was going to bollix up the works but good for the pigs. Throw them completely off their trough. Just at the right time, too. Maybe Hop'd be ejected by that fat-assed chief hog. But that wouldn't do! Hop *had* to be in the game right up 'til the buzzer! Had to be a player 'til the final whistle blew him away!

But as the pigs converged on the body, the Hoopmeister was still on the porch, speaking to that squat, swarthy doofus in black, the Walkers' private pig. Taking something from him. Turning him. This high-angle helicopter shot didn't cut it. Not in all this rain. Where the hell were the minicams? You couldn't tell exactly what was happening. You needed close-ups, goddamn it! But it looked like maybe Monique-the-Media-Babe's personal goon was the shooter. That goddamned wop flunky of hers was the fucking triggerman. It was all too much! Too far out! And it meant the Hoopmeister'd stay in the game. Hop'd be there for the final buzzer! There'd still be time to mess with his mind. Time to fake the jock off the Hoopmeister. Press and trap him! Take his head out of the game 'til the final surprise *really* did the job!

Pit Bull was supposed to've distracted everybody else. Wrecked everybody else's concentration—not his! The chase, the slick roads, the fishtailing, even the gate crashing—it was all great stuff. And he hadn't even considered this particular climax. Pit Bull snapping his chain permanently! That was the thing about live television. Sometimes the show turned out even more fabulously, even more marvelously than you planned or expected. Or even dreamed possible!

He removed his glasses, wiped his face with the front of his T-shirt, swigged some Mountain Dew, and loosed a long, cascading belch. Squinting up, he saw that a minicam was finally hot, shooting across the lawn. He breathed on his glasses, twisted his T-shirt to find a dry spot, cleaned the lenses, and put his glasses back on. There was Hop in his silly slicker handing over custody of Monique's hitman to one of the uniforms. Paramedics sloshed by them toward the Pit Bull. The body was barely visible among the legs of the pigs and vultures. Everybody but Hop was getting drenched to the bone, but no one seemed to notice.

He couldn't pull himself away from the show! He could watch it all night, he really could, but there was too much— more jingles, additional directives, the Big Surprise—far too much to do. This Pit Bullian media extravaganza had made him fall behind his *revised* schedule. It'd be well past dawn before he tied up the last of the loose ends. He gulped the rest of the Mountain Dew, shivered as the liquid rose in his throat, and gazed at his creations lined on the counter. The *Mayflower* was all ready for her maiden voyage! And this little flotilla was certainly ready, too—his *Nina*, *Pinta*, and *Santa Maria*! But he had so many other things to do before he could set them sailing. Well, at least he didn't have to listen to that little Bitch's yapping! That was one problem he'd taken care of expediently—if not elegantly. The kid, her now silent presence, still nagged him, though. Why the hell did she have to be so much like Sarah? She kept complicating everything, and thinking about her was the last thing he needed at the moment. He'd already decided her fate, hadn't he? It was a done deal. Wasn't it?

And what was this on the Videot Box now? The camera zooming in. Focusing. What a shot! A perfect shot! A definite keeper! There, standing above the melee, framed by the mansion's front entrance, back-lit by the silver-white walls and the scintillating chandelier was Monique-the-Media-Babe herself, gnawing on her knuckle as though she actually cared. The hulking Skywalker loomed on her right, and Bertie the Bagel slouched on her left. And there she stood regally surveying the bedlam, light coruscating around her, the Media Queen! The center of the universe he'd set in motion!

chapter 44

As rain beat on the windows at 9:20 P.M., Hopkins sat at the computer in Chief Mancini's office. He'd been called there fifteen minutes earlier when Paul Kim, monitoring the system, had received the message, **Hop, we gotta chat. Stand by. Right away!** Hopkins had replied, **Okay, we'll talk,** but there had been no further messages. The storm closed the room in, and, despite the thoughts whirling in his mind, he felt drained. He had seen death often enough during investigations, but the killing of Jack Bollinger still disturbed him. He hadn't liked the man, but he would never have wished him dead. And he had a sense that the killing had been, at least in part, his fault. It was as though the death had been orchestrated, and he, Hopkins, had been one of the primary instruments.

Anthony Ignacio was downstairs being processed, but Hopkins wasn't sure he would even be indicted. And there was no way he would ever be convicted of anything. Bollinger had clearly been the aggressor, and he had definitely been pulling an object from his trenchcoat pocket. It had only been a remote microphone, but Ignacio could not have known that. Indeed, Ignacio's lawyers would likely hammer the point that Ignacio had acted primarily to save Hopkins' life—the life of a police officer who had failed to react quickly to a possible threat of deadly force.

"You're sure he's still here?" Hopkins asked Paul Kim, who stood by the printer.

Kim blinked at the printout, took off his glasses, and fidgeted with the wire frames. "His tracks are still here," he said, "and he's always covered them before."

Time was running out, and Hopkins felt stymied again, frustrated by having to wait for Saville to make the next move. Staring at the screen, he realized that perhaps Adelman was right: he had nothing. Describing the perpetrator as a single white male, approaching middle age, living alone somewhere in the Chicago area, was ludicrously vague. Asking the public to report any suspicious single white male neighbors would produce not only thousands of irrelevant leads but a glut of ill-will. And even the more specific description of the misshapen hand would cause ire among the disabled and, in any case, help little, especially if Saville routinely disguised it as he had invariably disguised his other features when out in public.

Hopkins rolled his neck. He guessed that Saville was located close by, perhaps even in North Ridge, but the trails he'd left twice led into Chicago. And there was no guarantee, once the ransom was paid, that Saville would stay in the country, much less in the immediate area. He had obviously invested a lot of money, time, and energy in his so-called command center. But sticking around was risky, even stupid. And Saville, however sick he might be, was not stupid. Hopkins wondered if another investigator might have developed a sort of respect for Saville. He had not—not even a grudging respect. Saville had kidnapped and maimed a child. He'd murdered Cameron Bransfield and indirectly, if not directly, caused Bollinger's death. And he'd unceasingly manipulated Bollinger—and the rest of the media swarm, for that matter. Hopkins hadn't yet received a copy from WLN TV News of the e-mail message, but Saville must have told Bollinger about the ignition key, must have implicitly invited him to make a break in the Jeep. Saving Tonya Walker's life was paramount, but it wasn't enough. Saville had to be stopped. If he succeeded here, he wouldn't simply slink off forever into hyperspace. With forty-eight million dollars, he'd concoct some even more diabolic outrage.

The phone rang, startling Kim, who put his glasses back on before answering it. He listened for a moment, passed the receiver to Hopkins without a word, and stepped back by the printer again.

"Hoop," Ross said, "Adelman's on the line demanding to speak to you immediately."

"Okay," Hopkins answered. "Put him through." He listened to the line click twice.

"Tom," Adelman asked, "where the hell is Henderson?"

"At city hall conducting the evening media briefing," Hopkins answered. He swiveled in the chair so that he could keep his eye on the screen.

"Shit. That lunatic just sent four pages of directions. Single-spaced. Almost half an hour late. He wants three million deposited in each of sixteen banks beginning in the Far East and ending in Switzerland. And I'm supposed to wait for a confirmation each time. It'll take hours."

Hopkins heard Walker's voice in the background, low and fierce, shouting, "So what if it takes the whole night. Just do it, Bert. Pay the money and get Tonya back!"

Hopkins gazed over at the photographs on the wall. "It's Mr. Walker's call," he said flatly.

"I've got to talk to Henderson," Adelman said, his tone almost petulant. "The lunatic's threatening to put Tonya's head on a stick if *anything* goes wrong."

"Henderson'll be back after the briefing, Mr. Adelman."

"Have Henderson call me as soon as he returns," Adelman said before cutting off the call.

Hopkins hung up the phone, glanced at his watch, and then looked over at the dark twisting shadows of the rain-swept branches outside the windows. Waiting, doing nothing, was no longer an option. And goading Saville might cause him to make a mistake—or at least break his concentration. He cracked his knuckles and typed, **James Robert Saville, talk to me now. Or never.** As he stared into the night, nothing happened. The streaks on the panes were indecipherable runes; the waving branches provided no sign or signal, and the wind whispered no wisdom. Just as he pushed back the chair, the chat box filled—a torrent of words. **Never give me orders, Hop! I'm not some dipshit flunky you can boss around. And so fucking what if you know my name! Knowing it won't do shit, Hop! You're just like the rest. Trying to dick me around. Pretending all you care about is the kid. You're out of your league, Hop! Hopelessly outclassed! So shut the fuck up, and I'll tell you what to do when I'm ready!**

Moving closer to Hopkins, Kim stared at the screen. "Commander, ah, you . . . ," he began, but then stopped himself.

Call it off, Jimmy, Hopkins typed. **We'll get you help.**

Never call me Jimmy. It's James. James Robert. And I don't need help. Never have. You're the one that needs help, Hop! I don't need anybody. Not you or the Media Queen or J.P. or anybody!

Hopkins sat back and took a deep breath. "Well," he said to Kim, "you were right. And now we at least know he's hacked the FBI files, too." He leaned forward again and typed, **Let Tonya go, James!**

The kid?!? You think that's what this is about?!? What is it about, James? Hopkins typed.

"Revolution 9" snaked through Saville's headphones as he wiped the sweat from his face with his sleeve. He didn't have time for this. Felt sick again, like he might ralph all over the laptop. Hop knowing his name perturbed him—more, much more, than it should! He was inviolable, insuperable, but it still galled him. Hop had gotten to J.P., and the stoolie had, predictably, squealed—spouted straightaway! Life was a night flight—always. And you always flew solo. You alone were out there, beyond their realm, surfing beyond the serfs' comprehension. **You're too fucking dumb to get it, Hop!** he keyboarded. **Once a dumb jock, always a dumb jock. Wake up and smell the garbage, you stupid moron!**

Just as he finished, the screen read, **Try me. Explain it, James. You're the one that wanted to chat.**

Saville removed his glasses and wiped his eyes. Not chat. *Chat* wasn't the word. Instruct. Edify. Could Hop get it? No. Not a chance. Hop was a Terradicktal, turf-bound like all the rest. Bogged. Rooted in mire. Hop knew nothing of flight, of soaring far above the others! Of circumnavigating the globe in seconds! This was the stuff of legends! A watershed. A reconfiguration. A paradigm shift. Blazing trails—cyberpaths! The Terradicktals would never understand that all history would turn on this moment—B.S., Before Saville, and A.S. The media moguls were the most moronic mopes of all because they actually thought they got it. But they could only follow the path. They flamed, but never blazed! And he wasn't going to give the morons a map, provide them with a manifesto. No, they'd have to figure out for themselves, *if* they could, that all those fossilized ideas—land and race and class and beauty and athleticism and education and tradition—were meaningless in the new cyber-order. Indeed, there really was no new order at all, just wondrous chaos, awesome anarchy. And, irony of ironies, this monster that slouched to Bethlehem and back in a blink, was the true democracy, the real meritocracy, that all those morons had always been espousing. The brass ring was right there for anyone bright enough to grab it.

Hop was still feebly dribbling on the screen so Saville fumbled for his glasses and read, **Adelman's transferring the money. Let the girl go, James!**

The money? As if that was it! But it did indeed demonstrate that he'd made his mark, all right. No question about it. The legend of James Robert Saville was flashing across the land. Blazing radiantly! Absolutely incandescent! And it'd burn on, fueled by all that loot! The fucking Feds would make their lame attempts to freeze the accounts the ransom was being poured into. But with some quick prestidigitation, he'd launder the lucre. Send the scratch shuttling through the system 'til it settled, safe and secure—a cool mil in the coffers of forty-eight antigovernment activist outfits from the Ku Klux Klan to Greenpeace. Indeed, his Robin Hood machinations were undeniably elegant. He'd never need the shekels—siphoning bits of bread from banks galore was a cinch—but the forty-eight mil was a way of keeping score that even the government bozos could comprehend. And it was, naturally, the most impressive score ever. The Feds would eventually trace the loot, of course, but they'd have a hilariously hellacious time dealing with those activist psychos. It didn't matter whether they shaved their heads and sported silly mustaches or saved cetaceans, they all itched for some serious scratch. And he could count on those media morons, those pestilent peckers everywhere, to come great electronic gobs over all this moolah hoopla!

All he had to do was keep his focus and bench the Hoopmeister. **I've got promises to keep,** he keyboarded, **and miles**

to go before you sleep. Everything had been set up earlier, of course, but there was still so much to do. And there wasn't time for any systems checks. Not that he needed them. The bombs were virtually set, and these first moves were child's play; the feints and the finesse came later. He gazed up at the photo he'd posterized below the hanging monitor and the simple, sublimely scrawled message. On the phones, John and the lads were segueing into "Good Night." How appropos! **Night, night, Hop!** he keyboarded. **Say bye-bye to the little lady for me!**

chapter 45

Pushing the chair back from the computer, Hopkins said, "He's gone."

Kim stared at the computer for a moment and said, "Commander, he's ah, not covering his tracks."

"He's still gone. He knows it won't do us any good now." Hopkins shook his head. "Print out that chat box, Paul. I need to look over exactly what the guy said."

As Kim came over to the computer, Hopkins stood and stretched. His whole body ached, the stiffness running deep. "Keep an eye on things," he said, "but I don't think he'll be back." The first page of their conversation slipped out of the printer. "I'm going to make sure Dave's got the SWAT team . . ."

"Oh, no!" Kim interrupted. He began striking the keyboard. "Something's not . . . this isn't, ah . . ."

The lights flickered and went out.

"Damn storm," Hopkins grumbled. In the darkness, he

felt his way around the desk and past the Windsor chairs. He crossed the office, found the door, and opened it just as the auxiliary generator kicked in and the safety lights in the hallway went on.

Kim, barely visible in the scant light in the office, was still leaning over the keyboard. "Commander," he said over his shoulder, "the computer went out first, *before* the lights."

Hopkins stood half in the office, his hand still on the door handle. "What?" he asked. "What do you mean, Paul?"

Kim hurried toward him. "The server crashed!" he said, his voice cracking. He passed Hopkins and began trotting down the hall toward the officers and support staff milling outside the records office. "The whole system's crashed!"

Hopkins stood alone in the doorway, gazing first at the computer in the half-lit office and then at the darker windows.

"Hoop," Ross said as she jogged toward him carrying two flashlights, "the phones are dead."

"That son of a bitch," Hopkins muttered. "Paul thinks the server crashed, too—before we lost power."

"Jesus," she said, handing him one of the flashlights. "The electrical, the phones, and the computers." She looked up at Hopkins, but in the dimness the light was gone from her eyes. "Saville?"

"That bastard's had us set up all along." Hopkins shook his head to clear it. "Is Mancini back from city hall?"

"Not yet."

He flicked on the flashlight, strode over to the printer, and snatched the sheet that had already printed. Holding the flashlight under his arm, he folded the paper and stuffed it into his pocket. As he came back toward her, he said, "Let's see what we can do about getting this place running again." He took hold of her arm. "Meghan," he murmured, "his last words to me were to say good-bye to the little lady."

They stood in silence for a moment before she said, "I was already on my way to see you when all this . . ." She glanced along the hallway. "I've got to talk to you about . . . the messages . . . the ones on the computer."

"Concerning my little helper?"

She nodded again. "He didn't mean me," she said with a conviction that surprised him. "I got tapes of your first press briefing and of Bollinger's arrest."

McGinty's description of Saville's sister flashed through his mind. "Cari?" he asked.

"She's in both."

He stepped back, leaned against the door jamb, rubbed his face, and took a deep breath. "Jesus," he whispered, shaking his head and exhaling slowly. He slammed the heel of his hand hard against the wall, looked at Ross, and said, "I've got to get over there."

She put her hand on his shoulder. "I've already asked the Chief to assign a surveillance team to the house. And I contacted your ex. Told her protecting the lead investigator's family was routine in cases like this. I'm not sure she bought it."

Hopkins shook his head. "She knows better."

Ross lifted her hand and brushed back her hair. "You handle the rescue and the Walkers, Hoop," she said. "I'll spend the night with Cari."

Shortly after midnight, Hopkins stopped at the Walker mansion. The problems at the North Ridge Police Department had all been computer glitches caused, as far as Paul Kim could determine, by logic bombs planted not only in the police department's computer system but at Ameritech and Commonwealth Edison. Auxiliary power and cellular phones were being used, but Kim could do nothing to get the computer back on line—and the problems had hampered the final planning of the rescue operation.

Jones-Walker stood at the cooking island in the kitchen. The oven's exhaust fan sucked away the smoke from her cigarette. Wearing a blue and gray warm-up suit, Walker leaned against the French doors. Outside, the rain had eased, but the wind still gusted from the northeast, and he gazed through the drizzle at the swaying oaks and elms.

Hopkins wondered what was going through their minds after witnessing the shooting on their doorstep. "The rescue team's almost ready," he said. "As soon as there's a message from Saville or a break of some kind, we'll . . ."

"You supposedly understand this guy," Jones-Walker said, "why hasn't he contacted us?" Her hand quivering, she tapped the ash from her cigarette. "What the hell is going on?"

"I'm not sure," Hopkins answered. "He's probably waiting for Adelman to finish the transfers. And I doubt, Mrs. Walker, that anyone really understands him." He was beginning to sweat in the wool pullover he had put on before leaving the police department. Saville had always been punctual, and even his twenty-minute tardiness with the ransom directions worried him. "Mr. Adelman's completing the transactions now?" he asked.

"From his office downtown." As Jones-Walker answered, she blew smoke at the exhaust vent. "He'll call us here and Henderson at city hall when he's done."

"Maybe something's thrown the guy off," Walker said, still looking out at the slackening storm.

"Maybe," Hopkins answered. "I don't know. Bollinger's death or . . ."

"Or he's learned you know his identity?" Jones-Walker asked.

Hopkins nodded. "He knows," Hopkins said, "but he also knows it won't help us any at this point."

Walker turned and stepped away from the French doors. "What does this mean for Tonya?" he asked. "What does it do?"

Hopkins looked into Walker's face, which betrayed both fear and anger. "Truthfully," he said, "it can't help the situation. It may not hurt, but it won't help."

chapter 46

At 1:40 A.M., Hopkins drove past the ten
television vans parked across from North Ridge City Hall. Six
of the vans had their signal processors raised, and four reporters were broadcasting live in front of the massive four-
story building despite the hour. He turned the corner and,
after being waved through the police barricade, pulled into
the parking lot behind the building. Rescue vehicles, doors
open and engines running, lined the curb. After passing the
convoy—a dozen police cars, various vans, and two ambulances—he parked the Taurus in a fifteen-minute space near
the building's back entrance, got out, and stretched. A mixture
of fatigue and adrenalin made him lightheaded; his feet did not
quite feel as though they were touching ground.

The night air was dank and the pavement wet, but a pale
shrouded moon shone between breaking clouds. The helicopters' incessant beating was faint, and, though there were
well over a hundred people in the lot, they were subdued, al-

most quiet. Most of the FBI agents, NRPD officers, Illinois
state policemen, paramedics, and technicians stood silently by
their vehicles or spoke in small groups in low voices. The
sheer bulk of the stone and red brick city hall shielded them
from the television cameras out front. Erected a century before as a Jesuit prep school, the building had been renovated
in the 1970s when the city council, unable to raze the land-
mark after the school had closed, had taken it over in an attempt to centralize most of the town's services.

As Hopkins made his way toward the head of the convoy,
Milan Durovic, the North Suburban canine officer, accosted
him. A short, broad-shouldered man with a square face, he
held a tawny, droopy-eared bloodhound and a black Labrador
retriever on retractable leashes. "Any news, Hoop?" he asked.

Hopkins shook his head. "Not yet."

Durovic smiled broadly, baring his teeth. "You get us close,
Hoop," Durovic said, "and Sherlock'll find the girl." Nodding to the Labrador whose eyes looked almost red in the lot's
mercury vapor lights, he added, "And Joe Louis'll tell us if
there's any explosives."

David Banks, reviewing procedures with his SWAT team,
waved to Hopkins but didn't pause in his instructions. Brian
Murphy, the bomb disposal officer, sat alone on the back
fender of his van, hunched forward, an elbow on his knee.
"You all set, Murph?" Hopkins asked as he passed him.

Murphy tossed away the cigarette he'd been smoking,
stood, ground out the butt with his boot, and answered,
"Ready to go, Hoop."

When Hopkins approached the lead vehicle, a white, unmarked Caprice, Carl Henderson stepped away from his FBI
team and asked, "How're the Walkers doing?"

"On edge, but holding up okay," Hopkins answered. "Anything from Adelman yet?"

272 ~ j a y a m b e r g

"Talked to him ten minutes ago." Henderson's brown suit was wrinkled, his collar unbuttoned, and his striped tie loosened. "He said he's still got four more deposits to make."

"Looks like you're ready to roll."

"Have been . . ." Henderson switched the thick *Chicago and Vicinity Street Finder* from his left to his right hand and glanced at his watch. "For more than an hour. The waiting's starting to get to some of my guys."

Hopkins looked back along the line of vehicles. "I'll bet," he said.

"Hoop!" Meghan Ross called from the cement steps by the building's side entrance.

"Be back in a second, Carl," Hopkins said. When he met Ross at the bottom step, he asked, "Where's Cari?" After leaving the Walkers forty minutes earlier, he had spoken to both Ross and his daughter on the cellular phone he'd been issued after the shutdowns at the police station.

Ross pulled up the collar of her NRPD windbreaker and folded her arms in front of her. "Your, ex, uh, kicked me out."

"What?" Hopkins rubbed his eye.

"Right after you called, Cari and I were in the family room talking and watching TV with the sound off." She gazed at the group of FBI agents by the white Caprice and then looked Hopkins in the eye. "She told me I wasn't needed. That she couldn't sleep with all the commotion. With me in the house."

"Shit," Hopkins muttered. "That . . . I better get . . ."

Ross took hold of his elbow as he turned. "Hoop," she said, "we've got the place covered. The Chief's got Aaron Smith out front and Larry Hedlund in the alley."

"Hoop," Henderson shouted, "got a question for you over here."

Ross held Hopkins' gaze. "It's going to be all right."

"Yeah." He kicked a damp twig that had blown against the

bottom step during the storm. "Okay." Looking at her again, he asked, "Where the hell is Mancini, anyway?"

"Back at the station." Ross smiled ironically at Hopkins. "I think he's more comfortable trying to get the system back on line than he is here."

"You're probably right," Hopkins said, scuffing the sole of his shoe against the step. "Jesus, I hate this waiting." He put his hands in his pants pockets. "And I'd feel a hell of a lot better if you were with Cari."

"Hoop!" Henderson yelled again.

Ross squeezed his elbow. "I'll go back in the morning," she said. "It'll be okay."

"Good. Thanks." He gazed up at the clouds skimming above the building. "Just the same, I think I'll swing by there after I find out what Henderson wants."

chapter 47

When the cellular phone rang, Hopkins started awake. He had been dreaming of returning to the court after a time-out. His team was trailing by a point with four seconds remaining in a championship game in a gym filled with his opponents' maniacal fans. His teammates were shouting to him, spurring him on. He knew the play had been designed to get him the ball, but he wasn't sure what to do, what pick to cut off of, where to square up to take the shot.

Disoriented, he gazed out of the fishbowl. The office swayed for a moment. Realizing where he was, he placed his hands on his desk to settle himself. He was sweating, his back and neck itched from the wool pullover, and his right wrist was numb where his head had rested on it. He wiped sleep from his eyes and looked at his watch. It was 6:15 A.M.

He shut his eyes for a second before picking up the phone. During the night, he had twice driven by his wife's house, but neither time had the two officers assigned to surveillance noticed anything even remotely suspicious. Adelman had re-

portedly finished the transfers at 3:45 A.M., but there had been
no response from Saville. The more time had passed, the more
apprehensive Hopkins had become. He had been sure Saville
would send a message by dawn, but the sun was already well
up. Saville had to have been doing something, but he'd had no
idea what. He'd returned to the station at 5:30 partly to get an
update on the situation there but mostly because he could no
longer stand the inactivity at city hall or the ominous quiet
outside his family's house. At 6:05 he'd come into the fishbowl to get a file, sat down for just a moment—and then the
phone had rung him awake.

"Hopkins," he said into the receiver.

"Hop?"

Hopkins recognized J.P. McGinty's soft, quiet voice. Massaging the back of his neck, he answered, "Yes, J.P. What is it?"

"I've been trying to reach you for hours," McGinty said
breathlessly, as though he had been rushing somewhere. "That
number you gave me was out of order. I finally turned on the
TV. Found out your systems had crashed. For a long time, I
couldn't even get through on that 800 number for reporting
information related to the case." He paused, finally taking a
breath. "Eventually I spoke to a woman who seemed to know
you. She gave me this number."

Hopkins stood up and rolled his shoulders to alleviate the
stiffness. "Yes, J.P.," he repeated. "You have information?"

"I don't know," McGinty answered, his voice a whisper.
"I'm not sure. Remember I told you James always had secrets,
even as a kid. But he always gave hints you were supposed to
get if you paid real close attention to him. He always thought
nobody paid any attention to him."

Hopkins rubbed his eyes again. He wanted to shout *Get to
the point*, but he slumped back into his chair and opened the
drawer where he kept a plastic bottle of ibuprofen.

"Well, anyway," McGinty continued, "when I got home I

went through all James' old messages. I've kept a file, a morgue, of all the e-mail anybody's ever sent me. I'd gotten more mail from him than I'd remembered. It took hours."

Hopkins opened the bottle and shook out three caplets.

"And twice when James was talking about setting up his command center, he made a point of mentioning that it was a dump. One time he said, and these are his words, *I'm going to transform a true dump into a techie Taj Mahal.*"

Hopkins dropped the open bottle and caplets onto his desk. Standing again, he yanked the sheet of paper from his pocket.

"I don't know exactly what he was referring to," McGinty went on. "But the fact that he mentioned it twice may help you."

Hopkins read through the first page of the print out, which ended, **Once a dumb jock, always a dumb jock. Wake** . . . He felt an eerie certainty settling over him again. "It does," he said. "Thanks, J.P. You're a lifesaver."

"You think it'll help?" McGinty asked.

"Yes. Thanks, J.P.," Hopkins repeated, already hustling from the fishbowl. "You've been a terrific help!"

chapter 48

The wind rustled the tops of the trees as Hopkins drove through Deerbrook, the town in which both he and James Robert Saville had grown up. The morning sky was washed clean after the storm, but twigs and wet leaves littered the roadway. He had checked in with Henderson at North Ridge City Hall but hadn't told him or anyone else that he was following another of his hunches. When he arrived at the sprawling yellow brick and cement Active Disposal Corporation headquarters and yard, the sun was sparking the roof of the three-story garage and maintenance building. As he parked the Taurus in front of the main entrance, an old man in a baggy gray uniform was swinging back the heavy iron gate. Hopkins leapt out onto the pavement, still damp from the rain. The breeze did little to alleviate the putrid stench of soggy garbage. The roar of the diesel engines filled the air as the first of the garbage trucks headed toward the gate.

"Hey! Whatchu doin'?" the old man hollered.

As he jogged toward the man, Hopkins flipped his wallet

open to display his badge. "Don't let any of those trucks leave," he shouted.

"What's happenin'?" the old man asked. His beard was grizzled, and his two upper front teeth were missing. "My boss, he ain't gonna . . ."

Hopkins stepped past him and held up his arm to halt the approaching garbage truck. "I said, stop these damn trucks from leaving," he shouted at the old man. "Now!" He surveyed the area. The Active Disposal Corporation complex formed an **L** around the bend in the road. Offices comprised the short side of the **L**, and the maintenance building and garage formed the long side. A parking lot was across the street from the offices, and three wood-frame bungalows and an overgrown vacant lot stood across from the garage and maintenance building.

As Hopkins' cellular phone rang, a burly man in a gray uniform with the sleeves rolled up to reveal his biceps plodded over and growled, "What the hell d'ya think you're doin'?" The name VINCE and the word SUPERVISOR were stitched above his shirt pocket.

Flashing his badge, Hopkins answered the phone. He then slid the wallet back into his pocket and cupped his free hand over his other ear so he could hear above the diesels' engines.

"We just got a fax, Hoop, like a poem or something," Sky Walker said. "It's to Bert, but he's still not back."

"What's it say?" Hopkins asked, pressing his hand harder over his ear.

"Thanks so much, sir, Bagel Bert," Walker read,

"Bankruptcy and prison's bound to hurt.

"If you want to find . . ." He hesitated for a moment before continuing.

". . . the little Bitch,

"Check the garbage that you pitch.

"Follow that old rumbling truck,

"And all you'll need's a stroke of luck.

"When you get there with the Walkers,

"You'll attract a mob of gawkers.

"Do it smart, and do it fast,

"Or finding her will be a blast!" When he finished, Walker added, "It doesn't make any . . ."

"Yes it does," Hopkins shouted into the phone. The message had been sent to Adelman, but it was really for him. "He's sending us to the ADC yard."

"What?"

"No time to explain. Come to the Active Disposal Corp yard in Deerbrook." While the old man and the heavyset supervisor stared at him, he flipped the phone shut, flipped it open again, and tapped out the rescue team's emergency number.

"Hey, you," the supervisor grumbled, "you better tell me *now* why the hell you're holdin' up my trucks."

As soon as Henderson came on the line, Hopkins said, "Carl, we've got contact." He was almost shouting, but his voice was slow and calm. "It's a go. Get the rescue and SWAT teams over to the Active Disposal Corporation headquarters in Deerbrook. I'm already there. It looks like we're dealing with another bomb."

"A bomb? Here?" the supervisor asked. "What the fuckin' fuck?"

Hopkins closed the phone and, turning to answer the supervisor, noticed a new beige Chevrolet backing out of the driveway of the bungalow on the left, closest to the vacant lot. Two fishing poles were in the car's back seat, and the elderly, bearded man hunched at the wheel wore a floppy fishing hat low over his eyes.

"What's this shit about a fuckin' bomb?" the supervisor snarled. The old man in the baggy uniform stepped backward and began to sidle away toward the street.

Hopkins glanced at the bungalow for a second. It was a dilapidated one-story structure with a sagging roof. The aluminum siding was dirty; a yellowed shade covered the picture window to the left of the front door. The yard was untended, and a teeming jungle of unpruned bushes separated the house from the neighbor's. The garage, connected to the house by an enclosed breezeway, was new, as was a tall stockade fence that blocked a view of the house from the parking lot.

"I said, what's . . ." The supervisor jabbed Hopkins' shoulder with his thick index finger.

Hopkins brushed the man's hand away and looked again at the beige Chevrolet braking for the stop sign at the corner. "Jesus, shit!" he muttered, his heart racing.

The moment Hopkins began to run, the Chevrolet fishtailed around the corner and sped away. "Halt!" he shouted as, still sprinting, he pulled the .38 revolver from the holster clipped to his belt. By the time he reached the stop sign, the car was a block and a half away. He leveled the .38 but, knowing it was useless at that range, did not fire. "Goddamn it!" he swore at himself. "Goddamn it!"

He raced back to the Taurus, dropped the cellular phone on the seat, grabbed the radio, and yelled, "APB, Walker suspect, beige late-model Chevrolet, leaving Active Disposal Corp area in Deerbrook at high speed." He slapped the .38's butt against the steering wheel. "Repeat, APB, Walker suspect, beige Chevrolet, Deerbrook." He started the Taurus, skidded on the wet pavement, floored it past the parking lot up the street to the intersection, ran the stop sign, and jammed on the brakes. There was no car in sight in any direction.

chapter 49

Lights flashing but their sirens silent, the police vehicles rounded the corner and headed toward the ADC complex. Stepping out of the lead vehicle before it came to a complete stop, Henderson wore body armor over his suit and carried a helmet with a clear visor under his arm and a radio in his hand. "What've we got?" he asked Hopkins, who paced by the Taurus he'd again parked near the ADC main gate.

"In there." Hopkins pointed at the bungalow. "And there's a bomb set to detonate if we don't find her soon. But, be careful. His message was blatant this time. He *wants* us here."

"Cordon off both blocks," Henderson shouted to four NRPD officers crossing the drive. "Keep the media and any other gapers beyond the intersections." He turned back to Hopkins. "There's no report at all on the Chevy you saw. It's like it vaporized, vanished in space. You sure it was the perp?"

"Absolutely," Hopkins answered. "No old-timer'd go

perch fishing right after a Northeaster. And the guy took off as soon as I spotted him."

Banks and his eight-man SWAT team stood poised between the ambulances and the bomb-disposal van where Brian Murphy was unloading equipment.

Henderson raised his radio, then paused, staring at Hopkins. "What were you doing *already* here?" he asked.

Shrugging, Hopkins scratched his nose. "Saville mentioned garbage to me. And in his e-mail to McGinty a couple of years ago, he referred to a dump."

Henderson gazed at Hopkins for a moment before nodding. "The money's gone," he said. "All of it. We froze the accounts as soon as we got the listings from your buddy, Bert. But Saville somehow instantly transferred the money." Shaking his head, he smiled wryly. "We did pick up Adelman, though. He siphoned off an additional three million over and above the ransom demand, and we got him in the executive lounge at O'Hare's international terminal." As he moved off to direct the FBI agents and NRPD officers surrounding the bungalow, he turned and added, "The asshole had himself booked to Buenos Aires."

While Hopkins ordered all the ADC employees to stay behind the main gate, Henderson shouted for Durovic to bring over the dogs. A television news helicopter arrived as Chief Mancini's car pulled up. The helicopter hovered so low that the noise of its rotor blades drowned out most of what Hopkins tried to tell Mancini. The police chief got on his carphone and threatened the TV station, and the helicopter backed off and away just as a second helicopter flew low overhead. The TV vans lined the street beyond the police cordons, and the television reporters focused their minicams on the red Jeep Grand Cherokee that passed them and headed toward the ADC entrance. The Jeep parked near Hopkins' car, but the passengers stayed inside behind the tinted windows.

The ADC employees milled in the maintenance yard, pointing at the Jeep and straining to see what was going on across the street. The two dogs, seemingly confused by the noise and the odor of rancid garbage, circled Durovic yapping at each other.

Banks finished deploying the SWAT team around the bungalow. Brian Murphy slammed the bomb van's doors shut and followed Durovic, his assistant, and the two dogs across the street. Hopkins put on body armor and crossed the street with Henderson. Overhead, three television news helicopters circled like buzzards. Henderson spoke to Banks, who then signaled his team. They closed in quickly and, wary of a bomb at the front door, approached the windows, covering each other and moving stealthily along the walls of the house. Communicating with Henderson through the radios clipped to their black uniforms, the SWAT team positioned themselves for the attack. Then, on a signal from Banks, the officer crouching on the front porch sprang through the picture window into the house. Simultaneously, two other officers rolled through side windows. Banks disappeared around the back of the house.

Nothing happened for the next thirty seconds.

Then Henderson's radio crackled, "All clear. First floor secure." The front door swung open, and Banks waved them in. Hopkins and Henderson followed Murphy up the creaking front steps and into the house. Glass fragments were scattered across the bare hardwood floor of the large front room. Henderson and Murphy rushed toward the back of the house where the dogs had begun baying, but Hopkins lingered for a moment in the living room. All four walls were lined with cinderblock and unfinished pine plank shelving filled with what looked like more than a thousand paperback books neatly arranged by category. Most were science fiction and thrillers, but a few were about subatomic physics and cosmology. The room was devoid of furniture except for a forest green Laz-E-Boy reclining chair and a floor lamp in the corner. A copy of *Stranger in a Strange Land* lay on the arm of the Laz-E-Boy. Four black corner-mount Bang & Olafson speakers hung near the ceiling.

Hopkins entered the dining room, where shattered glass was strewn below the thick maroon drapes. A card table and one chair stood in the center of the room on an old frayed Oriental rug. No pictures hung on the walls, but two more speakers were suspended near the ceiling. The small bedroom off the dining room was littered with glass shards. The only thing on any of the walls was a single black-and-white poster of John Lennon gazing from behind his rimless granny glasses. Sweatshirts, shirts, bluejeans, and corduroys hung in a neat row in the closet. Bins on the overhead shelf held sleeveless T-shirts, underwear, and socks. There were no shoes at all.

Henderson leaned in the door, glanced at the poster and said, "Another one of Mr. Lennon's well-adjusted fans, huh?" He gestured with his radio. "*Both* dogs are going berserk back in the kitchen."

The kitchen was so clean and bare that it looked like it might never have been used. The counters were completely empty; there were no utensils or dishes or pans visible anywhere. Henderson stopped by a closed door. Across the kitchen near the sink, the house's back door was open to the enclosed breezeway leading to the garage.

Durovic had the bloodhound by its collar, holding it back as it yapped at the closed door. "Hoop," he said, "Sherlock's telling us the girl's here."

"Or, at least, been here," Henderson said.

Durovic nodded toward the retriever set at point and added, "And Joe Louis, he says we got us a bomb."

"Okay," Hopkins said. He glanced at Henderson. "It's your call."

"You can take those dogs out of here now," the FBI agent said over the barking. He turned and asked, "Murphy, what do you think?"

Brian Murphy stepped past the dogs. "If it's anything like the device the guy used in Chicago, I'll have it disarmed in two minutes. He squared his shoulders, tapped the door with his knuckles, and inspected the two hinges. "Maybe less."

Henderson turned his back to the door. "Everybody out," he said. "It's all yours, Murphy."

Back outside, Hopkins updated Chief Mancini and then crossed over to the Grand Cherokee. As he reached the driver's door, the window slid down. Walker wore wraparound sunglasses and a wide brimmed hat. Jones-Walker sat in the passenger seat rolling an unlit cigarette between her trembling forefinger and thumb and staring through the windshield. "The dogs picked up Tonya's scent in the garage and house," he said. "But the door's booby-trapped. There's an explosive device of some sort behind the basement door."

Walker nodded.

"How much longer?" Jones-Walker asked. She looked at Hopkins, her eyes bleary, the veneer of cold toughness finally gone completely.

"A few minutes," he answered. "Just a few minutes."

"You're sure she's there?" she asked, again staring out the windshield.

"I'm sure she's been there. And I can't see why he'd move her."

Jones-Walker nodded slowly, her attempt to smile dissolving in tears.

Almost twenty minutes passed before Murphy finally radioed the all-clear. As Meghan Ross drove the department psychologist up the street in the black Nissan, Henderson led

Hopkins back into the house. The basement door was open, and wires leading out of a device covered with duct tape had been snipped. A section of the door Murphy had cut away with a cordless saber saw lay on the floor tiles.

Murphy waved toward the stairs leading to the basement. "Follow me," he said. As he started down the carpeted steps, he added, "The guy tried to get cute. Set a second device on the door down here. Much more sophisticated. But I got it." He flipped the light switch at the bottom of the stairs. "He may be some sort of computer guru, but he's a minor-league bomber."

As Henderson stepped under the dismantled device taped above the doorway, he murmured, "His command center."

"The goddamned command center," Hopkins repeated as he entered the all-white fourteen-by-eighteen-foot room. The console with its wheeled armchair and incredible array of electronic equipment ran along the wall to his left. To his right, hats, beards, glasses, and other disguises lay on a series of white prefab shelves next to the costumes hanging trimly from a rack.

"She must be in there," Henderson said, nodding toward the door in the opposite wall.

As Murphy crossed the room, Henderson stopped and pointed to a photocopied senior portrait of Cari Hopkins taped to the wall above the computer screen. The caption, scrawled in black marker, read, SHE LOSES, TOO. SAY, BYE-BYE, HOP! The television suspended from the ceiling above the photo was turned on without sound. The image jiggling on the screen showed an aerial view of the house they were in.

"Oh, God!" Hopkins muttered as he stared at the picture.

Murphy ran his hand along the door, touched the handle lightly, stared down at his boots on the carpeting, and yelled, "Shi . . . !"

The explosion hurtled Hopkins against the wall.

He slumped by the doorway to the stairs, gasping for breath. The room had gone black. His ears rang, and the picture of his daughter tore at his mind. Smoke poured over him and rushed up the stairwell. His forehead and cheek were warm and damp; splinters stuck to his body armor. Each time he took a breath, pain shot through his ribs and back. Choking, he rolled over and moved his arm until he touched Henderson's prostrate body. The FBI agent lay on his side, unconscious, breathing erratically.

"Officer down!" Hopkins shouted. Pain wracked his chest and back. "Officer down!" He could barely hear himself.

Pain surging along his spine, he crawled beneath the acrid smoke. He found Murphy lying on his back, but when he located the bomb technician's wrist he could detect no pulse. He moved his hand up the torso until, in a pool of blood, he found Murphy's neck twisted at an acute angle. "No! Christ, no!" Hopkins shouted over the rush of smoke. He tried to wipe away his own blood trickling into his right eye. "Officer down!" he yelled again, but he knew it would do no good. As he turned his head so that the blood dripped away from his eye, he thought he heard faintly through the jangling in his ears, a small voice screaming somewhere close by.

chapter 50

James Robert Saville sat on the edge of the king-sized bed in his Highland Holiday Inn room gaping at the console television the exact size of the monitor that had been suspended from the ceiling in his now-defunct Command Center. A cheese Danish and a cup of coffee rested on the nightstand. He wore only his underwear. His traveling ensemble, a dark European-cut worsted wool suit that Bert Adelman would envy, hung in the closet, and his raincoat lay over the back of the desk chair. That raincoat had perfectly covered his right hand the evening before as he'd strolled through the lobby with his fine black leather briefcase in his left hand. He'd checked in, the fashionably dressed businessman—just as he had half a dozen times before in the past four months—and then changed disguises and slipped out through the underground garage and back to the Command Center for the finishing touches on the Big Operation.

Though his heart was palpitating and sweat was beading on his neck and forehead, he'd been watching the finale unfold with real satisfaction, even awe, at what he'd wrought. The pigs scurrying about by the garbage dump. The SWATTING of his Command Center. The arrogance with which the FBI Hottentot and the Hoopmeister reentered the little house. The bubbling anticipation—and then the jostled image and the smoke billowing from the windows, rising toward the camera like a pagan offering. The madcap scuttling about as the *Santa Maria*, the third surprise, the real surprise, the Big Surprise, knocked the socks off the bastards!

He tried to slow his heart, regulate his breathing. That close encounter of the worst kind with the Hoopmeister had, he was forced to admit, shaken him. Not that it had *really* caused a problem. He *always* planned for contingencies, and he'd had another vehicle and disguise—a red Ford pickup, dark wig, sunglasses, and, just for fun, a Bulls cap—waiting in the rented garage in the alley three blocks from the bungalow. The squad cars had screamed right by, the pea-brained pigs rutting far too wildly to stop him. But still! How the fuck had Hop gotten there *before* he'd sent that last little ditty? The Hoopmeister had proved—surprise, surprise—*almost* a worthy adversary. It was all history now, of course. Hop was a footnote. A footnote and a doornail! This should be a moment of pure ecstasy, of sweeping grandeur, of unencumbered soaring—but the fucking sweats just wouldn't stop.

It had been quiet for a while, and Tonya Walker hadn't been sure if she'd only imagined voices out there in the Beast's cave. The pasty Beast himself hadn't been back since he'd taped the box to the door and run wires below the door and under the cave's carpeting. She crouched in the corner, holding the mask of her father's face, her own face low against the wall and floor, making herself as small as possible. She didn't want the Beast to see that she'd worked the tape from her mouth. She hadn't yelled again, but she'd needed to breathe better—and clawing the tape down to her chin and neck hadn't taken that long. She pressed herself harder against the floor. She couldn't stand the thought of hearing that squeaky voice threatening her again or of the punishment that would follow if he discovered what she'd done.

The blast pancaked her against the floor and wall, dazing and shocking her. At first there was only a deafening noise in her head and bits of tile and plastic raining on her. But then the smoke caused her to gag. She had no idea what had happened, but she was overwhelmed by the sense that even this shrunken white-dark world, the only world she still knew, was flashing apart. And she began to scream.

Then someone was there next to her. A shape that wasn't the Beast's, longer, thinner, lit by fire, coming close through the smoke. It's mouth moved, but she could hear nothing in this shadowy, stormy cloud.

She couldn't stop screaming. A large hand touched her head lightly, and another ran over the tape wrapped around her, skimmed down her body to the straps on her ankles. A man's hand, strong and large. But soft, too, the touch of care and comfort and relief. She stared at the unknown face and strained to hear as the mouth moved.

The hand left her head, and her right ankle jerked as this smoke-blackened phantom sawed at the straps with a pocketknife. Her throat was scratchy, her breath coming in long fitful gasps when she stopped screaming. She looked again into the man's face, saw pain there as the strap jerked with the cutting. She could suddenly swing back her right leg. The man was slicing the straps from the wall. The sawing continued, and dimly she began to hear his voice, almost catching a choked, huffing howl of pain. And she was free.

The large hands gathered her, lifting her from the tiles. And she was borne up from that white dark world, through hot smoke, into the Beast's cave. She clung to the man, her face buried at his neck in some hard, bulky clothing he wore. Something, his blood, was wet on his collar, but she nestled her head against it. The voice was alternately wheezing and speaking, the words broken by the clanging in her head and the rush of fiery air, ". . . all right . . . Tonya . . . don't worry . . . -ther and father . . . make it . . . dad's out . . ."

Her father's friend bumped into something that rolled away. Stumbling, they crashed into a wall or a door. Then they were climbing through the swirling smoke. Voices were all around, shouting as they emerged into light. Her eyes burned, and whenever she tried to open them, the brightness stung her. Someone tried to take her from her father's friend, but she screamed and molded herself against his neck and shoulder.

They came clear of the smoke, passing quickly out a doorway into open air, the leather straps swinging below her feet. Sirens blared, and a repetitive hammering somewhere above her mixed with the clamor in her head. Her eyes fluttered, closed, opened again for a second. Men in uniforms were everywhere, shouting her name, cheering her. A lady in a uniform put a bathrobe, *her* pink bathrobe, over her back. Her father's friend slowed near an ambulance. She looked up, her eyes still stinging. Her father was there, reaching out his arms toward her. And her mother was beside him. They were both nodding and smiling and crying.

chapter 51

Disbelief. Shock and disbelief. Over there on the Videot Box, Hop was hobbling out onto the front porch. And the kid was clinging to him—not hanging limply in his arms! He had deliberately, quite consciously, directed the blast outward, leaving her survival to fate. He'd figured the odds against her at six-to-one—fifty-fifty on the blast, which was, of course, perfectly fair, but three-to-one against the morons actually reaching her quickly enough afterward. Just the sort of longshot the Bagel couldn't help but bet on. And she'd beaten the odds. But Hop couldn't have survived. There was no way he should've escaped the blast. No way! The moment he set foot in front of that washroom door, he should've been a goner, a stain they'd have to wipe from the Command Center wall. The image of his endangered daughter searing in that jockey brain of his as the explosion ripped his head off. At least he *looked* like Mr. Death, bloody and battered and bent.

James Robert Saville tried to stay calm. Hyperventilating in this homely Holiday Inn just wouldn't do. He wanted to run, to hide, but he kept himself planted at the edge of the bed. He mustn't panic! Not now. Late in the afternoon, when the coverage became redundant, he was hopping to St. Louis—dull, bourgeois St. Louie, where they'd never expect to meet him—and then taking wing across the pond. He was flying on a Dutch passport, had jetted back from Europe on it two weeks before. Skipped across the pond on another bogus passport to check his safe houses and then slipped back west on this one the next day. Nobody was going to question its authenticity. Nobody. And taking on the Dutch identity had been such a nice touch, too. No one really knew what the fucking Dutch looked like except that they were generic Western European whitebread. And people were just as clueless about the Netherlands except for iniquitous Amsterdam and windmills and chocolate and fingers in dikes—all of which he could handle just fine in his practiced, nasal, proto-European accent. And he'd become so adept over the years at subtly hiding the hand, making it absolutely invisible, that he'd routinely mesmerized store clerks and ticket-takers and all the other nonentities without any of them ever noticing. He was flying high, all right, free as the singing blackbird whose moment had most definitely arrived.

So why the flickering ticker and the icy snakes slithering down his back? Because the kid knew his face? So what if she provided one of those wretched composite sketches, and the pigs faxed it around the world. Across the fucking universe, for that matter. They'd never catch up with him. Never. They'd be looking for James Robert Saville, not him. Not an urbane Netizen like him. Two weeks in a Baden-Baden spa, a little eye tuck in Amsterdam, maybe a skin graft, and she wouldn't know him if he visited her at fucking Walkerville on the Lake!

There on the Videot Box, the Hoopmeister was passing the kid to that Skywalker putz. And Skywalker was smothering her in those gargantuan arms of his. And Monique-the-

Media-Babe, the goddamned Media Queen, the fucking Media Bitch, was standing there with them, sobbing, playing the part. But deep down, he knew, she was the Ice Maiden still, recording it as always, incapable of immersing herself in the moment.

So let the kid live, goddamn it! After all, he'd *allowed* it to happen. And nobody was going to forget James Robert Saville. Ever! There'd be TV specials and gabfests with celebrity psychobabblers. And magazine articles by overeducated idiots. And instant books like the ones that kept popping up during that O.J. travesty. Certainly a major motion picture. And at least a couple of made-for-TV flicks. Later, an anniversary show perhaps, recapping every act right up to the finale. And a five-year retrospective prying again into all of the morons' lives and marveling once more at the genius of it all. The tabloids would never let go of James Robert Saville. Never! He'd be elevated to the pantheon with Elvis and Jackie O. Only, unlike those two deities, he'd still be very much alive, still flying, and savoring every little morsel of the fame he so richly deserved.

After handing Tonya Walker to her father, Hopkins watched him hug her. A paramedic, without taking her from her father's arms, began to cut away the duct tape. A second paramedic tried to take the mask from her, but she yanked it back and pressed herself harder against her father's chest. Jones-Walker stood next to them and, tears running down her cheeks, hugged her husband and patted her daughter on the back. The helicopters hovered overhead, beating away the rising smoke as their cameramen shot the Walkers' reunion.

Hopkins had no idea what he'd done with the Swiss Army knife after he'd cut Tonya's bonds. Dizzy from the smoke and anxiety and exhaustion and the pain in his ribs and back, he felt his legs giving out. As he began to stagger away, Sergeant Banks put his arm around him and led him toward the second ambulance. "Hoop?" Banks said as he waved his free hand at a paramedic, "We got Henderson. Reached him okay down there. But Murph . . . Murph didn't . . ."

Hopkins leaned his hip against the ambulance's hood but couldn't put any pressure on his back. Shaking his head, he said, "I know . . . the bomb . . . the third . . ."

"You got the girl out, Hoop," Banks said. "You got the girl." He turned toward three of his officers as the paramedic, a dark-haired man with a mustache, started to dab at the gashes on Hopkins' forehead and cheek with a sterile cloth.

Brushing the paramedic's hand away, Hopkins said, "Not now, I've got to . . ." He tried to walk away but made it only around the side of the ambulance before collapsing on the curb. His mind reeling, he pulled himself up until he was sitting. He patted his pockets but couldn't find the cellular phone, had no clue when he'd lost it.

The paramedic, whom Hopkins didn't know, stooped next to him and said, "You're in no condition to go anywhere, Commander Hopkins." He placed a surgical pad over the wound on Hopkins' forehead.

Standing now, James Robert Saville wiped his face and neck with a cool washcloth. His legs quaked, and his T-shirt was soaked with sweat. He stared at the Videot Box, where the thrashed and pummeled Hoopmeister was lurching and pitching about. And there was that hulking bald flunky of his hugging him, practically dragging him toward the medicos, all of it live and on camera for all those millions and millions of morons! The hell with it. Let the Hoopmeister have his thirty seconds of fame. *Inevitably*, Hop'd suffer the rest of his pathetic life. Thanks to the proficiency of American Taxi's licensed delivery service, the *Mayflower* would be arriving at any moment! It was supposed to've produced Hoop's *terminal* thought, but, maybe, this way was even better. Alive, the Hoopmeister'd go on paying big time, just like all the others, knowing he'd been debilitated, impotent, incapable of saving his own daughter. The heartrending debt compounding with each successive year!

All he himself had to do was regain control. Regulate his breathing. Stop the sweats. Sit tight right here in this tacky hotel room until he finally flew away, up and away, far away from the masses and their desperate little lives.

Looking around, Hopkins saw Ross coming toward him. As he called out to her over the din, pain streaked across his back. When she knelt next to him, he took her wrist and said, "Smith and Hedlund, they're still at . . ."

She shook her head. "The Chief called them off when you sent out the APB on Saville. They went after the Chevy."

Hopkins squeezed his eyes shut, but the spinning only got worse. "Get a phone," he said to Ross, opening his eyes and looking at her. When the whirling continued, he placed a hand on the ground and tried to fix his gaze on the ADC garage across the street. "I need a phone."

She did not ask why. Running her fingers along his arm, she said, "I'll be right back, Hoop."

When she returned with a cellular phone, the paramedic had staunched the bleeding from his cheek. As the paramedic set a surgical pad over the wound, Hopkins tapped his ex-wife's number on the phone. Behind them, Walker climbed into the first ambulance, still holding his daughter who would not loosen her grip on him. Jones-Walker entered after them, and the driver swung the back doors shut.

"That's enough," Hopkins said to the paramedic who was dabbing drying blood from his chin and neck. "I'm okay." He wobbled to his feet, felt bile rising in his stomach, and leaned his hip once more against the ambulance. His skin was clammy, and the bedlam around him kept going in and out of focus. When his daughter answered after the second ring, he said, "Cari? Cari, is that you?"

"Dad?" she asked, her tone befuddled.

He coughed, waited for another wave of nausea to pass, and asked, "Are you okay?" He could not raise his arm to cup his other ear, but he could make out the sound of a television in the background.

Ross stood nearby, staring at him and chewing on her lower lip.

"I'm watching TV," Cari said. "I've got the TV on, and I just saw you . . . What's . . . ?"

Losing his balance, Hopkins slapped his hand against the side of the ambulance. "Where's your mother?" he coughed.

The ambulance carrying the Walkers drove off, trailed by two of the helicopters.

"At the door," Cari answered. "There's some delivery guy, a cabbie . . ."

Hopkins' stomach turned. He leaned over and vomited on the pavement. His heart raced, and he could not breathe for a moment. He shut his eyes again and said, "Get your mother. Right away, Cari!"

Her tone still confused, Carie answered, "But the delivery guy, he . . ."

He opened his eyes and gazed up at the smoke swirling off to the southwest. "Get her now, Cari!" he shouted into the phone. "And get out of the house!" His heart was pounding, and he could do nothing to calm himself.

Paramedics began wheeling Henderson out of the bungalow's front door. Hopkins' breath was shallow. "Put the phone down, get your mother, and leave the house," he said. As he spoke, he looked at Ross. "The delivery, it's . . ."

"The kidnapper?" His daughter's voice filled with fear. "You mean, he's the kidnapper?"

"I don't know!" Hopkins yelled. "But the *package*, it's from him!" He could not stop the hammering in his chest. "Get out! Run!"

He waited, hearing his daughter yelling, then waited longer until he was sure he heard only the reporter's voice on the television. And then he sank to the pavement, the world blurring, reeling away from him.

Epilogue

As the gibbous moon rose, it paled and shrank. The lake undulated, but there was little wind and no surf. A straight shimmering path of moonshine crossed the water to the breakfront where Hopkins sat. Gnats he couldn't see brushed his face and arms. Water sliding against a sunken barge to the north produced a deep tolling. A month had passed since he'd stumbled free of the burning bungalow cradling Tonya Walker, but he could still not sit normally. Although the three ribs broken in the bomb blast were healing, there was also disk damage, and an operation might eventually be necessary. There was little solace for him at the lakefront, but, immersed in thought, he didn't move from the rock.

The media frenzy had continued unabated. Barely an evening passed without some special report on some aspect of the Crime of the Century. The television networks and newspapers ran daily stories regurgitating the scant information known about James Robert Saville and speculating about his psyche and motives. A photographer in one of the helicopters had caught with a three-hundred-millimeter lens the exact moment that Hopkins had handed Tonya Walker to her father—and the photograph had already become a cultural icon. Hopkins, resisting all attempts to make him the country's newest instant hero, had retreated from the badgering reporters, but Sky Walker's every move was broadcast live. He had come back to play for the Bulls, leading them with a vengeance to the NBA championship. He had dominated the four games the team had swept, tearing rebounds from above the rim and slamming dunks that twice shattered backboards. But there had been no joy; he had not smiled once, and he had left the Bulls victory celebration without a word to the media.

After two weeks off, Monique Jones-Walker had returned to WLN but not as the news anchor. She was doing a series of segments on health-care reform—reports that didn't require her to engage in any repartee with her colleagues or make any references to her daughter's kidnapping. On camera, she seemed aloof and regal; her face, limned by tragedy, was even more beautiful.

Tonya Walker had seldom left the house in the three weeks since she had been released from the hospital. She had neither returned to gymnastics nor gone anywhere else without her father and two new bodyguards. The psychologists said that she would eventually recover, but Hopkins wasn't so sure.

James Robert Saville had disappeared without a trace. Tonya Walker's description of him had circumnavigated the globe within a few hours of her rescue, and by early afternoon scores of reported sightings had begun to pour into the FBI. Although hundreds of leads were still coming in, none had produced any hard evidence. But Saville would resurface from cyberspace at some point, Hopkins knew. He might already be lurking in the FBI computers or North Ridge police department's revamped system—or skulking in some new command center, fabricating some further abomination.

Still hospitalized with multiple fractures and internal injuries, Carl Henderson had already undergone seven surgeries. Though he had a long, slow recovery ahead of him, both he and his doctors were optimistic that he'd eventually be able to return to his job. Given the prosecutors' contention that Bert Adelman would flee from prosecution, Adelman had been held over for trial. Adelman had stepped down from both Walker Management and the Skywalker Foundation, but he had repeatedly insisted he would be exonerated once all the facts of his financial dealings came to light. Anthony Ignacio had also left the Walkers' employment—whether he had quit or been fired was an ongoing debate in the media. Having only been charged with involuntary manslaughter in the shooting of Jack Bollinger, he had gotten himself an agent. He was already working the talk-show circuit, expounding on the need for personal security for anyone famous or near famous—a service his new firm just happened to provide.

Hopkins looked down at a tiny wildflower near his shoe, barely visible in the moonlight, that had taken root in whatever dirt and sand had blown into a narrow cleft in the rock. The flower's pale violet petals held sparse light. The package delivered to his daughter by the unwitting taxi driver had contained a bomb hidden in a gift-wrapped *Hoop Dreams* video cassette. According to the FBI experts, the device was designed to maim rather than to kill. Tonya Walker's abduction and Saville's madness had, ironically, bound Hopkins more deeply to Cari. They'd talked almost every morning before she went off to her job as a sports camp counselor. And, he was looking forward to the week they planned to spend together canoeing in Michigan's Boundary Waters—if he'd healed enough before she left for college. Reporters had begun pestering her for interviews about her father; agents, noticing how photogenic she was, had promised that if she told her father's story to the tabloids and the TV newsmags she could make enough money that summer alone to pay for her college education.

At work, Hopkins felt mostly numb. He went through the motions but cared little for a job he had relished before. He had lunch and dinner in the police department's cafeteria where he could avoid the reporters that still hounded him whenever he ate in any of the local restaurants. Only Ross, who still sometimes anticipated his thoughts, could reach him. She'd stopped over at his apartment a few times in the evening, but too often they'd lapsed into long silences, lost in their own thoughts about the kidnapping, the bombings in Chicago and Deerbrook, Jack Bollinger's death, and the child-hood that had compelled James Robert Saville to return to North Ridge to exact his revenge and enact his media extrav-aganza. Hopkins was aware he harbored a deep, inexorable anger toward Saville, but he didn't consciously dwell on it. More than anything, he felt incomplete. Saville was still out there somewhere because, ultimately, he, Hopkins, hadn't done his job well enough.

He waved the gnats from his face and gazed for a time at the tranquil lake. As the moon rose, the path of light widened, glittering across the black water. Four bright spots glimmered in the eastern sky near the moon. Three of them, airplanes, faded, but the fourth, Mars, hovered blinking in the night.